Someone was lurking in the bushes...

Meliana heard a movement to her left. She crouched, breathed carefully, concentrated. She should have brought a knife, she realized. She kept still and forced herself to remain calm. Her heart was slamming so hard she felt certain whoever was there would hear it. She searched the darkened ground for a weapon. A stone was the best she could find, but she needed something to defend herself in a struggle.

What if it was *him?*

It had to be him...waiting to pounce. Had he followed her? It was possible. He'd done a number of other bizarre things. Like stealing her underwear.

She waited a full thirty seconds. The frogs seemed to grow louder with each second that passed. The sound of rustling bushes reached her again. Someone was directly behind her. Still in a crouch, Meliana spun. As she did, a man's arm wrapped itself around her shoulders and a hand came over her mouth....

JENNA RYAN

DREAM WEAVER

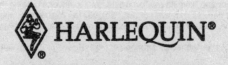

HARLEQUIN®

TORONTO • NEW YORK • LONDON
AMSTERDAM • PARIS • SYDNEY • HAMBURG
STOCKHOLM • ATHENS • TOKYO • MILAN • MADRID
PRAGUE • WARSAW • BUDAPEST • AUCKLAND

ISBN 0-373-88696-9

DREAM WEAVER

ABOUT THE AUTHOR

Jenna Ryan loves creating dark-haired heroes, heroines with strength and good murder mysteries. Ever since she was young, she has had an extremely active imagination. She considered various careers over the years and dabbled in several of them, until the day her sister Kathy suggested she put her imagination to work and write a book. She enjoys working with intriguing characters and feels she is at her best writing romantic suspense. When people ask her how she writes, she tells them by instinct. Clearly it's worked, since she's received numerous awards from *Romantic Times BOOKclub*. She lives in Canada and travels as much as she can when she's not writing.

Books by Jenna Ryan

CAST OF CHARACTERS

Meliana Maynard—A stalker is sending this gifted Chicago surgeon white roses.

Johnny Grand—Meliana's estranged husband. Two years undercover for the FBI damaged his mind and his marriage.

Julie Denton—Meliana's best friend and a Chicago police officer. She predicts the stalker will become murderous.

Sam Robbins—Julie's awkward stepbrother. He has a strange mental gift, and a big crush on Meliana.

Charlie Lightfoot—Meliana's friend is a psychologist with powers of his own. He predicts great danger for Meliana.

Zack Crawford—Deputy sheriff in Blue Lake, where Johnny lives and Meliana used to spend her vacations.

Nick Hohlman—A surgical nurse who fought hard to become part of Meliana's team.

Chris Blackburn—An FBI agent. Once Johnny's friend and partner, he admits to being in love with Meliana.

Tim Carrick—Johnny's phantom neighbor in Blue Lake. His wife simply vanished one day.

Sheriff Owen Frank—He enforces the law in Blue Lake, but only when necessary.

Prologue

I am not crazy!

There, that's out of the way. Sometimes people tell me I am, and it makes me furious. But I don't want to think about that, or I might do something unpleasant.

I'll think about Meliana Maynard instead. Beautiful, exotic Meliana. I've been watching her for a very long time now. I know her routine, her habits, even some of her quirks.

I've watched her jog on the shore of Lake Michigan and in the park. I've seen her at the hospital where she works. She wears blue scrubs when she's operating and a white lab coat when she isn't.

She has black magic hair—that's dark, dark brown with just a hint of red—but it's her eyes that are the real magic. They're silver-gray, like the lake on a rainy day when the sun pokes through and shines on it.

I love her. I don't care that she married another man. I would if they were still together, but she left him six months ago, so it's okay. Sort of. She came to her senses and did the smart thing, the right thing. We can be together now. Or—well, soon.

She has an amazing body. I took some of her lingerie. Six pieces, and every piece as lovely as she is. I think she wears sexy lingerie all the time. There was a lot of silk and lace in her drawer.

There were a lot of photographs, too, pictures of Meliana on her wedding day. I wanted to tear the man beside her to shreds.

It's odd, but I find myself staring at a scalpel she used once. I see it covered in blood. I'm starting to shake. She has a mind of her own, my Meliana. She's very strong.

The shaking is getting worse. All I can see is blood.

I've been spinning dreams about her for many long months. I've woven the threads of them back and forth in my mind until now, finally, I've created the perfect picture of Meliana and me.

And yet I worry. I see blood. I shake. What if she doesn't want me? What if she thinks I'm crazy? What if she doesn't love me?

What if the blood is hers?

Chapter One

It was going to rain. At the moment, the air was warm and sultry as late summer stroked lingering fingers over the Chicago area, but there were black clouds suspended above the lake and strong traces of red and gold on the leaves.

Labor Day had come and gone. Children were back in school, the tourists older now, couples for the most part, looking for both excitement and nostalgia as their vacation time wound down.

Meliana Maynard wasn't looking so much as listening to her neighbor Chris Blackburn's thumbnail account of the attempted break-in on her midcentury town house.

"Your alarm went off when the guy tried to jimmy the back door." Chris cocked a thumb over his shoulder. "He must have burned rubber across your lawn. Cops showed within four minutes." He grinned. "That's gotta be a first, right? I flashed my ID and went inside with them, but I don't think whoever it was made it past the back stoop." His grin widened as he rested both arms on her shoulders and set his face close to hers. "So how was your day, sweet cheeks? Did you cut into anyone worth mentioning?"

"A cute sixteen-year-old with a ruptured spleen and a guy with a gunshot wound to his right leg. Sorry, no gory details on that one." Meliana looked past Chris at the pair of approaching detectives. "Hey, Julie."

The female of the pair smiled. She had straight, chin-length blond hair, a squarish jaw and bright haze-green eyes. "Are you going to check your place with me, Mel, or hang out all day with that fed?"

"He's being supportive," Meliana said, but she tapped Chris's arms with her index fingers and got him to drop them. "What do you think—did he get inside?"

"I doubt it." With a nod to her partner and another head motion at Meliana, Julie started up the rear stairs. "I always think it's weird when people try to break and enter town houses—them being so close together and all. But you're on an end, so I suppose he figured he could pull it off. What are you doing, Blackburn?" she asked over her shoulder.

"Supporting a friend, Detective Denton." He quirked a brow. "You got a problem with that?"

"I've got a problem with most feds, and you in particular. If Mel needed the FBI, which she doesn't, her husband, your former partner, would pull rank on you in a minute. Go home and watch the Sox get their tails whipped."

Chris's brow went higher. "Aren't you in Homicide these days? I don't see any dead bodies around here."

"It's called looking out for a friend, Blackburn. Although you seem familiar with the concept, this isn't your turf. Go away."

Despite the situation, Meliana's amusement rose. Julie and Chris had dated once, and it hadn't gone well. They'd butted heads, tossed a little too much alcohol into an already volatile mix and very nearly wound up having their own private kickboxing match.

"That's enough, you two. Do you have any idea who it was?"

"Not a clue. This neighborhood's been pretty clean lately."

"Except for the car thieves," Chris remarked from behind.

"She still has her car, doesn't she? I'll go through the house with you, Mel, but it looks like the guy bolted when he heard the alarm."

"Which is exactly what I said earlier," Chris countered with a smug air.

Meliana jabbed his ribs. "Stop needling her, Blackburn, or I'll think you've been spending time with Johnny."

Chris snorted. "No one's been spending time with your hubby—sorry, ex-hubby, Mel. He lives like a hermit up at Blue Lake. Last time I saw him he had one beer, two eggs and a few scary-looking slices of white bread in his fridge."

They were separated, not divorced, Meliana reflected, but she let it go. "Eileen Crawford cleans house for him. She'll stock his fridge. Did anyone look in my cookie jar? For money," she added when Chris opened his mouth. "I keep extra cash inside for emergency pizzas."

"God, you eat as bad as Johnny." Julie pushed the door open. "It's a miracle you two lived long enough to get married."

"She dug a slug out of his chest is why they got married," Chris said.

"Nice try, but how we met isn't why we got married." Meliana scanned the living room. "Seems fine here."

It was the same in the bedrooms, the dining room, the bathrooms and the kitchen. Even her cookie jar rattled with loose change.

"A twenty, two tens and a chewed five-dollar bill. My neighbor's new puppy's teething," Meliana explained, screwing the lid back on. "The only drugs I have are run-of-the-mill aspirin, and my wine cooler still has seventeen bottles inside. I'd say he took off."

"Good." Julie closed her notebook. "I can write my report and be home by seven. Hot date." She grunted in Chris's direction. "Thankfully, not with a fed. You know, the only one of their kind I've ever been able to tolerate is Johnny, and even then there were times when I wanted to shove his ID up his—nose. Shut up," she said before Chris could speak. "I'm leaving, Mel. If you find anything missing, call me on my cell."

Through the kitchen window Meliana watched the storm clouds creep inland from the lake. The premature darkness reminded her of her wedding day when thunder had rumbled in the background of the outdoor ceremony and lightning had ultimately struck one of the three trees on the perimeter. She had to admit, no matter how it had ended, her relationship with Johnny Grand had been anything but dull.

"What are you smiling at?" Chris lounged against the counter and threw a tangerine into the air. A shrewd brow went up. "Johnny?"

She laughed. "I swear that lightning bolt was an omen."

"You think it was funny?"

"In retrospect. Come on, Chris, we were amazing for a while."

"And then Johnny went undercover."

"Yes." She sighed. "He did." Tossing her purse onto a chair, she headed for the stairs. "I need to change. I'm having dinner with the head of surgery and his wife tonight."

Chris followed her up. "All by your lonesome?" He clucked his tongue. "Not good, angel face. But no fear, I happen to be free."

"I'm not. I have a date."

He caught up with her and handed the tangerine over her shoulder. "That's not very nice, is it? Choosing a stranger over a friend and neighbor who's been there for you through thick and thicker?"

"If that's an offer of help, I accept." Amusement danced in her eyes as she turned. "It's a blind date, with the head of surgery's wife's nephew. You go in my place, tell the geek you like men who giggle and I'll go for a nice long run on the beach."

"On second thought, I might be getting a migraine."

"Yeah, I figured." She started for the bathroom, then paused and backtracked.

"What?"

She regarded her top dresser drawer. It was open almost a full three inches. She always closed her drawers, not because she was a neat freak but because she'd gotten a puppy recently and he'd chewed several pieces of her clothing to shreds. On the other hand, the puppy had pretty much grown into a dog at this point.

"Mel?"

She tipped her head to the side. "That drawer was closed when I left this morning."

Chris followed her gaze. "You think some crook bypassed your video equipment and laptop to poke through your drawers?"

"Not really. I'm sure it's…" She opened the drawer, froze, closed it. "Nothing."

"That nothing sounded like a whole lot of something to me." Chris pulled on the handle, peered inside. Then he looked at her. "You keep roses in with your underwear?"

"One rose," she corrected. "Long stemmed, white, with a sprig of baby's breath." She picked it up and stared. "It's the fifth one I've gotten in the past month."

"I WHIPPED UP A BIG BATCH of chili and a pot of spaghetti sauce, divided them into servings and labeled the containers." Eileen Crawford drew air pictures as she spoke. "They're in the freezer. You can cook pasta, right? Of course you can. There's fresh milk in the fridge, bread, vegetables and two big packages of cold cuts. Vacuum-sealed, so don't open the second until the first one's gone. I'll be back on Tuesday to tidy up the bathrooms and such. Will you be all right until then?"

Sometimes Johnny swore the woman was beamed from Mars to his doorstep twice a week as a test of earthling patience. Eileen had been cleaning houses for the residents of Blue Lake for twenty years. She was a heavyset woman with a faded Maine accent, curly blond hair and more nerve than anyone Johnny knew. And he knew or had known a great number of nervy people.

But that was in another lifetime, another world, one he didn't care to visit these days.

He tried to ease the woman politely out the door. "Thanks, Eileen. I appreciate the food and the clean sheets."

She shifted her handbag to her other shoulder. "You're just like my Zack when it comes to keeping house. Where clothing lands is where it stays. Has he been around to see you lately?"

Johnny fixed a smile on his face and kept it there as he nudged her forward. "Not for a week or so."

"Well, Sheriff Frank's been out of town. He belongs to some order of brethren or other and they convene every year at a big hotel, so Zack's been pushed a bit more than usual. I think there was some function he had to attend in Woodstock today. It's all go with you law enforcement types. Constantly busy."

How busy could one of two deputies be in a town with less than fifteen hundred year-round residents and the tourist traffic down to boaters, backpackers and fifty-five-plus couples?

"I'm sure he'll get some time off soon."

"When he does, you two should go bowling, or head over to the grill for a game of pool." Eileen set a hand on her hip. "You're so practical, the pair of you. All I want is one grandchild before I retire, and what does Zack do? He dates a tourist for two weeks, then drives her down to O'Hare and says goodbye. Doesn't get her address, home or e-mail. I bet he never even thought to ask for her phone number."

"Maybe she wasn't the right one." They were almost at the door. "Move, Shannon," he said to his curious Irish setter. "Eileen wants to leave."

The big dog barked and began sniffing the woman's leg. She halted and rolled her eyes. "Doggie treats! I never gave them a thought. I'll run some out here first thing tomorrow morning."

"Shannon likes soda crackers. She can snack on those instead."

"Crackers? My God, Johnny Grand, did you treat your wife like this?"

Now it was Johnny's turn to stare. "Excuse me?"

She strengthened her grip on her shoulder strap. "I'm sorry. That was out of line. I just can't help wondering why a couple as lovely as you and Meliana broke apart. Your wife's a skilled surgeon, and yet she bandaged more knees and treated more stings and bites whenever she came up here than Dr. Fell—rest his soul—did in all his time on the lake. The woman's an angel."

Wanna bet? Johnny thought with equal parts humor and regret. "She has her moments," he agreed.

"How did you meet?"

Oh, no, she was settling in. "It's a long story, really long. I'll tell you about it another time. Right now…" The phone rang behind him.

"I'm expecting a call," he lied. "An important one."

She patted his arm. "You take it, then, and I'll let myself out."

"Walk her to her car," Johnny ordered Shannon in a low voice. He picked up. "Yeah, Grand here."

"I know you're there, Grand, but you should be here."

Johnny waited until Eileen was out of earshot before turning away. "Julie? Why the hell are you calling me at—" he squinted at the burled wall clock that had come with the house "—eight at night?"

"Your wife got a rose."

He watched as Eileen's '81 Taurus sedan rolled off. "What?"

"Actually, she's gotten five roses in four weeks. Long stemmed, white, from a—ha-ha—secret admirer. And those weren't funny ha-ha's."

Johnny sat on the arm of the sofa. "What were they?"

"Worried. I take it your good buddy Chris didn't call?"

"About roses? No."

"Okay, here's the deal. Someone tried to break in to your—her town house today around five. We thought the alarm scared the guy off. Everything looked okay inside. But later, after we'd left, Mel found a white rose in her lingerie drawer. It isn't the first one she's received. It is the first one that's really violated her space. The other four didn't involve a break-in. Also…" She took a breath and Johnny heard the faint shudder beneath it. "Some of her lingerie's missing. She figures five or six pieces. One of them is that bustier thing she wore under her wedding dress—you know, the strapless bra slash corset slash garter belt number."

Johnny swore. "Did she call you?"

"Yeah, but only this time. She didn't mention the other four flowers until today. Blackburn was with her when she opened the drawer, but I figured—and I was right—he'd be as likely to contact you as cut off his foot."

Johnny searched the low tables for his car keys. "What are you doing about it?"

"There's not much we can do. We dusted for prints, but you know as well as I do we won't find anything. We'll also talk to her neighbors. So far, though, it seems like you bought into a complex where people mind their own business. Are you coming down?"

"Yeah." He checked under the sofa cushions for the keys. "Don't tell Mel, okay?"

"You know, I really hate it when people say that to me. She's my friend, Johnny. She kept me from getting hysterical when I thought my mother was having a heart attack. Then she very calmly ran the tests and removed her gall bladder. I'll give you two hours before I blab."

"You're all heart, Jules."

He spotted his keys in a ceramic bowl beside the door, grabbed them along with his jacket and whistled for Shannon. "Do me another favor, okay?"

"What is it?"

"Ask Mel if she's gotten anything else with those roses."

IT WAS NINE O'CLOCK when Julie reappeared at her door. Meliana greeted her with a canny "You called him, didn't you?"

Julie reddened just enough for her to see. "You can't possibly know that."

"Yeah, right, because I don't know you at all, do I? We only got arrested together in Mindanao and had to spend ten days in a sinkless hellhole shouting at anyone who'd listen to us that, no, we weren't soliciting and we certainly hadn't been using the act as a cover to deal drugs."

"That's what you get for carrying white powder in your purse."

"It was a free sample of Oscar after-bath."

"Which we couldn't make them understand, because they didn't bother to run any tests and we didn't speak the language—which I thought you said you did."

"I speak Hawaiian, Julie. That's a big linguistic step from the Philippines." Because she really wasn't annoyed, Meliana let the door swing open. "Is he coming down?"

"Unless he forgets to gas up. Always a possibility."

"Hey, he's my husband—I'll make the nasty cracks." Linking her fingers loosely behind her back, she watched her friend stride along the short corridor, pause, then glance from side to side. "Chris isn't here, Julie. I sent him out with patrolman Dick—"

"Dirk."

Meliana smiled. "They're talking to Mrs. Feldman. She's the only bona fide snoop in the area."

"Everyone I know lives with curtain twitchers. What makes your neighbors so special?"

"Not special, professional. Most of the people around here don't get home until six or later."

"No latchkey kids?"

"Busy on their computers. Chris made the rounds, Jules. No one saw a thing."

"Mmm, well, as I see it, there wasn't enough time for the guy to have hauled butt up to your bedroom, planted the rose, swiped your lacies and hightailed it back out before we got here. That means he either did the deed while you were home and occupied, in which case he'd have had fairly free access, or he knows your security code."

"Which he rearmed, then set off on the way out?"

Julie started for the stairs. "He stole your underwear, Mel. You can't expect rational behavior." She glanced up. "Is that thunder?"

"There's a storm on the lake. Perfect backdrop for a murder mystery."

"You need to date again," Julie decided.

"I had a blind date lined up for tonight. That's why I'm not as upset as I probably should be about the break-in."

"You're as sick as your underwear thief. Is this the dresser?"

"Top drawer. White rose lying on a folded black slip. Patrolman Dirk bagged it."

"Was it hothouse?"

"I saw a few spots on the petals. I'd guess garden grown."

"Thorns?"

"Shaved off." Which unsettled her and had her rubbing her bare arms. "God, I hope he's not spying on me."

"They often do."

"It's creepy. " Meliana drew her fingers across her throat and fought a chill. "I don't want to be a bug under a microscope."

"It's a burden, I'll admit." Julie sat on the bed and let herself sink back into the padded headboard. "Tell me the truth, Mel—are roses the only thing this guy's left for you?"

"That I'm sure of, yes."

"Of course, this could just be the beginning of a more frightening agenda."

"That's reassuring."

"I'm a cop. I deal in facts."

"So do I, but I don't tend to approach patients' families and tell them I'll be gutting their sons and daughters." She heard wind howling around the eaves. "Andy McRae says it's going to be a brisk fall."

"And he knows that because…?"

"He maintains the lawns and gardens in the complex. Means nothing, Julie. Your mother knows as much about flowers as he does."

"Whereas you and I know nothing." A wry expression invaded her features. "I wonder what Johnny knows?"

"More than me and less than your mom." She heard

the door slam open and bang off the wall downstairs. "Ah, good, a looming confrontation. I should have gone ahead with that date."

Johnny rushed in as if he expected the intruder to still be there. He had his keys in his left hand and a big red dog at his heels.

Delighted, Meliana went to her knees. Shannon barked and jumped on her. "I didn't think you'd bring her."

When he realized there were only the two women in the room, Johnny regrouped and shot Julie a dark look. "That was a short two hours."

"Hey, don't blame me." Julie stabbed a finger at Meliana. "She guessed. Count yourself lucky Blackburn didn't find out. He'd have been a wall in your face before you got up the stairs."

"He'd have been flat on his ass in the downstairs hallway."

Meliana ruffled Shannon's silky ears. "I love it when men do the testosterone thing. Johnny, do you even try putting your clothes together?"

He frowned, glanced down at his jeans, T-shirt and jacket. "What's wrong with them?"

The brown jacket looked as if he'd slept in it, the red T was torn and frayed at the hem and his jeans were the oldest pair he owned. Meliana hid her amusement. "Nothing, I guess. Knee-jerk reaction. I see Shannon swallowed your last hairbrush."

He moved his lips in a perfunctory smile. "I wasn't thinking personal aesthetics when I jumped in my truck and raced down here. Is the rose gone?"

"Off to the police lab to be mutilated. Are you limping?"

"Eileen Crawford cleaned today. I tripped over the magazine rack."

"Which she undoubtedly put back in its proper place. This isn't a big deal, Johnny." Meliana was going to repeat that until she believed it. "Some pervert likes roses and underwear. He left one and stole the other. Maybe he just wanted something pretty to wear."

"Or maybe he'd rather you wore it for him."

"You're not going to be nice and let me delude myself for a few hours, are you?"

Instead of answering, he looked around the room. "You painted."

"Julie and I did."

"It's called coconut cream," Julie told him. "We thought it was more soothing than the scary harvest gold that came with the place and Mel let you keep because you apparently grew up in a time-warp bungalow with parents who still aren't aware that several decades have passed since the mid-seventies."

"She means the walls looked dated." Meliana stopped an excited Shannon from hopping onto the bed. "That's a white-on-white quilt, handmade by Johnny's grandmother, Shan. You didn't have to come all the way to Chicago, Johnny. I'm having the security code changed tomorrow. And I have a dog here most of the time."

His frown deepened. "Where is Lokie?"

"Visiting my cousin in Joliet."

He made a disgusted sound. "The kids'll rip her ears off."

"If they do, I'll kick Joey's butt from here to Honolulu. She'll be fine. I taught her how and when to bite."

Julie chuckled. Then she sobered and craned her neck. "Damn. Blackburn's coming back."

"With his sidekick Dick?" Meliana teased.

"Dirk."

"Trying to lighten the mood here, Jules." Climbing to her feet, she ran her fingers through Johnny's rumpled hair. "You look like you lost the battle with a wind machine." When his eyes— rather stunning eyes, she acknowledged—narrowed, she let her hand fall. "I don't think I mentioned this, and I'm not sure if it's relevant or not, but white's my favorite color."

"Yes, we know that," Johnny said.

"Lokie's a Samoyed, also white. I found her tied up on the front porch right after you moved to Blue Lake six months ago. The vet figured she was maybe five months old."

"I thought you said she was a gift."

"She was. There was a ribbon around her neck with a card attached to it. It said: 'A beautiful puppy for a beautiful woman. She's called Lokelani.' I thought the Raymonds left her for me when they moved. There were always new dogs popping up over there. But then the roses started coming, and I started to wonder."

"You think the rose guy gave you a dog?"

She regarded them both, her husband the FBI agent and her friend the cop. "White dog, white rose." She drew a deep breath. "The white dog already had a name and, FYI, Lokelani just happens to be Hawaiian for 'heavenly rose.'"

Chapter Two

They had a brief and mildly unpleasant run-in with Chris in the downstairs hallway. Johnny and Chris had been friends of a sort once. Then Johnny had gone undercover for two years and a great many things had changed.

"He was hitting on you at our wedding," Johnny said as he helped Meliana into his SUV. "And he jumped on the first town house that came up for sale in our complex after we moved in."

"He likes vaulted ceilings."

"He likes you."

"I like him back. But like isn't love, and I've told him that at least a dozen times."

"Chris Blackburn has the ability to be selectively blind and deaf when it suits his purpose."

Meliana grinned. "Unlike another person in this vehicle, right? Will Shannon be okay while we're gone?"

"I gave her food, water and a big plate of soda crackers."

"You're corrupting her, Johnny." Propping her foot

up, she retied the lace of her sneaker. "Do you know where you're going?"

"Where, yes. Why, no. Charlie Lightfoot's a nutcase."

"Wrong. In actual fact, he solves nutcases."

"By picking up psychic vibes from objects, then translating them into emotions and, occasionally, physical traits."

"Hey, it's highly unlikely the cops will get anywhere with this. There were no prints and no help forthcoming from Mrs. Feldman or anyone else. I want to know who stole my lingerie and why, beyond the obvious, the color white seems to be significant. I know." She cut off his protest. "White denotes purity, innocence, virtue."

"Virginity."

"Uh-huh, well, he missed the boat on that one years ago. And I was never pure, innocent or especially virtuous."

"You were a navy brat."

"Base life had its moments, Grand. My mom made captain before she turned thirty-five. I thought it was pretty cool growing up with a parent who flew jets and got to order a lot of other people around."

"You're a chip off the old navy block, Mel."

"Did you know she's a commander now?"

"Does she know you're a top-notch surgeon?"

"A noble and worthy profession, but not the one she wanted for me. Unfortunately, I'm not as fond of flying or of the navy as my mother is."

"How's your *nui kaikunane,* Maleko?"

"Very good," she congratulated. "My big brother

Mark's fine. He's doing some kind of undercover work in Honolulu. Last time I saw him he looked like a cross between a Gypsy and a pirate. Big gold earring, long hair, slick clothes."

"Is your mom okay with that?"

"She wasn't especially happy when he left the navy after only four years, but he's a great cop."

"He has the right instincts. My division leader says any time Mark wants a job, it's there for him."

"He'd appreciate that. Turn left here."

"I remember where Lightfoot lives, Mel. My brain didn't burn out totally on that assignment."

But more damage had been done than could be easily repaired, Meliana thought with a pang. She changed the subject. "Charlie's become a fixture on the South Side scene. He broke up with a woman last year because she wanted him to move away from there. He loves his apartment."

"And his Deadhead music and his incense. He tried to analyze Mark's captain's dreams at our wedding, Mel. He's lucky the guy was so drunk he didn't give a damn."

"You're such a stickler. Charlie's brilliant. Okay, maybe he did a few too many psychedelic drugs in the early seventies, but you like harvest gold and avocado green."

"I grew up with them."

"I grew up with a father who embezzled money from a pineapple factory, but I manage to keep my fingers out of the hospital funding pot. Honest to God, Johnny, you're so by-the-book in some ways and so fly-by-the-seat-of-your-pants in others. It's like there's two people living inside your head."

"One head, Mel, two sides to my brain." He turned on the radio.

Meliana studied her husband's profile. He was gorgeous, always had been, through good times and bad. His hair, somewhere between brown and dark blond, was unkempt and far too long to be considered FBI standard. He had an incredible face, all lines, planes and angles, a devastating mouth and eyes the color of smoked charcoal. Friends used to tease them that if their kids didn't have some form of gray eyes, it would be absolute proof that Meliana had been unfaithful.

Never could have happened, she reflected on a wistful note. She'd loved Johnny Grand with everything she had inside her—and that had been a considerable amount. Johnny said Chris had been hitting on her at their wedding. She believed him, but hadn't noticed. She still didn't, even in retrospect. All she remembered about that day was being deliriously happy and grateful that her father, on parole after having served six years of his ten-year sentence, had been permitted to attend.

"Summer's heading south," Johnny commented over the rain and music. "There was a bite in the air at Blue Lake, and a lot of the birds are gone."

She continued to study him. "Do you get bored up there?"

"Sometimes. Then I remind myself that being there's essential to my mental rehab, and I replace a shingle or two."

"Does it work?"

"As rehab?" He moved a shoulder. "You tell me. Do I seem less stressed than before?"

"At the moment, yes. But not when you flew into the bedroom earlier. I'm not going to get paranoid about what happened, Johnny. I'll talk to Charlie, get Lokie back, change my alarm code and leave the rest to Julie."

"What about the card that came on Lokie's collar?"

"I have it somewhere. I'll dig it out. Turn here."

She indicated a narrow street that read more like a downtown alley. Rusty fire-escape ladders hung from dilapidated brick and concrete buildings. Many of the windows were blacked out and the darkness and rain only reinforced the sinister atmosphere.

"It's great here," Meliana remarked. "Like Al Capone meets *West Side Story*."

"In Dracula's dungeon."

"This is an old part of the city. You should see Los Angeles after sunset."

"I have."

And New York and Miami and Cartagena and Mexico City. "I'll call ahead." She punched her colleague's number on her cell. "Heads up, Lightfoot," she warned. "We're here." She slid her gaze to Johnny. "Yeah, okay, I'll tell him."

Johnny stared straight ahead. "I don't want to know."

"He says for you not to use the bathroom, and no matter how suspicious the tea smells, it's only a Chinese herb blend."

"You believe that?"

"I'm due in the O.R. at 11:00 a.m. I need to believe."

Johnny, who'd had more than a few strange conversations with Charlie Lightfoot since the separation, cast dubious eyes over the ravaged balcony railings. "Babe, I hope you know what you're doing."

"THIS IS PRETTY." Charlie held Meliana's black slip up by the straps and grinned like a fool. "Where'd you get it?"

"New York City." Meliana sat cross-legged on his sofa—at least, Johnny assumed there was a sofa under the massive Native American blanket. "Do you feel anything, Charlie?" Her eyes sparkled. "Other than hot and bothered?"

"That's top of the list, Mel." He ran a ringed hand over the silky fabric. "I see you at a swanky cocktail party. Nope, sorry, wedding reception."

Johnny frowned. "Who got married?"

"One of the surgical nurses, last July. That slip's been washed half a dozen times since then. How long do vibes linger?"

Charlie drank his tea laced with God knew what and winked at them. "Depends on the strength of the memory. Did you have fun?"

"No."

"Ah, well, bad's as weighty as good." Eyes closed, he fingered the lace trim. "Relax, Johnny," he advised. "This isn't black magic. It's just a little tap I sometimes have into a part of the brain most of us don't use."

What could he say to that? Johnny watched Meliana

sip her tea while she in turn watched Charlie psycho-
analyze her slip.

To be truthful, he didn't dislike Charlie Lightfoot. He
just felt a little edgy around the guy. But then, he felt
edgy around most people these days. Thus his requested
leave from active duty and a solo retreat to Blue Lake.

Charlie pressed three fingers to the headband he ha-
bitually wore. If he started humming, Johnny thought
he'd have to leave the room. He might have to get out
anyway. The air in the cramped apartment was ripe
with the smells of simmering herbs, strawberry incense
and two grizzled old terriers.

Charlie sat barefoot on a faded Persian carpet,
across from Meliana. He wore a cotton T-shirt with a
peace symbol on the chest, worn jeans and three
earrings in his left lobe. His hair was as long as
Johnny's, although there wasn't quite as much of it,
and it was much darker—almost the same color as
Meliana's, in fact.

Different heritage, though. Johnny drank the beer
Charlie had given him and slid his gaze to his wife.
Charlie Lightfoot was half Blackfoot, half French.
Meliana was one quarter Hawaiian on her mother's side
and 100 percent drop-dead gorgeous. Johnny had fantasized about her hair while he'd been undercover. It
was very nearly black, extremely thick and just the
slightest bit wavy. It skimmed her collarbone these
days, though when he'd met her five and half years ago
it had actually been several inches longer.

"Calhoun," Charlie said clearly.

"That was the groom's name." Reaching out, Meliana gave the slip a tug. "Forget weddings."

"Maybe you need to be in it for the vibe thing to work," Johnny suggested.

"Always a possibility." Charlie stared unblinking at the fabric. Johnny had no idea how he did it. His head was throbbing, and his eyes stung from the herbs and incense. And Jethro Tull on scratchy vinyl in the background wasn't helping.

He massaged his temples. "Do you need the rose?"

"Could be." Charlie bunched the slip and breathed in. "Sounds lunatic, I know, but this really does work sometimes. Tell me about the other roses, Mel."

Johnny moved his lips into a smile. "Yes, tell both of us."

She set her cup aside. "They appeared in different places each time. I found the first one four weeks ago on the driver's seat of my car. The second showed up ten days later on my desk at the hospital. The third was in my locker, which wasn't locked—yes, I know, Johnny, not smart—and the fourth found its way into my lab coat pocket. He must have slipped it to me while I was making my rounds. It could happen," she said with a shrug. "You bump into people all the time in hospital corridors."

"Nurses, orderlies, patients?" Charlie assumed.

"Other doctors, maintenance workers, visitors." Meliana sighed. "Sorry. Unless I'm in the O.R., I interact with a lot of people on a daily basis."

"No surprise there. Hey, can we put this on hold for

a few minutes? I need the bathroom, and mine's out of commission. Lucky for me, I've got an obliging neighbor downstairs."

Johnny's head was beginning to buzz. It was a bad sign. He blocked the images that wanted to creep in and focused on Meliana.

She wore jeans tonight, faded blue with a leaf embroidered on the hem of her flared left leg. Her T-shirt was pale yellow and short. Though he hadn't gotten a good look at it yet, he could envision the tiny gold ring she wore in her navel.

She'd had it pierced on their honeymoon. He'd had his left earlobe done. The rings had been engraved with the same design as their wedding bands.

God, it felt like years ago that they'd been lounging on that beach in Papeete. They'd eaten dinner at an outdoor restaurant, watched Polynesian dancers, then returned to their cabana where it had been his turn to watch her do a hula just for him.

She'd been good, damned good.

He rolled the cold bottle of beer across his forehead and decided it might be wise to block that memory, as well. They were separated now, a nightmarish fallout from his last assignment. He'd changed, he knew it, and so did Meliana. He'd been coiled up inside when he'd returned, prone to fits of inexplicable rage. He'd feared becoming violent. He'd feared hurting Meliana.

The nightmare was over, yet, oddly, much of what had happened in the two-year interim was still available to him only in fuzzy snippets.

What the hell, he wondered in exasperation, had he been thinking, accepting a two-year undercover stint on the street?

He swore, then looked around as two pairs of eyes landed on him. Charlie had returned without him noticing it. "Sorry," he said. "I'm bummed about the flowers." Not a total lie. "Come on, Lightfoot, what sort of guy does stuff like this?"

Charlie resumed his modified lotus position. "Your basic pervert'll indulge himself from time to time, but it isn't always that drastic a scenario. Could be someone who's lonely, a teenager with a crush. The lingerie, though, that goes deeper. Now we're probably talking obsession, deviant thoughts."

"How deviant?"

"I can't…" He halted, raised his head. He had Meliana's slip in his hands again. "Razor blade," he said. "I see a flat razor blade being used to slice off the thorns."

Meliana glanced at Johnny. "The thorns were removed from all the roses."

"Who's using the blade?" Johnny wanted to know.

"I don't know, but he's doing it on an old plank board, like barn wood."

Johnny's lashes lowered in suspicion. "Are you sure you've only got herbs boiling in those pots?"

Charlie laughed. "Positive. And they're the kind you can consume without seeing pink elephants. I'm blank now, Mel. I think that's it for tonight."

"I'm impressed." She braved one of the cookies he'd set out, and with it between her teeth reached for her slip. "Grateful, too." She took a bite. "I know you get tired of the quack stigma. These are good, by the way."

"Demerara sugar's the secret. You can unwind now, Johnny," he said without looking over. "Black magic's done."

Johnny tipped back his beer to finish it. "Chris Blackburn uses a flat-blade razor to shave."

"So does your father," Meliana pointed out.

"My father lives in Indianapolis."

"Chris didn't steal my lingerie, Johnny."

"He knows your alarm code."

"He's FBI."

"Doesn't mean he isn't twisted."

The look she sent him told him clearly what her thoughts on that subject were.

A delighted Charlie shifted his gaze from one to the other. "Really cool, guys. Don't keep anything bottled up inside."

"Yeah, well, that's only one bottle opened." Johnny pushed out of his chair. "We have several more."

"And apparently the number's growing." Standing, Meliana kissed Charlie's cheek. "Thanks for the magic. Are you at the hospital tomorrow?"

"Day after. I'm holding a clinic on suppressed aggression, if anyone here's interested."

Johnny ignored the remark and located his keys. "You should let him touch Lokie while you're at it."

Charlie adjusted his headband. "Your dog? Why?"

"He was a gift," Meliana explained. "Possibly from the rose guy."

"A live gift, huh?" Charlie's brow furrowed. "I'm not sure I like that."

"Like it or not, she's mine, and I'm keeping her. Thanks again."

"Yeah, me, too," Johnny echoed.

Charlie caught his arm as he started to follow Meliana out. "Keep an eye on her, man. I don't like some of those last vibes I got."

Better and better, Johnny thought.

He took the rickety stairs to the front door. If you could call it a door. It looked more like a piece of dented metal with a faulty latch. It was a miracle the guy lived to hold clinics.

The rain had stopped. He caught up with Meliana in the parking lot. "I wasn't looking for a fight, Mel. I just have trouble believing in psychic power."

"Uh-huh…" She was standing dead still.

His brows came together as he regarded her. "Problem?"

"I'd say so." Taking his wrist, she turned him so he was facing his SUV. There, written in bold white block letters across the front windshield were the words LEAVE HER ALONE!

HER 11:00 A.M. OPERATION was postponed, first by a gunshot wound, then by an acute appendix in an overtaxed E.R. Meliana didn't mind the extra work. It kept her from thinking about roses, underwear and warnings written on the windshield of an SUV.

What if this wasn't a harmless crush? The question

whispered repeatedly in her head. It had already followed her into her dreams and haunted her through an early-morning breakfast.

Johnny had been adamant. He intended to spend the night in Chicago. Meliana had told him he could stay with her, but he'd negated the idea before she'd even gotten the words out.

It stung a little, but she understood his reasons well enough not to argue. There'd been a suppressed sort of violence about him when he'd finished his assignment, one that neither Meliana nor Johnny had been able to deal with.

After their visit to Charlie, Johnny had left Shannon with her and gone next door to sleep at Andy McRae's house.

In his prime, Andy had managed a large garden shop in the city. Now a nimble eighty-two, he was paid by the people in Meliana's complex to maintain the grounds. He loved his current job and did it very well. He was short and paunchy, had knobby knees and wore soda-bottle glasses. Meliana loved him. His fuzzy white hair and sweet grin reminded her of a handmade teddy bear she'd had as a child.

Johnny had told her to scream if she saw or heard anything suspicious. That included Chris Blackburn, should he happen to show up unannounced.

Times changed, Meliana reflected as she took a final stitch to close the appendix patient's incision. One day Johnny and Chris had been allies, the next enemies.

"That's it, Nick," she said to the nurse beside her.

"This guy's lucky. Ten more minutes and that appendix would have ruptured."

"Luckier than he knows," Nick Hohlman replied. "Ten minutes sooner, and Welcher would have been the one to cut him open."

"Welcher's strictly day surgery, isn't he?"

"In a perfect world, yes, but we've got two residents off sick, and two other surgeons on vacation."

Meliana watched her patient's breathing as the mask was removed. "Who scheduled that?"

"One's on emergency leave. Dead grandmother, I think. The E.R.'s been backlogged for days. How about some coffee when we're finished?"

She checked the monitors. "Looks good from here." She thanked her assist and the rest of the team. "I love it when an operation goes well."

"You love that Nick remembered to bring your Ella Fitzgerald disk down." One of the other nurses wheeled the instrument tray aside. She grinned under her mask. "Not that I'm complaining. I had two surgeries with Dr. Bergen yesterday. He likes opera. If we hadn't been so understaffed, I'd have developed a stomach bug and gone home to my squabbling kids."

Nick retrieved the disk while Meliana made one last check of the patient. "This guy won't be in recovery long," she predicted. "He looks like a fitness freak to me."

"If he gets a look at you," Nick predicted, "he'll rip his stitches out so you have to do it again."

"You men are so superficial." She removed her gloves and followed the gurney through the swinging door. "I never fell in love with any of the doctors I knew growing up, and two of them were incredibly hot. My mom's chiropractor looked like a soap star."

Nick preened. "I've been told I could model."

"I have some charts to update, Nick. Let's do the coffee thing later, okay?"

"No problem."

He pulled off his cap. White-blond hair spiked up as if by magic. He was what Julie would call a pretty boy. At twenty-eight, he had more peach fuzz on his face than whiskers. His eyes were lake-blue, his features verging on soft, his spiky hair, minus a serious amount of gel, baby fine.

"Mel?"

She turned at the sound of her name, spotted Johnny and felt her amusement kindle. He still had clothes at their town house. He'd dug out fresh jeans and a blue T-shirt that was faded almost to white. His sneakers actually matched today, though she had no idea how he'd managed that.

"I see you found a hairbrush," she said by way of a greeting. "Johnny, have you met Nick? He's one of our best surgical nurses."

"Best nurse works with best doctor. I'm here until seven tonight if you change your mind about that coffee. Nice to meet you, Mr. Maynard."

Neither Meliana nor Johnny corrected him, but Johnny did send the man a speculative look as he walked off. "Does every guy you know have a thing for you, Mel?"

"I doubt if Nick has a thing for any female, Johnny. Rumor is he's gay."

"Don't believe everything you hear, darling. Why is it so cold on this floor?"

"Because the AC system's been acting up, and until yesterday it was eighty-two degrees outside."

"It's sixty-two now and dropping. Did I hear your nurse friend mention coffee?"

Meliana removed her cap. "There's usually a pot in the doctor's lounge. Five's warm, we can go up there." She started for the elevator. "Did you talk to the people in Charlie's apartment block?"

"Running the list, that would be a cat lady named Summer, a guy who makes his own vitamins, a bus driver, a stripper and two old women who've lived in the building since they were twenty."

"Isn't there a man who studies reptiles?"

"He's in New Mexico until Thanksgiving. No sublet. Only the cat lady had anything to tell me, and it wasn't about the writing on my windshield."

"Please don't say one of her cats got run over."

"Went missing." Johnny offered her a smile. "I'm under strict orders as an agent of the government to whom she pays her taxes to keep an eye out for a fur ball named Fluff."

"Did you get a description?"

"I got the hell out of there. She has twenty-seven felines, Mel, in a one-bedroom apartment. Eight of them were abused by their previous owners. They don't like men, and five of them have claws like grizzly bears."

"At least Summer's heart's in the right place." Meliana glanced back along the corridor as the elevator door slid open. "I think Nick took my disk."

"Ella?"

"Her greatest hits."

"Maybe he's planning to return it to you tonight, at home."

"And maybe you're looking for ulterior motives where none exist. Nick's more likely to want you than me."

"Thanks for that."

She pushed five, then patted his cheek. "Take it as a compliment."

"I took the card that was attached to Lokie's collar to the police today, but I'm not holding my breath they'll be able to make anything of it."

"It looked computer generated. Obviously this guy wants to remain anonymous. Would you rather go to my office for coffee?"

"Why? Do I seem uncomfortable here?"

She laughed. "You act in hospitals the way I act around open heights."

"White-knuckled."

She pressed seven. "I want this to be nothing, Johnny. I could've convinced myself it was if I hadn't seen the writing on your windshield last night. He followed us to Charlie's place."

Johnny leaned against the wall while the large elevator worked its way upward. "He was warning me last night, Mel, not you."

"That doesn't make me feel better. And don't say

you're trained to deal with stuff like this. No one's ever really equipped to handle an unstable person. It's like playing dodgeball with a bottle of nitro."

The doors opened. Warm air flooded in and with it the smell of lavender.

"Better than disinfectant," Johnny remarked. "How do you stand it? All the death and sickness and open wounds."

She turned left. "You put it into perspective and remind yourself you're here to help people feel better, to make sure they live instead of die."

"And when they die anyway?"

"Then you try and remember the ones who didn't."

"Sounds like a tall order to me." His brows came together. "Did you change offices?"

"I got a window when Dr. Morrison retired. He left his coffeemaker. It usually works." She regarded him in mild concern as he scanned the desk, the filing cabinet and her new lake view. "I think you should go back to Blue Lake, Johnny. Today. This guy, whoever he is, probably won't do any more than he's already done." She hoped.

"In other words, you think I'll flip out if I stay in Chicago much longer."

"The unofficial recommendation was for you to avoid work-related stress for a while."

"It's been six months, Mel."

"You were undercover for two years." And the eight brief times she'd seen him during that period had shown a marked deterioration, both in his attitude and his demeanor. He'd been less and less Johnny Grand and more and more John Garcia, cold, hard and abusive. Not to her, at least not physically, but in every other way.

"I was…" Johnny began, but Meliana set a finger on his lips and glanced at her pager.

"I have to go to the nurses' station. Coffee's in the cabinet under the machine. I might be a few minutes."

"I'll wait."

He had that stubborn look on his face. She'd seen it too many times to bother arguing. There were other, more effective ways to get around Johnny when he dug in.

"Oh, good, Dr. Maynard, you're here." The desk nurse came to the counter. "Mrs. Lund's been rescheduled for three o'clock. There's a cyst on two that Dr. Hilton wants to go over with you, and this came up an hour ago from Main Reception."

She handed over a padded brown envelope.

"No return address," Meliana noted.

"At least you can figure you're not being sued. Law firms make sure their names are front and center. Anyway, I think this was hand delivered."

Meliana glanced toward her office. Then she thanked the nurse and took the envelope along the hall to the solarium.

There were two patients in wheelchairs enjoying the plants and filtered sunshine. Meliana kept her hand steady as she opened the flap. There was no street name on the mailing label, no stamp or express post tag. Had it come from inside the hospital or out?

Mood music played softly in the background. Several more jarring sounds thrummed in her head.

Her stomach clenched as she removed a pair of silver-white stockings, tied with a white ribbon and topped with a white bow. Attached to the bow was a small white card.

"I'm going to change my favorite color," she murmured, and drew a curious stare from one of the patients.

She turned toward the window, breathed in and read the message.

Accept this token of my love, Meliana
Accept my love.
Accept me.
We are meant to be.

Chapter Three

Johnny returned to Blue Lake late that afternoon. He'd felt something black and ugly pressing in on him, a stream of memories and reactions he was neither prepared to handle nor capable of offsetting.

He needed to breathe, to recenter himself and find his focus. It wasn't so much that he'd lost it—his world since he'd met her had been Meliana—but having been immersed in a seductively evil role for so long, he tended to stray into rather unpleasant areas from time to time.

He phoned Julie as he drove north.

"She's holding something back," he said. "She's a good actress, but I could see it in her body language, in the way she was moving and walking."

"I'll talk to her," Julie promised. "You're only an hour away, Johnny."

"I'll be back tomorrow. I just need a little time to chill and think."

He ended the call and ordered himself to be steady. He could chill out over the past while he thought about the present.

What did this rose guy want from Meliana? How far would he go to get it? Was Meliana in danger?

Johnny frowned, glanced in his rearview mirror. He should have stayed in Chicago, should have taken his wife out for dinner. He could have worked on her until she'd agreed to come to Blue Lake with him.

Easily said in retrospect, not so easily done with Meliana. When she was on call or the hospital was short staffed, a bulldozer couldn't budge her from the city.

The lakeside house was dark when he arrived. He unlocked the door, went in and switched on the first lamp that came to hand. He was heading for the fridge and a cold beer when a pair of headlights slashed across the front window.

Johnny recognized the shape of the cruiser, made it two cans and dropped onto the sofa.

"Door's open, Zack," he said through the screen.

"I took a chance and swung past on my way back from Woodstock." Deputy Zack Crawford caught the beer Johnny tossed him. He looked around the tidier-than-usual main room. "Either Meliana's back, or my mother's been here. I'm guessing my mother."

Johnny rested his head on the cushions. "I'm in trouble. She's started making dinners and freezing them for me."

"She needs someone to fuss over, and I've been out of town a lot lately."

"Business?"

Zack sat on the ottoman and popped his beer. "You could say that. I'm taking a course—paramedic training. I signed up in late spring and still have a fair distance to go, but when I'm done, I'll be able to get out of here and down to the city."

"Why not train to be a cop?"

"Being a deputy's what I fell into, Johnny, not what I wanted. It's all about saving people's lives, right? I'm tired of slapping kids' wrists in the summer and making sure old Harry Riley gets home from the bar in the winter. Just do me a favor, and don't tell my mother."

"She doesn't know?" Johnny took a long drink. "How'd you manage that?"

"I lied."

"Good a way as any, I guess."

Standing, Zack crossed the floor to the large side window. He had a build similar to Johnny's, lean and rangy, with long legs and blond-brown hair. That's where the resemblance ended. Zack's eyes were green and his nose was slightly skewed from a bad break in high school. He brushed his hair back from a cleanly sculpted face, had a quick grin, a bad knee and a small scar on the left side of his jaw.

"What are you looking at?" Johnny asked when Zack peered around the blind.

"Just wondering if you can see Tim Carrick's place from here. Mrs. Wilmot at the post office swears she saw him walking naked in the woods last week."

"Tim's the hairy guy with the beer gut, right?"

"Have you seen him around?"

"Not naked, but yeah, I see him all the time on weekends. He was loading his pickup with old crates last Sunday."

"Strange guy." Zack sipped his beer. "You see him up here, you think he's a hillbilly, right? But he's a salesman during the week. Pharmaceuticals. He walks naked in the woods, glares at everyone he meets, then takes off to the city and pushes his company's pills on anyone who'll listen. It's no wonder his wife left him."

"Was she the woman I used to hear shouting in Spanish?"

"Portuguese. Her name's Vivianne. Meliana knew her. She was half English, half Brazilian. They watched *Wheel of Fortune* sometimes over at Tim's place when Mel came up for the weekend. She took off about a year ago."

"Back to Brazil?"

"Miami, I heard. Tim doesn't talk about her, and most of us are too weirded out by the guy to press. Man, I tell you, I like it here, but I won't be sorry to lose this place. Small-town dynamics and all. You're lucky you're FBI. People hesitate before poking their nose into a federal agent's business." Zack regarded his watch. "Ten-thirty. If I want out, I'd better hit the books."

"Are you on duty tomorrow?"

"Four hours' worth. Phil and I are pulling part-time shifts right now. Sheriff Frank got back from his Shriner's convention in Gary today. I'll catch you later, Johnny. Keep an eye out for Tim."

Just what he needed, Johnny reflected, a nudist neighbor who liked to walk in the woods. A man who no longer lived with his wife. A guy with two different and distinct sides to his personality.

Disgusted with himself, Johnny got off the sofa and

made a circle of the room. He shouldn't be here. He'd given in to a moment of panic and flown. He could handle city life—he'd done it for years. Meliana had urged him to go, he'd felt the pressure building in his head, he'd caved and fled. What a wuss he'd turned into.

He gnawed on the side of his lip, glanced at his jacket, then released a breath and snatched it off the hook. Keys. Where? He searched the room twice, felt his pockets. There was nothing except an old shopping list inside.

He checked the top of the fridge, then his computer desk. He had e-mail, he noticed and gave the mouse a tap.

It wouldn't be Mel. She preferred the phone. And his supervisors in Chicago weren't likely to…

The thought dried up, simply vanished when the message appeared on screen. His blood turned to ice as he read it.

MELIANA'S MINE.
YOU TOUCH HER, YOU DIE.

MELIANA WAS UPSTAIRS in her home office, reviewing the file of a patient scheduled for surgery the next day, when she heard the commotion outside. Her brows went up as she checked her desk clock. Twelve minutes past midnight?

The men's voices grew louder. She recognized them, and for a moment rolled closer to the window to listen.

"Fat lot of help you've been, Grand. You hang around for less than a day, then rush back up to your lakeside retreat so you can bury your head in the sand. If that's your plan of action, you should stay there and leave the dirty work to those of us who can handle it. Man, do you think about anyone but yourself these days? Some creep waltzes in here, plants a flower in your ex's lingerie drawer and steals some of her stuff. The cops shrug their shoulders, you take off and, meanwhile, some sicko's running around with only his crazy brain cells functioning. It's depraved."

"Done yet?" Johnny asked when he ran out of breath. Meliana recognized the tone. She closed her eyes as she heard Chris's muffled "Oomph."

However, knowing Chris as she did, she imagined he'd given Johnny a hard shove or two to punctuate his earlier points.

No matter what he'd been through, Johnny wouldn't use his fists unless he was pushed right to the wall. In the case of Chris Blackburn, that wall might be mere inches from Johnny's back, but he still wouldn't have precipitated a physical fight.

Shannon reached the front door ahead of her. Lokie, who'd been returned to her that evening, lagged behind.

"Coward," she accused, and gave the dog's head a scratch.

Lokie barked and sniffed her hand for a treat as she opened the door.

"Who do you think you are?" Chris demanded, red faced.

He was broader than Johnny and taller by about three inches, yet somehow Johnny's presence always managed to dwarf him. Still, Chris outweighed Johnny by a good forty pounds. In an all-out fight, that could present a problem.

Motioning for the dogs to stay back, Meliana leaned on the doorjamb and regarded the pair of them.

"This is my house, and you're trespassing." Johnny pitched his voice lower than Chris. He wouldn't shout unless it was absolutely necessary. "Go home, Blackburn."

Chris responded by shoving him again. "This is Mel's house. You moved out, remember? She lives here, I live two doors down and you have no business being here."

Meliana caught the gleam in Johnny's dark eyes and cleared her throat. "Don't like to spoil your fun, guys, but you're making a lot of noise for this time of night."

"Andy wears earplugs." Chris shot Johnny a hostile look. "He's the only neighbor within range, and anyone in the park at this time of night doesn't care what we're doing."

"I care."

"Yeah, well, I caught your ex skulking in the bushes."

"He's not my ex," Meliana reminded him. "Johnny has every right to be here, Chris."

Johnny rested his butt on the iron rail. "Nice try, though. Now tell her what you were doing."

Chris's fingers twitched. "I was checking the place for perverts."

"By sitting in the backyard and staring up at her

bedroom window? He was waiting for you to go to bed, Mel," Johnny said with contempt.

Meliana hooked his arm and drew him toward the door. "You're like two kids fighting over a toy. Thanks for the thought, Chris, but I'm fine. You can take off."

The look he sent Johnny smoldered. "I'll hear if she screams."

Meliana held fast to Johnny's arm while Chris stalked away. "Let it go, okay? You copped an assignment he wanted. He resents you for it. Maybe it even scares him a little, seeing how it affected you. He could have been the one who almost got swept under. The outcome might have been worse if it had."

"Blackburn's got a granite skull. He'd have come out of it just fine."

"Now you're flattering him?" Meliana urged the dogs inside and closed the door. "This balled-fist stuff you guys do totally baffles me. Are you friends or not?"

"Not. One guy wants another guy's wife, he's no friend."

"Remove me from the picture. Closer then?"

"Unlikely." Johnny scowled. "Maybe. I don't know. Are you all right?"

"Sure. Why wouldn't I be?"

"No more roses?"

Guilt and a trace of renewed fear trickled in, replacing amusement. "Not so far." She rubbed her palm on the leg of her jeans. "Do you want coffee?"

He hesitated. "You were working, weren't you?"

"Homework for an op tomorrow. I'm clear on the details. Why did you come back?"

"Because I felt like a wimp for leaving."

"You plowed a fist into Chris Blackburn's stomach. I wouldn't call that wimpy."

In the kitchen doorway he stopped, brows raised. "You changed the appliances."

"They were my grandmother's."

"Were?"

Meliana opened the stainless steel fridge. "She died fourteen months ago, Johnny. I was going to tell you when your assignment was done, but—well, I didn't."

Johnny swore, raked a hand through his hair and began to pace. "I liked her."

"I know. There was no funeral, only a memorial service on Maui. She wanted me to have her appliances. They were brand-new, and she knew how much I love to cook."

"Hell." Johnny dropped onto a tall counter stool. "I should have been there."

She pushed two plates, a knife and half a coconut cake into his hands. "Don't beat yourself up over something you can't change. No one expected you to come, least of all me. I knew you were FBI when I married you. Anyway—" she ran a teasing finger along the line of his jaw "—I wasn't alone." His expression went from blank to suspicious so quickly that she laughed. "My brother was there, and Julie flew over with me."

He narrowed his eyes. "You want me to tell you what I'm thinking right now?"

"No." Because he wasn't doing it, she picked up the

knife and sliced into the cake. "But I think I should tell you something."

"Good or bad?"

"You decide." She licked frosting from her thumb. "The rose guy sent me a pair of white stockings, tied with a white ribbon and bow."

Johnny trapped her chin. "It was this afternoon, wasn't it? When you left your office."

"The package was hand delivered, or at least hand placed. No one downstairs remembers receiving it. Reception said it just appeared. Probably true."

His eyes held steady on hers. "Did you give it to Julie?"

"Not yet. I handled everything carefully—not that I think there'll be prints."

"Where's the stuff?"

"Upstairs in my office." She waited a beat, then added. "There was a card."

"Damn it, Mel."

She raised the cake knife. "Don't give me that look. I'm not being stupid, and I'm not taking this lightly. I just wasn't sure if I wanted to tell you first or Julie."

"What did the card say?"

She sighed. "'Accept this token of my love, Meliana. Accept my love. Accept me. We are meant to be.'"

Anger sparked in his eyes. "And you sat on this?"

One thing Johnny Grand had never been able to do was browbeat her. She leaned forward on her elbows and said clearly, "Yes, I did. Make a fuss, and I'll take my cake and leave you here in the dark."

Johnny regarded her for several long seconds, then

made a sound in his throat and reached into his back pocket. "This came for me today while I was here in Chicago. I sourced it to a South Side Internet Café."

Meliana scanned the brief message. It was more malevolent than hers and, as a result, far more frightening.

"He threatened your life." She glanced at the living-room window, visible across the open island. "Why do I think he's serious?"

"Because people like this exist, Mel. Always have, always will."

"Why choose me? And you?"

"Because you're beautiful, bright and talented. And he figures I might be in the way…." He paused, looked away. "I think."

She was quick enough to follow his sudden shift of thought. "This has nothing to do with your work, Johnny. Anyone who might want to hurt you the way you're thinking would simply put a bullet through my head."

"Not everyone uses a simple approach, Mel. One guy I was involved with prefers torture to a shot in the head. His name's Enrique Jago. If something's illegal, he'll take it on. He pimps his own wife to business associates. My contact thought he might have made me near the end."

"Did he?"

"I don't know. I didn't think so, but I could be wrong."

She quashed the tendrils of uneasiness in her stomach. "Why would he send me roses? It's a form of torture, I'll admit, but there are much nastier versions if he's really into it."

"He's different with women."

"In what way?"

Johnny leaned forward, trapped a strand of her hair and brought it to his lips. His lashes shielded his eyes as he replied in flawless Spanish, "To invoke terror in the heart of a woman is to be granted power over her. Total power. The power to choose whether she lives…" Using her hair, Johnny tugged her forward until their lips touched. "Or whether," he whispered against her mouth, "she dies."

The last thing Meliana wanted to do was kiss him. It would get her all tangled up again, and she still wasn't untangled from their separation. But she let herself tumble in because that's how it had always been between them. A quick fall followed by a fiery meltdown.

She opened herself to him, let him explore while she touched him, tasted him, inhaled him—and tried very hard not to let reason sneak in.

He slid a hand into her hair, cupped her head and held her in place while he quite literally ravaged her mouth.

Deep kisses, she thought in a daze. They numbed her mind and sent her emotions spinning out of control. Only Johnny could do this to her. Only Johnny had ever really done anything to her. Only he had ever hurt her.

She wanted to push against his chest, but she didn't rush it. The heat of him made her want to slide in deep and stay there. It wouldn't be a safe or secure place, but it would be exciting. And Meliana lived for excitement. Or she had once.

She pressed her palm to his heart, felt it beating hard

and fast against his ribs. "Johnny, stop," she managed, and drew back. "Just—stop."

He did, with an effort that was visible even to her blurred mind.

He closed those stunning eyes of his and let his head fall forward. "Sorry," he said, then gave a soft laugh and breathed out, "No, I'm not."

In his real life he'd never been much of a liar. Meliana collected what composure she could and stepped away. When she saw the dogs staring at them with lolling tongues, she found her sense of humor and felt a smile work its way across her lips.

"We had to go and complicate a perfectly workable situation, didn't we?"

"I did it, Mel. You just…"

"Tripped and fell against your mouth?"

"If it keeps things level, yeah."

She hesitated a moment, then brushed the hair from his face. "Nothing's ever been level for us, Johnny. Not then or now."

"And we're doing our utmost to see that it stays that way." He flicked a finger between them. "This is why I slept at Andy's last night and will again tonight."

She glanced next door. "He'll love you for waking him at this hour. Andy's sleeping habits tend to follow the sun."

"He got a parking ticket last week. I'll ask Julie to fix it. That'll square us. Can I take the cake?"

She nodded, but stopped him before he could leave. "It wasn't your fault, Johnny."

From the doorway, he regarded her. "Tonight or overall?"

"Both. I don't need to blame you for anything."

"You never did." He sent her a miserable look and wrapped his fingers briefly around the door frame. "But I do."

SHE WOULD KEEP HER BALANCE, Meliana promised herself. She repeated that every time her thoughts strayed into dangerous territory for the next three days.

Johnny hadn't meant to mess with her head, or her emotions, but how could he not when she'd loved him so much it hurt. Still did love him, if she was honest with herself. Always would, no matter how divergent their life patterns became.

He'd worried that she would grow to fear him. Although she never had, she'd glimpsed the violence inside him. They'd fought, bitterly, when he'd returned. Over what, Meliana couldn't say, but at the root of it had been both a lifestyle and an alter ego he'd embraced just a little too fully for a little too long.

Determined not to dwell on that now, she went about her business as usual at the hospital.

She made her rounds, turned the envelope, stockings and card over to Julie, covered the overload in the E.R. and even sat in on one of Charlie's clinics for twenty minutes during an afternoon break.

The man was amazing. She knew serious skeptics who were willing to give his methods a try.

"He's a whacko genius." Julie came up behind

Meliana, who'd paused in the doorway to observe Charlie's newest group. "Do you think he does hypnotism?"

"I doubt it." Meliana swiveled her head. "Are you looking to get hypnotized?"

"No, I'm looking first for you, whom I've found, and second for Sam, who's been complaining of headaches again."

Sam Robbins was Julie's stepbrother, a quiet young man with a talent much more freakish to Meliana's mind than Charlie Lightfoot's. He was one of those rare people who could scan a page in a phone book and memorize it instantly, names and numbers.

"Sam's probably downstairs unloading food trays." Meliana gave Charlie a quick wave before closing the door. "I'll talk to Elizabeth Truman in Neurology. Maybe she can schedule a round of tests. It could be that Sam's brain takes too much in at one time and can't cope with the overload of information. Tell him to stop reading for a while."

"Maybe I'll send him fishing with Johnny up at Blue Lake. No praise intended, and no idea why, but Johnny's really good with Sam. Must be a big-brother thing."

"You're worried about him, aren't you?"

"A little. Don't forget, his father died of a brain aneurysm."

"I'll talk to Liz," Meliana promised. "So what's the deal with the stockings?"

"Zip so far. Whoever this guy is, he's taking all the necessary precautions. Is Johnny still around?"

"He went back to Blue Lake. Broken pipe in the downstairs bathroom. Eileen Crawford found it when she came to clean." She nodded forward. "There's Sam now."

"With an overstuffed cart as usual."

"It's a long way down to Food Services." Meliana grinned. "He's saving himself a trip."

"Sam!" Julie called.

He halted so abruptly he almost rolled the cart into a housekeeping trolley.

"Head in the clouds," Julie muttered.

"Hi, Sam," Meliana greeted. She saw him press his temple under a messy cap of dark curls. "Headache?"

"They come and go." He sent her an affable grin. "Julie says it's all the junk food I eat." The smile faded and he stared at her lab coat. "Your pager's going off."

"It is?" Surprised, Meliana felt her pocket. "I don't hear it."

He regarded her with innocent brown eyes. "That's because it hasn't…"

When the device began to beep, Meliana and Julie both frowned at him.

"It just—came to me," he said and checked the cart for slippage. "I need to get this downstairs. Later, okay?"

Meliana started for the nurses' station. "This is a new thing, right?"

"I have no idea." Julie strode along beside her. "Do you think— He couldn't be, like, psychic or something, could he? I mean, we use psychics from time to time on impossible cases. My captain half believes they're for real."

"That seemed pretty for real to me," Meliana said. "Problem?" she asked the duty nurse.

"You're needed in Emergency, Dr. Maynard. We've got a four-car pileup with injuries."

"On my way. Try not to see it as a burden," she said to Julie as they took the elevator down. "Call it a gift, and let Neurology check him out."

"Yeah, sure. Mel." Julie caught her wrist as the door opened. "I'm only a little spooked about Sam. I'm worried about you. This rose guy could be totally deluded. At the very least he's got a big problem. And you're sitting right at the heart of it."

I'M ANGRY. I've been that way for days now. It's not Meliana's fault, it's her ex-husband's. Except he isn't her ex yet, which is partly why I'm angry.

I warned him to stay away from her. He didn't listen. I'm going to make him listen.

Meliana will understand. She has to. I don't know why she lets him into her house. It's her house, not his, not anymore. They're finished. Meliana's mine now. My dream will come true.

I won't let him come back into her life. I hope she understands that. I can't believe she'd want him back.

I think I might have to hurt him.

Chapter Four

"I've heard about Blue Lake." Nick followed Meliana out of the O.R., whipped off his cap and held her Ella Fitzgerald disk up between two fingers. "I burned this a couple nights ago, along with Coldplay and Janice Joplin."

"That's quite the combo, Nick."

"I have eclectic taste. But actually, I did Janice for Dr. Lightfoot. That's why I mentioned Blue Lake. Word is, he's thinking of buying a retreat outside the city, and he knows you have one there."

"Bit of a story attached to that, but yes, I do."

"Can I ask you a personal question?"

"Sure." She slid her gaze sideways. "I might not answer it, though."

"Are you and your husband together or separated?"

It hurt more than it should by now. "We're not together, Nick."

He beamed. "That's twenty bucks to me."

Meliana wasn't surprised. Bets based on gossip

flowed more freely around the hospital than tap water. "Who's the loser?"

"A guy in Administration. So—I'm having a wine-tasting party next weekend. You're invited. I plan to cover California, France, Italy and Australia."

"If I'm off the duty roster, I'll think about it." She paused outside her office. "Do you know Sam Robbins?"

"Only through you."

"Have you ever sat and talked to him?"

"Once or twice. He seems a bit Forrest Gump–like to me, but I know he shot through business administration in college."

"He'll be running Food Services in a few years," Meliana predicted, "whether officially or not."

"Do you want me to invite him to my party?"

"I want to know what it is about him that makes his memory so instantaneous and so incredible."

"Ah, you'd like me to ask my grandfather what the deal is with someone like him." Nick tugged on his spiky hair to straighten it. "No problem, but I'm not sure, even with all the studies he's done on the human brain, that Granddad will have an answer for you. Sometimes life just throws people a weird curve. Like Dr. Lightfoot and his touchy-feely stuff. Granddad thinks Lightfoot's a quack. But I'll ask about the memory thing for you. Next Saturday night, okay?"

"I'll do my best."

They parted company at the elevator. Inside, Meliana checked her watch. It was after seven. She'd been working steadily since 9:00 a.m. She could handle that.

However, she hadn't been able to reach Johnny at Blue Lake since yesterday, and that was a worry.

She could call Eileen or Zack or even the sheriff, but if he was simply looking for down time, Johnny wouldn't appreciate being monitored.

She mulled it over and decided to try one more time. In her office she picked up the phone and punched his number. Twenty rings later, she stared at the handset and sighed. "Where the hell are you, Grand?" Vexed with herself more than him, she skirted her desk. "Why do you care, Meliana? Separated, remember? Time to let go."

Her chair was rolled partway out, angled toward her computer. She swung it around, then hissed in a breath and took a quick backward step.

A single white rose lay crosswise on the seat.

SHE MADE IT TO THE HOUSE at Blue Lake before 9:00 p.m. Only one light burned inside, a lamp on a table next to the front door. Meliana considered, then knocked. "Johnny?"

There was no answer. At her side, Lokie and Shannon barked.

She tried again, louder. "Johnny, are you here?"

"Yes, I'm here."

His voice came from behind her, and she spun. Whatever she'd planned to say dissolved in her throat. He was covered with mud and grease, he had a rag wrapped around his right hand and he looked thoroughly out of sorts.

It had to be the expression on his face that caused her lips to twitch. "Problem?" she asked in her most ingenuous tone.

The look he sent her had a decided bite. "Where do you want me to start? With my truck, the gusher in the toilet, or the fire?"

"Fire?" She grabbed the dogs' collars to keep them from jumping on him. She sniffed, but smelled nothing except trees and lake water. "Where?"

"In the shed."

She glanced around his arm. "It looks fine from here."

"Check out the far side, Mel. It's toast."

She kept a firm hold on the dogs. "How did it start?"

"Local fire chief's gonna let me know that when he figures it out, which should be by next Easter. Until then, I'm guessing arson."

Something twisted in her stomach. "Arson's a pretty drastic conclusion, Johnny. It could've been someone smoking in the woods."

"It could also have been a gas bomb."

"Right." Meliana gave up. "What happened to your truck?"

"Two flat tires, with only one spare to replace them. And it wouldn't start."

"Someone got under the hood."

"Unless a squirrel made off with three of my spark plugs and disabled the carburetor."

Meliana pushed both dogs to a sitting position. They wanted to hunt the bullfrogs that were croaking in the reeds by the lake. "Stay," she ordered and had to trust that Lokie would follow Shannon's lead. "This day's really not improving. What about the gushing toilet?"

Johnny blew at the hair in his eyes. "That could have

happened on its own. The plumber who fixed the broken water pipe Eileen discovered also runs Eddy's Spaghetti House. He had a party of twenty booked in for dinner last night. I sensed his mind was on his meat sauce while he was here. He capped the geyser and told me to use the upstairs bathroom until he can get a better look at the problem."

"Right. Fire, spark plugs, toilet. Now tell me why your answering machine and cell are turned off? I've been calling since last night. I even e-mailed you this afternoon."

He rubbed his grimy hands in distaste. "My cell's dead, Eileen moved the answering machine so I walked through the cord and tore it out of the wall, and you never use e-mail to contact me so I tend not to check it. I called you twice at the hospital today. Despite the usual runaround, I got the impression you were in surgery pretty much nonstop. That meant you were okay, so I didn't leave a message." Concern crept in as he cocked his head to survey her. "Did something happen after my last call? Has Chris…?"

She waved him off. "Nothing like that. Chris is out of town until Monday."

"Some hero."

"I don't need a hero, Johnny."

He took a step toward her, a dangerous step, to her way of thinking.

"I got another rose," she told him. "At the hospital, in my office. Sometime between four and seven this evening."

His head fell back, and he gave a humorless laugh. "Not in tune with the cosmos at all, are we?"

"I thought you didn't believe in that sort of thing."

"What I don't believe is how easily this guy slips in and out of your world. Home, office, car. No one sees him...." He stopped. "No one saw him, right?"

"I asked all around the seventh floor. No one noticed anything unusual."

"So either he's ridiculously lucky or he sees all and knows exactly when to leave his goodies. Or steal them, as the case may be."

For the first time, Meliana detected the smell of scorched wood. Her gaze traveled around the open yard to the shed. "You think the rose guy burned the shed and disabled your truck, don't you?"

"I think it's very likely."

"So do I." The knots in her stomach tightened. "He's watching me, Johnny, and he doesn't like you. You need to stay here, and let Julie do what she can in Chicago."

"I know cops, Mel." He closed in on her, but was thankfully too dirty to touch. "Julie's a cog in a big regulation wheel. She won't be able to do much, no matter how good her intentions. Flowers and petty theft don't amount to a great deal in the eyes of the police."

"Julie's a friend."

"I'm your husband."

She lifted her hair from her neck so the lake air could reach her skin. "We're separated, Johnny, and you're not supposed to be involved in any kind of investigation right now. On a more dangerous note, you're also supposed to be discreet about any action you undertake, in case someone you were involved with as John Garcia did happen to make you."

He used a knuckle to tip her chin up. "You've been talking to Blackburn, haven't you?"

"Not about you." She let her hair fall. "I watched you change over time, from the man I married to a man I stopped recognizing as my husband. I didn't grow up in a bubble, Johnny. I've seen people get sucked into bad situations. With you, I saw an evolution. It wasn't healthy, and it certainly wasn't pretty. You seem so much better these days. I don't want you to slide backward."

"I won't."

"You could. John Garcia's a part of you now. You created a persona, and for two years it became your reality. You lived it, breathed it, worked it. When they pulled you out, the FBI considered putting you in a witness protection program. They would have if you hadn't been so adamant that your cover hadn't been blown."

"I didn't think it had."

"But now you're not sure. Enrique Jago might be out there looking for revenge. And what would he do? He'd stalk me. He'd distract you. He'd make you look in my direction when really it's you he wants."

Johnny lowered his lashes. He was silent for a moment. Then, with his mouth mere inches from hers, he said, "This stuff's coming off the top of your head, isn't it?"

Absurd amusement rose in her throat. It had to be his delivery coupled with his speculative expression. He'd always been able to make her laugh at the most inappropriate moments.

"This isn't funny, Johnny." Although she had invented most of what she'd said on the fly. Suddenly, though, she couldn't remember why or think of anything other than the fact that she wanted to jump him.

The knuckle under her chin slid along her jaw until all of Johnny's fingers were wrapped around her neck. "Tell me again how I get sucked into bad situations."

She felt a shiver work its way upward from her belly. "You're the worst possible situation for me, Johnny. We agreed on that six months ago."

His lips grazed hers. "And your point is?"

Impulse kicked in. Knocking reason aside, Meliana grabbed him by the front of his shirt and yanked him against her. "I hate you, Johnny Grand."

"Me, too," he said and, angling his mouth over hers, began to devour.

SHE WOULD HAVE GONE UP to the loft bedroom with him, and he would have taken her there in a second, but both dogs began to bark, and the headlights that swept over them preceded the blast of a horn.

"Okay, you two, knock it off," Julie called out the car window. "You've got visitors, and one of them had her most recent date interrupted by a friend whose underwear got scoffed."

Johnny hated to think what he'd have done at that moment had his other persona been in place. But he was

Johnny Grand, making out with his wife in the front yard of their summer home. A snarl was the nastiest reaction he could manage, and only Meliana heard it.

He saw her silvery eyes twinkle as she whacked his hands away. "He got me all dirty," she said to Julie, then added a softer "Though I could have handled getting a lot dirtier" for him.

Johnny ground his teeth. He was grateful he'd worn loose-fitting pants. He swung to face the car, saw two doors open and scowled. "What are you doing here, Lightfoot?"

"Don't sweat it. I bumped into Julie at the hospital after Mel left. We got to talking about roses, silk stockings and e-mail threats, so I tagged along."

Meliana gave Charlie's cheek a peck. "Are you going to feel out Johnny's computer?"

"It'd be a first. As it happens, I'm also on the lookout for somewhere to hold a series of clinics I'm having, examining the effects of a tranquil environment on the super-stressed mind."

"Already been done a hundred times," Johnny said.

Charlie tapped his temple. "Not my way, it hasn't. Any ideas for a group of, say, fifteen, Mel?"

"There's the Blue Lake Inn or Reddings on the Lake—that's a motel. Or you could rent a house. Lots of people here own large properties that they rent out in the off-season. That'd be about now, actually."

"Sounds good." Charlie nodded past her. "Why's Johnny all dirty?"

Julie lifted her head. "I smell burned wood."

Johnny started forward. "It's been a long day. I'll close up my truck. Mel can explain."

"Mel can tell them what happened," Meliana agreed. "She can't really explain." She pushed the dogs toward the house. "I'll make coffee, Charlie, and show you the computer while Johnny cleans up."

"I'll make coffee," Johnny mimicked, heading for his truck. "We'll have a party. Charlie can feel up Johnny's computer. Oh, hell," he swore as another set of headlights bounced along the road toward him. "Why not invite everyone we know."

Zack braked and climbed out. "You look as ticked as I feel." He wiped his hands on an old towel.

"You look dirtier than me," Johnny countered. He slammed the hood of his truck. "Is there a problem in town?"

"Five vehicles got rolled into Stokes' Bog last night. Phil and I have been there since dawn helping to haul them out. We managed four, the fifth's stuck on something. And you wonder why I'd rather be a paramedic. How's your busted pipe?"

"Capped." Because he didn't feel like picking them up and it wasn't supposed to rain, Johnny kicked his tools under the SUV.

Zack leaned on the top of his car door. "Sounds like you've had a lousy day, too. I was hoping for a beer."

Johnny had been hoping for a whole lot more than that. "Mel's here." He searched his pockets for his keys. "And some friends from the city."

"Rain check, then." Zack raised a hand at Meliana,

who'd come onto the porch. "How are things?" he called out.

"Busy," she called back.

Julie appeared behind her. Johnny saw the poke she gave Meliana, and the action eased his foul mood. "You might as well come in, Zack, and save Mel the trouble of persuading you."

"Hey, I don't mind being persuaded. Who's the blonde?"

"Julie Denton. City cop. Not married."

"My mother'll be pleased to hear it." Zack whipped down the towel he'd draped over one grimy shoulder and tossed it into the cruiser. "I figured this day had to improve at some point."

"You'd think so, wouldn't you?" Johnny agreed. Then groaned as the house, indeed the entire lakefront yard, went black.

THE POWER FAILURE LASTED fifteen minutes. Meliana and Charlie sat cross-legged on the sofa and by candlelight watched the other three argue about the source of the problem.

Johnny assumed it was the breaker box, the obvious choice. Zack figured the outage might involve the whole lakefront area, and Julie mentioned the word *sabotage*.

Fortunately, a minute after that word left Julie's mouth, the lights popped on. The music Meliana had been playing resumed and the ceiling fan began to grind.

"You like blackouts, don't you?" Charlie asked while

the mini-hubbub continued around them. "I bet you're a fan of old horror movies."

"I like suspense," Meliana agreed. "Psychological terror as opposed to blood and gore."

"Yeah, she sees guts being spilled every day," Johnny put in from the kitchen.

"He'd have passed out if we hadn't tranquilized him when he was shot." Meliana spoke just loud enough for Johnny to hear.

"That's right, you operated on him, didn't you?" Charlie shed his jacket as the heater kicked in again.

Meliana's eyes sparkled. "I was a resident, overworked and exhausted. It was 2:00 a.m. We heard a cop—sorry, FBI agent—had been shot. No one knew how bad it was. I'd just finished stitching up a knife wound, so I was it."

"I wouldn't have passed out." Johnny handed Charlie and Zack a beer, Julie a hard lemonade and Meliana the soft one she'd requested. Someone had to drive the others home—apparently.

"He threatened to faint like a girl." Meliana moved her glass in a triangle between Zack, Julie and Charlie. "Have you all met?"

Julie hit the sexy button, smiled and shook her hair. "Zack and I introduced ourselves."

"And I met Zack last year," Charlie said. "I followed your neighbor up here one day after Christmas. Read him the riot act over doling out samples of his company's pills to anyone who stuck out his or her hand."

"Tim Carrick gives sample medications to patients?"

Meliana swirled her lemonade while she digested that. "I should be surprised, but I'm not. I imagine he figures if they like what he's offering, they'll ask their doctors to prescribe it. Or is he looking to make private deals?"

"He's not that stupid," Zack said. "He doesn't give out samples as such. According to Tim, some thief lifted a bunch of boxes and other containers from his case one time when he was in Chicago."

"A generous thief, who distributed the packets to anyone he felt needed them." Charlie shook his head. "Carrick did the deed anonymously, knowing his company's name was on the label, but my guess is the order to do it came from a higher source within said company. Either that or he's an out-and-out dealer."

"Did you mention any of this to the chief of staff?" Meliana asked.

Charlie chuckled. "Every time I see him, although lately I've noticed he tends to dart down side corridors whenever our paths threaten to converge."

Zack perched on the arm of Julie's chair. "What got Charlie hot was that some poor woman wound up taking an unprescribed handful of antidepressants."

"They were far stronger than anything she needed." Charlie made circles in front of his headband. "She was in la-la land for three days. Her husband thought I'd set the dosage, so he called me. It took ninety minutes of questioning for me to figure out that she got the pills from the source—that being good old Tim. I tracked Carrick to his home, couldn't find him, went to the sheriff's office." Charlie chuckled. "The sheriff was having ants exterminated from the jail cells, so he told Zack to deal with it."

"Sounds like Sheriff Frank. He likes to delegate," Meliana added in a stage whisper to Julie.

"He's retiring next year." Zack arched a brow in Julie's direction. "If you're looking to get out of the rat race, Blue Lake's going to need a new sheriff, and neither Phil nor I are in the running."

Meliana rested her head on the sofa cushions. "Why not?"

"Because Phil's too lazy, and I want out."

Julie smiled. "Just don't plan on leaving too quickly, okay?"

Meliana smiled at her friend's come-on. She didn't use it very often, which meant she liked what she saw.

While Charlie examined Johnny's recent e-mail and Julie and Zack took turns flirting with each other, Meliana wandered over to join Johnny in the kitchen.

"What do you think?" She angled her head at the burgeoning twosome. "Good fit or bad?"

"I give it till Christmas—unless Eileen pushes too hard and sends them flying off in opposite directions."

"She means well."

"So did my mother."

"Both your mother and your father asked me to date you before you did."

"I was in pain."

"There's no pain after one of my operations. You were embarrassed because you knew I'd seen your reaction to all the blood."

"I thought I was going to die."

"I told you you weren't."

"And I figured, what does a kid—a beautiful kid, I'll admit, but still a kid—know about gunshot wounds? I thought the E.R. was so backed up they were down to letting first-year med students loose with carving knives."

"Scalpels. And you hassled me so much, I considered stitching your mouth shut before we started."

"Yeah, right. I—" He broke off, bent low and stared through the kitchen window.

"What?"

"Someone's out there."

Her breath stalled. "Are you sure it's a person, and not a bear?"

"Not unless the animals have started wearing plaid jackets."

She leaned over him, but saw nothing except black trees. "It could have been a kid."

"One with a pipe bomb. Or a white rose." He straightened, set his hands on her arms. "I want you to stay here and keep the party going."

"No."

"Mel…"

"Lady said no, Johnny." Charlie strolled in and winked at Meliana. "I've never known her to change her mind."

"Someone's outside," Meliana told him.

"Where?" Zack and Julie joined them.

Johnny rolled his eyes. "In the trees near the shed. Maybe we should all go out and look, make lots of noise, give him a good head start."

"Or maybe," Julie suggested, "we should dispatch ourselves one by one and see if we can surround him."

"Was it Tim?" Zack asked.

"This guy wasn't naked."

Meliana pictured their hairy neighbor. "Good so far," she remarked.

Charlie was already at the back door. "I'll go this way."

"I'll take the side entrance." Johnny motioned Zack to the front.

They crept out in unison.

Julie retrieved her gun from her purse. She checked the cartridge. "I was really hoping to catch a break tonight, but no such luck, it seems."

"Bad day?"

"Not personally, but a patrolman I know found a woman in a downtown alley under the El. Someone strangled her with a scarf, then dumped her behind a bunch of garbage cans. I saw the pictures. She was a graphic designer, really pretty, late twenties, pale blond hair. It always shakes me up when I see something like that. I thought coming up here would be therapeutic, and I have to admit it started out that way. I mean, Zack is awfully easy on the eyes."

"Mmm, awfully. Speaking of which..." Meliana glanced at Julie's gun. "Johnny's got excellent distance vision. There probably is someone out there. So why—" she secured her hair with an elastic band "—are we still in here?"

They left by the kitchen door. Nothing and no one moved, not even the tallest branches. Water lapped the shore and the small boat dock. Insects sang and the frogs continued to croak, but beyond that there was little sound.

Meliana let Julie pass her. She had the gun, after all. But then she heard a leaf crunch and she halted. "Julie," she whispered.

No answer.

She crouched, breathed carefully, concentrated. She heard a movement to her left, someone passing through the bushes.

She should have brought a knife, she realized. She breathed carefully, kept still, forced herself to remain calm. Her heart was slamming so hard she felt certain whoever was there would hear it. Or she'd sneeze and give herself away.

She searched the darkened ground for a weapon. A stone was the best she could find, but she had a good throwing arm. She could inflict damage in a struggle.

She'd lost Julie, had no idea where Johnny was and didn't want to move yet in case the flower guy—it had to be him, didn't it?—was waiting to pounce.

Why?

Because he'd followed her up here. It was possible. But would he go that far to watch her? Why not? He'd done a number of other bizarre things. Like stealing her underwear…

She waited a full thirty seconds. The frogs seemed to croak louder with each second that passed. She glanced at the house and hoped she'd latched the door so the dogs couldn't get out.

The sound of rustling bushes reached her again. Someone was directly behind her. Still in a crouch, Meliana spun. As she did, a man's arm wrapped itself around her shoulders and a hand came down over her mouth.

Chapter Five

Panic leaped into Meliana's throat—and vanished a split second later. She bit the hand over her mouth and would have taken a swing at the face behind it if she'd been able to maneuver herself around.

"That's ten years gone, Johnny." She settled for plunging her elbows into his ribs and went from a crouch to her knees to face him.

He nursed the side of his wounded hand. "You have a wicked bite, Mel. I didn't want you to scream."

"I never scream." She brushed bark and leaves from her jeans. "Did you find him?"

"I found these." He dangled a pair of bubblegum-pink panties in front of her. "I'm thinking they're not yours."

There was a teddy bear embossed on the front and a skinny strip of lace around the waistband. "They might have been when I was ten. Where did you find them?"

"Behind the shed, on that patch of grass by the rock wall."

"Secluded spot. Pink panties. Says teenagers to me." Relief lightened her mood and had her looking around the small clearing. It was beautiful in northern Illinois, peaceful, rural and visceral. The seasons were well defined in this part of the country. You knew when the slide from summer to autumn began and when autumn dipped into winter. For someone who'd spent much of her childhood in Hawaii, the natural shifts were breathtaking.

She picked up a leaf and twirled it. "I'd miss this if I left here."

On his feet and squinting into the darkness for the others, Johnny swung back. She glimpsed shock in his features before he masked it. "Are you thinking of leaving?"

"No, but opportunities come up from time to time. I was offered a position in Dallas several months ago."

"Why did you turn it down?"

She couldn't bring herself to tell him the truth, so she shrugged. "Because I realized you were nearing the end of your assignment—and I like Chicago. I like the Great Lakes. You love it here. It felt wrong."

They heard branches cracking, followed by a young man's voice.

"We weren't hurting anyone, Zack. We're both seventeen. That's old enough for you to butt out."

Two teenagers appeared between the trees. Zack and Julie followed. "Your intruders," Zack remarked.

"No plaid jacket," Johnny murmured. He raised his voice. "Did either of you see anyone near my house a few minutes ago?"

"We were kinda busy, man," the boy retorted.

The girl gave him a hesitant look. "I think I saw someone." When the boy glared at her, she lifted her chin. "Well, I did, and I'm gonna tell Deputy Zack. There was a man. He was wearing a black knit cap and a plaid coat. He had a shovel or a stick or something in his hand. I saw him go past us. I thought he might be heading for your place." She smiled at Johnny. "But like Troy said, we were kinda busy."

Meliana looked around. "Where's Charlie?"

"Yo, over here." A panting Charlie Lightfoot was bent double at the far edge of the clearing. "I got a funny flash and circled back to the house. It was fine, dogs were barking at each other. No flames," he said to Johnny.

"But," Meliana prompted.

"The two vehicles that were parked near the lake—that would be Zack's cruiser and Johnny's truck—are, as we speak, floating in it."

IT WAS BEDLAM, and Meliana was in the thick of it. Zack thought the culprits must be the same ones who'd rolled five other cars into Stokes' Bog the previous night. Johnny wondered about Tim Carrick. The kids just wanted to leave.

"Let's call it a full-moon syndrome come early and send for a tow truck," Meliana suggested.

"It's punks," Julie said, then reached into her bag for her ringing cell. "I see it all the time in Chicago." A moment later she was whirling away, firing questions at the person on the other end.

"Sam's been hurt," she said when she punched off.

"He was up on seven at the hospital, checking supplies in the food cupboards, and someone jumped him. His wrist's been sprained." She jabbed a finger into Meliana's arm. "He was in the lounge next to your office."

THIS HAD TO BE the strangest night of her life, Meliana reflected ninety minutes later. Cars in the lake, kids in the clearing, Julie's stepbrother with a sprained wrist and no idea who'd attacked him in the lounge.

"I didn't see anything," Sam told Johnny, who'd returned to the city with them. "One minute I was counting cream containers, the next I was lying half in, half out of the cupboard." He blinked baffled eyes. "I heard footsteps, slow and steady, like a metronome, but that's all."

"Did you check your office, Mel?"

"There's nothing out of place." Or in place where it shouldn't be, she reflected gratefully. "Sam's gone over this several times, Johnny. I think you should let Julie take him home. You can talk to him again tomorrow."

"Yeah, sure." He gave Sam's shoulder an affectionate slap. "Take it easy, slugger."

Sam grinned. "You, too."

"Food," Meliana said before Johnny could open his mouth. "I'm hungry, you look beat and there's nothing more we can do, either here or at Blue Lake. Zack's dealing with the vehicles, and Charlie's gone home to mull over his Blue Lake clinic options. What do you say to Cantonese on the beach?"

"I say you're forgetting what state we're in. This

isn't luau weather, Mel. There's heavy fog on the lake, and the needle's dropped below fifty-five degrees."

"Wimp," she teased. "Let's do Addifah's, then. It's dark and exotic, and it suits the fog."

It took them half an hour to reach the South Side restaurant. At 1:00 a.m. and with an early morning under her belt, Meliana knew she should be dead tired, but she felt oddly revved, no doubt due to all the excitement and the uncertainty surrounding it.

Because she wasn't on duty for the next two days, she ordered an ouzo and settled cross-legged on a large floor cushion.

"What did you think about the kids?" Johnny picked at the herbed bread.

"The boy was annoyed, the girl was embarrassed. That's normal. The guy in plaid with the shovel was interesting. I suppose he might have been digging for truffles."

"Yeah, right. You don't think he might have rolled two vehicles into the lake instead?"

"Yours couldn't have been fun with two flat tires."

"The property slopes downward from where it was parked. It would have rolled easily enough."

"What about Sam?"

Johnny toyed with his glass. "That bothers me. He could have been hurt, and we have no idea why. There was no flower, no gift, no card. So did the rose guy whack Sam, or was he up at Blue Lake, or neither?"

"I like my full moon theory best."

"That's because you were born during one."

"I was born during a blue moon, a rather rare occurrence."

"For a rather rare woman."

She held up a warning finger. "Don't you dare try to charm me, Johnny Grand. I'm too jumpy to fight it."

"Sounds like a golden opportunity. Wanna dance?"

"This music's for belly dancing."

"I'm game—but we don't have to do a belly dance just because the music says we should."

"Were you born contrary, Johnny, or did that trait develop later in life?"

"I was nothing but trouble growing up. When I wasn't pretending to be James Bond, I was fighting duels or squaring off with a black hat at high noon. Come on."

He took her hand and drew her to her feet. Since the kebabs and rice they'd ordered would probably take a while, Meliana let him coax her onto the small tiled floor. Two men in fedoras and a single elderly woman watched them.

"You're all wound up, Mel." Johnny's fingers kneaded the muscles in her neck. "Relax, okay? Forget tonight."

"Like you're going to?"

"Solving problems is part of my job. Yours is sewing people back together."

"Like Dr. Frankenstein." Johnny had wonderful hands. Meliana wanted to purr, but stopped when a thought struck her.

"Maybe it's someone I operated on. White could be considered a clinical color..."

"It *is* a clinical color...."

"Only the stark version. There are plenty of warmer shades. White rose, white stockings, white ribbon, white dog. What if it's all hospital related?"

Johnny pulled her closer and continued to knead. "It'd be worth a check of your patient files."

"I did some work up at Blue Lake while you were undercover. No operations, but a lot of patching up at the clinic whenever I was in town."

"Do they keep computer lists of patients there?"

"I saw a computer. It looked old. But they'll have some kind of filing system…. What are you doing?" His mouth was almost on hers. The scent of his skin and hair was already making her crazy. "Johnny…"

He swallowed the rest of her objection. Except it wasn't really an objection so much as a token murmur.

He ate her up, body and soul. She couldn't think straight when he kissed her. First there was sensation, a fierce kind of hunger, followed by a desperate need for more.

His tongue dipped and sampled and explored. She savored every moment, every new touch. She breathed him in and let her hands slide downward, over his chest to his waistband.

She almost forgot where they were. The music had a mystical quality that made her want to gyrate. She moved her lower body in a slow, seductive rhythm against him until he hissed in a breath and dragged his mouth away.

"Not fair, Mel."

Her heart was racing, she could barely breathe. Her fingers were on his fly. They were in a public place.

Did she care?

A smile stole across her lips. "You started it, Grand," she said into his mouth. Then she took pity on him and eased back. "You know how much I love erotic music, and belly dancing isn't so far removed from hula."

In fact, she had no idea if the two were connected or not—unlikely—but the clouds in his face began to clear at her humorous tone.

She felt a tug of sadness. Poor Johnny. He'd lost more than his direction on the streets. He'd forgotten how to have fun.

He still seemed a little shell-shocked, so she took his hand and led him back to their low table.

When he sat cross-legged on the floor, as was the custom at Addifah's, he shot her a look that spoke volumes about his physical state.

Meliana leaned forward on her elbows. "Take your own advice, sweetheart, and loosen up. Things might not be as dire as they seem where this rose guy's concerned."

"My truck's in the lake, Mel. So's Zack's cruiser."

"Five other vehicles are in Stokes' Bog."

"And Sam?"

"He could have slipped and simply thought he'd been pushed."

Their food arrived, a variety of colorful and aromatic platters. "You really believe that?" he asked when the server left.

"Why hurt Sam?" she countered.

"You said he had a premonition about you being paged."

"And you think the rose guy feels threatened by that? First of all, how would he even know about it? And second, one snippet of foresight is hardly proof positive of ESP."

"Sam's a little off the map, Mel. A nice kid, but behind that affable facade is an unusual brain. That's not my point, though. Sam could simply have been in the way, as you said."

"You mean the guy wanted to get into my office and Sam was working next door. Fine, but there was no rose in my office."

"Maybe Sam's being there threw your admirer off."

"Maybe, possibly, might have, could have—there's nothing concrete in any of this, Johnny. It's all speculation and conjecture." She worked a tomato off the skewer. "Anyway, if there is a psychic threat involved, it would come from Charlie, not Sam." She stopped the tomato halfway to her mouth. "You don't think Charlie's in danger, do you?"

"Lightfoot can take care of himself. You're the one I'm worried about."

Meliana used her fingers to dip into the rice bowl. "Put a knife in my hands and watch me defend myself."

He sampled a chunk of lamb from her skewer. "That'd work for a frontal attack, but what if he blindsided you?"

"He could only do that if he was someone I thought I could trust."

"Exactly." His eyes met hers and held fast. "So where did Chris Blackburn go, and when does he get back?"

CLICK, CLICK, CLICK.

Mad, mad, mad.

They're together. I saw them. They kissed. She touched him. This is bad.

Meliana, you didn't fight him off. Why not? You didn't even struggle. You kissed him back.

I don't know what to think, but I know I need to be calm. They didn't see me because I wasn't supposed to be there. They can't know who I am. They have their guesses, but they don't know.

I'm going to think this through.

I'm going to do something about it.

MELIANA DECIDED TO WORK Sunday. That allowed Johnny to return to Blue Lake and gave her the distraction she needed from the upheaval around her.

Sam was fine, taped up and back on the job by Monday. Johnny's SUV and Zack's cruiser were extricated from the lake. No more roses or other gifts appeared. By the following Thursday, she'd fallen back into her regular work groove, with only thoughts of Johnny to disturb her.

She went for dinner with Julie, turned down two movie invitations from Chris, jogged in the park during daylight hours and survived a baby shower for a friend and coworker.

The shower tapped her out emotionally. When she got home she changed and, with Shannon and Lokie beside her, went for a short run through the neighborhood.

It started to rain before she got back. Perfect, she

thought with a glance at the starless night sky. Now she'd have wet dogs running all over her cream carpets and hardwood floors.

"Mel!"

She was so absorbed in her thoughts that she almost tripped.

"Hey, whoa. You okay?" Chris caught her from behind. He was wet and breathing hard. From a thirty-second sprint to catch her?

She shook her head as she bounced in place. "Pretty feeble, Blackburn. I thought you FBI types could run mini marathons without getting winded."

He sucked in air. "Depends which branch you're attached to. I do a lot of desk work these days, and bench-pressing weights doesn't improve stamina."

The rain, which had been a gentle patter for several minutes, began to stream down.

"Can we go inside?" he shouted above the deluge.

Nodding, Meliana and the dogs jogged up the walk to the front door. She was inside and out of her sneakers by the time Chris arrived.

"Stay," she ordered Lokie.

Shannon had already plopped down in the corner. She eyed Chris, but made no move to jump on him. She was Johnny's dog, all right.

Lokie barked once, yawned and settled in beside her new canine companion.

Meliana found towels in the closet and, still grinning at Chris's lack of stamina, began rubbing Lokie's fur.

The ends of Chris's hair dripped on the floor as he

squatted down. "I hear you and Johnny hung out a lot last week."

Now, who had he heard that from? Meliana raised a questioning brow.

He lowered his eyes. "I talked to Julie about your lingerie thief. I had to pry information out of her, but it sounds to me like one, your thief and admirer is more than just nuts and two, you and Johnny have been getting pretty cozy since all this stuff started."

He brought his eyes up for the last part of his statement, and the implication in them halted Meliana mid-fluff.

"You can't be serious." She stared at him, half amused, half astounded. "You think Johnny's behind this?"

"He wants you back."

"That's irrelevant. He's Johnny. You know, your ex-partner, Johnny, who saved your butt more than once."

"Not as often as I saved his."

"You're being stupid, Chris. Johnny's—" She searched for the right words, then settled for "—Johnny."

"He *was* Johnny. He was also John Garcia, a man deep into serious drug cartels for two years. He got way down inside, Mel, farther than anyone expected. You go that far down, you don't surface without major scars."

"I've seen the scars, Chris."

"Some of them, sure, but who's to say there aren't more than anyone knows about, more than he'll admit. Are you going to tell me he hasn't been acting a little weird around you since this rose thing started?"

"I'm not going to tell you anything."

"You got Lokie six months ago, right?"

"So?"

"That's how long you've been split up." He cocked a thumb toward the door. "Johnny walks out, you dust off your hands. It's over. Then, bam, a dog appears."

Exasperated, Meliana wiped Lokie's paws. "You're crazy, do you know that? Not to mention delusional. Johnny and I were together for two years. There's no way he'd do any of this freaky stuff, no matter how deep he went undercover."

"So why did you split up?"

"None of your business. Your turn, Shannon."

The dog's tail swished. She kept her dark eyes on Chris and growled when he reached out to touch Meliana's arm.

Meliana offered him a smile. "She's a good guard dog. That's why Johnny left her with me. Come on girl, up."

Shannon obeyed, but barked as she did so. Meliana started to dry her fur, then noticed the large white envelope the dog had been lying on and paused. "Ahh."

"What, ah? You think because—" Chris spotted the envelope and broke off. "What's that?"

Did she want to know? She picked it up and regarded the label. "It wasn't mailed."

Chris glanced at the door behind him. "Someone must have shoved it through the slot."

"Yeah, right." She braced and tore open the flap.

There were pictures inside, eight-by-ten photographs, six of them. She didn't touch, but shook them onto a dry patch of floor.

"What the hell…?" Chris bent over with her. "When were these taken?"

He sounded more angry than shocked. Meliana sat back on her heels. "Recently. At Addifah's."

"You were doing that at Addifah's?"

"We were…" As she nudged aside the first five photos to reveal the last shot in the series, all her muscles, including her vocal cords, seized.

Chris leaned forward. "Half of this shot is whited out," he said. "I see you, but there's no Johnny."

"No," she echoed. "No Johnny." She used her hand to keep Shannon from nosing her way between them. "He's been— erased."

Chapter Six

Johnny dreamed about deadly weapons and men with icy smiles, flashing their teeth while they pressed the barrels of their guns against his throat. The darkness around him moved. Like a whirlpool, it sucked at his legs and tried to pull him down. He was caught in a vortex of leering masks, bullets and cash, crates of cash, filled with hundred-dollar bills. Crates that skimmed the ceiling.

He needed air. He wanted Meliana. He had to find his way home before he forgot who and what he was.

He saw himself in a small, airless room. It felt like Miami. Someone was screaming in Spanish. Someone else was swearing in English. His head throbbed. Do the deal and get out was his only thought. He had forty-eight hours of between time. He could fly to Chicago and see Meliana. He'd have to be careful, though. He was trusted, but he was still an outsider.

The lack of air fogged his brain. He saw roses now and crudely scrawled messages, like graffiti on a dirty brick wall. He heard whispers of silk, then whispering people. A hand came from somewhere to cover his mouth. The white rose in his mind took on mammoth proportions. It wove through a sea of faceless bodies and twined around his legs. He wanted to warn Meliana, but he couldn't speak. He didn't know where he was.

He couldn't breathe!

He woke with a gasp and an up-punch that made stinging contact with something hard.

"Take it easy, Johnny. It's me. It's only me."

The voice was familiar enough that Johnny fell back onto the mattress, kept his eyes closed and let his lungs fill with blessed air.

"If you're not part of the nightmare I was having," he warned, "you're in serious trouble."

"You're the one with trouble, pal." Meliana's brother, Mark, gave his arm a backhanded swat and motioned toward the west wall. "Someone's prowling around your property with a flashlight."

Johnny pressed his fingers to his burning eyes. "Is he wearing a plaid jacket?"

"All I saw was a shape and a light."

Johnny forced himself to sit up. The dream lingered and with it a strong feeling of nausea. "What are you doing here, Mark?"

At the window and peering out into the rain, Mark replied simply, "Julie called me."

"Figures. What time is it?"

"Three a.m. I caught the milk-run flight out of Honolulu. I don't see anyone now, and whoever he was, he seemed to be heading into the trees."

"The woods are open to everyone in this state," Johnny

said with only a hint of sarcasm. He glanced down and realized he'd fallen asleep in his clothes. "Shouldn't you be giving Mel a heart attack instead of me?"

"If I did that at this hour, she'd think I was worried. Anyway, I drove past the town house. The porch light was on. Everything else was dark and quiet. Julie said you'd been up here for the past few days, so I assumed things had settled down."

"My guess is the guy's taking a brief time-out. I'm not counting on it lasting." Johnny switched on the bedside lamp, propped his eyes open and studied the man across from him.

The genes in Meliana's family never failed to amaze him. Her mother was beautiful and so, as men went, was her brother. Meliana had said Mark looked like a cross between a pirate and a Gypsy these days, and she was right. He even had a large gold hoop in his left ear to prove it.

"You working a smuggling op—" Johnny rolled his head to ease the tension in his neck "—or some cooperative venture with Vice?"

"Both, but we're still in the early stages of the setup. My captain has a sister of his own. Plus, I have a few things to do in New York. Timing's good. I can afford to disappear for a while."

"You're lucky." Johnny stood, swayed, steadied himself. "You make better coffee than I do. Brew a pot, and I'll fill you in on what's been happening."

"I got the gist from Julie. All I need are the details—and your take on the situation."

Did he even know what his take was? Johnny wondered. He knew his gut feeling was bad, but then his instincts might be as screwed up as his head these days.

He started for the stairs. He heard the rumble of an old pickup truck outside, pictured his hairy neighbor loading boxes into the back and glanced in the direction of the man's house. "Tim Carrick's place is west of here. It was probably him you saw prowling around. Count yourself lucky it's too cold for him to be doing it naked."

"I'll leave that one alone," Mark said with a smile. "Talk to me about Mel, Johnny. Who do you think's behind the roses, the messages and the theft?"

Chris Blackburn's face sprang to mind, but Johnny kept the thought to himself. "My guess would be some starry-eyed patient who's got more problems than Mel was able to repair with stitches."

"Too vague," Mark decided.

"Tell me about it." Because his eyes didn't want to focus properly, Johnny wandered toward the kitchen half-lidded. He tried not to think about how much he missed his wife. On top of everything else he loved about her—and there was a great deal—she made a killer pot of coffee.

"You're dragging your feet," Mark noted from behind. "It's not like you. Maybe you should have a chat with that Bohemian psychologist friend of Mel's."

"We've had several already. He recommended I borrow his Jimi Hendrix CDs."

"How about trying to work things out with Meliana?"

"The suggestion was made."

"And?"

The floor was cold under Johnny's bare feet. He didn't want to talk about his marriage right now, not even with Meliana's brother. "Look," he began, then banged his foot into a chair, swore and bent to deal with the pain.

If he hadn't, he reflected later, either the projectile that came hurtling through the kitchen window or the long splinters of glass would have blasted him in the face.

The crash brought his head up and back. He squinted into the night. It had been raining earlier, but it wasn't now. With Mark directly behind him, he scanned the shadows of the open yard. His gaze came to rest on the trees beyond it.

"Do you see anyone?" he asked over his shoulder.

"No."

Johnny glanced down, spotted the projectile. He detected a familiar sound and shook his head. "Put it away, Mark. There's no point searching. We tried it last week, five of us, and got nowhere." He gnawed on his cheek, let his gaze travel sideways, toward Tim Carrick's place. "I heard a truck when we came downstairs."

"Approaching or leaving?"

"Not sure, but I heard it."

Mark stuffed his gun back in its holster. "What'd he throw?"

"A rock." Already crouched, Johnny regarded it. "The messages are getting more malignant." With his knuckle, he spun the rock around so Mark could read the words.

IF YOU TOUCH HER AGAIN
I'LL KILL YOU!

"MARK'S HERE? In Blue Lake?" Meliana wasn't sure
why that struck a humorous note, because God knew
there was nothing remotely funny about the situation,
but she felt a chuckle rising. "My own brother came to
you before he came to me? I always thought you two
were closer than you let on. Where is he now?"

"In town, talking to Zack."

The humor faded. "About last night's rock?"

"And some guy he saw skulking around outside."

She accepted the coffee Johnny pushed on her.
"Shouldn't you be the one doing that?"

"He wanted to scope out the area. I let him because—" Johnny set his mouth close to her ear "—I got
a call from Julie."

"The pictures?"

"Yes, the pictures." He clamped a hand around her
nape so she couldn't sidestep. "Why didn't you phone
me?"

She stared into his eyes, undaunted. "Because you
specifically told me to call *her* if anything happened."

"Call her, yes, but call me, too."

"Why? So you could worry? Or break the land speed
record getting back to Chicago? Come on, Johnny. The
photographs appeared last night. Julie came over and
took them. She made copies, which, against her better
judgment and mine, I brought to show you. Now you
tell me someone tossed a rock through your window

early this morning and almost hit you in the head with it. One of the pictures this guy sent shows only a creepy silhouette where your image should be, and he threatened openly to kill you. Any way you look at it, right now you're in more danger than I am."

"For the moment, maybe," he agreed, "but tomorrow could be a very different story."

That prospect had occurred to her. She couldn't disguise a shiver. "You think he'll turn on me."

"He might, he might not. He's not exactly sane, is he, and once disillusioned…" Johnny kept his hand where it was, but loosened his grip. Part of Meliana had been hoping he'd draw her in and kiss her. His gaze slid to the far wall. "How well do you know Tim Carrick?"

The question surprised her. She twisted her head, and he let his hand drop. "I knew his wife better. Vivianne was hot-blooded and hot tempered, and I never understood why she married Tim. He reminds me of a hairy little troll, except I think he's more bluster than action, if you know what I mean."

"He's not as uncivilized in Chicago as he is up here?"

"He has manners." She sipped her coffee, paused and frowned into the mug. "He doesn't always use them."

"Is he naturally strange?"

"More than taking nude hikes strange? He creeps me out when he stares."

"What does he stare at?"

"Mostly women's breasts."

Now it was Johnny who stared, and his expression made a laugh bubble up in her throat. "Lots of guys do it, Johnny. They're just more subtle than Tim. It's a burden we females have to bear. We could belt them, I suppose, but I prefer to let them know I've noticed and watch them squirm."

"You're a sadist, Mel."

"I only do it in blatant cases."

Johnny circled the room, snapping his fingers softly as he went. Meliana noted the agitation behind it and caught his hand. "Tim's a little weird, but I don't think he'd send me flowers or steal my lingerie."

"Have you ever treated him at the Blue Lake clinic?"

"Once for a bump on the head—actually a mild concussion, and another time for a badly burned arm."

Johnny halted. "Burned how?"

"On his kitchen stove, he said. I'd have guessed blowtorch if you'd asked me. Johnny, stop scowling. Tim lives here, not in Chicago."

"He's in Chicago every week."

"So are lots of people from Blue Lake, including Zack and Sheriff Frank."

Johnny's eyes landed on the copied photos. She saw the frustration in his face. She read it more strongly in his body language.

"The guy followed us to Addifah's, Mel."

"Johnny, don't."

"Don't what? Get upset? Passed that point days ago." He glanced up at the loft. "I'm coming back to Chicago with you."

"Mark will be there," she reminded him.

"So will Chris."

"You're being difficult. Chris isn't giving me roses. Why bother with subterfuge? He asks me for dates all the time."

Johnny's head swung around.

"And I turn him down," Meliana added before he could speak. She didn't have a temper as such, but her patience was beginning to wear thin. "Come on, Johnny, we're separated, remember? Chris can ask me out as often as he likes without stepping on your toes."

"Has he kissed you?"

She laughed. "You can't be serious." Then she sobered. "You *are* serious." She recalled Chris's accusations from the previous night and softened her tone. "No, he hasn't. Tried, yes, but I'm not interested." She sent him a pointed look. "Satisfied?"

"Not until this rose guy's caught. How's Sam?"

"He's fine—on the job as usual. No funny premonitions." She paused, sidetracked. "It's Friday, isn't it?"

"Is it?"

He looked so tired that she had a strong urge to hug him. Instead, she pushed him onto the sofa and sat beside him. "One of the surgical nurses, Nick—you met him—is having a wine and cheese party tomorrow night. I'm thinking of going. Do you want to come?"

"As a show of solidarity?" He ran the fingers of both hands through his hair and held it back for a moment while he considered. "I guess I could. Does this nurse have a digital camera?"

"Johnny…" Grabbing his chin, Meliana turned his head to face her and gave him a resounding kiss on the mouth. "Shut up."

AUTUMN SWEPT IN with a vengeance. The afternoon turned wet and windy with the threat of an even greater storm moving in from Lake Michigan. Meliana let Johnny and Mark talk her into watching a movie on DVD Friday night. Julie dropped by halfway through, asked Johnny about Zack, then promptly started discussing police tactics with Mark.

"Now, there's a match that fits." Johnny loaded more beer into the fridge. "Zack's too wholesome for Jules."

Meliana removed a tray of sausage rolls from the oven. "Is the Zack you're talking about the same one I know?"

"What do you mean?"

"The guy was a hell-raiser in school, Johnny."

"Not according to Eileen."

"Well, yeah—except she's his mother and doesn't see him in actual white light. You know, the way your mother doesn't see you as you really are."

He regarded her blank faced. "What are you talking about? I'm an only child. How could my mother not know me?"

"Knowing isn't seeing. Your mom sees her baby, not a warrior."

He lowered his lashes in suspicion. "What do you see?"

"Once upon a time? Johnny Angel. Now I'm not sure. But we were talking about Zack. He only took the job of deputy sheriff because Owen Frank got tired of arresting him for teenage pranks and misdemeanors and decided that a combination father figure and career goal might straighten him out."

Johnny stared. "How do you know all this?"

"I'm gregarious by nature. People talk to me, though once you get him going, Sheriff Frank'll talk to anyone. Zack can hold his own with Julie as easily as you and Mark do. And Chris," she added, popping a mini sausage roll into his mouth. Since he couldn't protest while chewing, she went on to muse, "You know, it suddenly occurs to me that I'm surrounded by cops."

"Most people in your position would see that as a good thing."

"I don't imagine the rose guy does." She tipped her head to one side. "Unless of course, he's a cop himself."

It was the wrong thing to say right after mentioning Chris's name. The look on Johnny's face told her as much. By the time the movie ended, Johnny was mentally pummeling his former partner.

The whole evening would have taken on a gloomy air if her brother hadn't been there to lighten the mood.

On Saturday, Meliana and Mark jogged through the park in the rain. Meliana kept a close eye on the thundercloud brewing to the north.

"You know Johnny still loves you, right?" Mark asked when they paused to stretch out their calf muscles.

Meliana bent her knee and pulled her leg up behind her. "I know lots of things about Johnny. It's what I don't know that's the problem."

"He's not himself, I agree, but he'll get there. You're not dealing with a naturally dark mind here, Mel."

She repeated the exercise with the other leg. "You know a lot more about what went down with him during his time on the street than you let on, don't you?"

"We talked some. Don't ask me to betray a confidence, Mel. I don't want to be placed in that position."

Because she'd been in a similar position herself and hated it, Meliana sighed and changed the subject. "Do you remember Chris Blackburn?"

"The fed who hit on you at your wedding?"

Exasperated, she retied her dripping ponytail. "Did you talk to Johnny about that, too?"

"Didn't have to. I saw him doing it. We weren't all as oblivious as you that day. Blackburn was drunk and crushing flower petals the last time I saw him."

Meliana stopped midtwist. "What kind of flower?"

"Whatever you had scattered around. Orchids, roses, carnations, gladioli. I don't think his actions then are symbolic of the current situation. He was simply angry and taking out his frustration in a nonviolent way."

"You sound like Charlie Lightfoot." She shook her arms to keep loose. "I'm worried about Johnny, Mark. He won't back off, and whoever this rose guy is, he's getting angrier every day."

"Or crazier, as the case may be."

"It seems like hurting Johnny is uppermost in his mind right now. He's unbalanced. The decision to hurt could become an obsession."

"I promise you, Johnny'd prefer it that way."

"He might, but I don't." She detected a movement across the street and twitched her shoulders. "Let's run, okay?"

"One more time around the park?"

"Please." She started off. And had to force herself not to look back at Chris, who was standing half-hidden by a curtain as he watched them through his living-room window.

"YOU'RE SURE YOU CAN BRING guests?" Julie rearranged her hair in Meliana's en suite bathroom. "Nick won't mind?"

"He said I could bring anyone I wanted to. There's plenty of wine, and he has a very large cellar at his disposal tonight."

"Must be nice."

"His grandfather's both a published psychiatrist and a connoisseur of fine wine. I think Nick disappointed him careerwise, so developing an appreciation for vintage grape was a form of appeasement."

"I've heard of the great Dr. Hohlman. Brilliant mind, brilliant man."

Meliana shimmied into a pair of black pants. "Charlie doesn't think so. You're ringing," she said, and pulled a black V-necked sweater over her head.

Julie punched her cell phone as they went downstairs. Johnny was there with Mark and the dogs. All four of them were engrossed in the American League pennant game.

"I don't know why you bother watching." Meliana

took the remote from Johnny's hand. "The Yankees always win."

Mark finished his beer. "Ever heard of a dark horse, Mel?"

"Not this early in the series." She snatched the half-full bottle away before Johnny could reach for it. "You're not supposed to pour wine on top of beer. You'll defeat the purpose of the party."

"Party in a dungeon," Johnny remarked. He ran the side of his hand over his mouth and his gaze over her body. "Nice outfit, Mel. Black's good on you. Nick'll be impressed."

"Not if we're late, he won't."

"I've heard of a Dr. Hohlman," Mark said. "He's been on TV, hasn't he?"

Meliana checked her mascara. "A couple of times actually, but he's a bit of a stiff."

Johnny stood. "Charlie uses that word."

"Only in conversational context—which is more pleasant than the medical slang."

Julie punched off. "I have to go. There's a shortage of officers downtown tonight—and a civvy found a body five blocks from the station. Apparently he threw up on her. Should be a lovely mess. Beg a bottle of anything from Nick for me, Mel. I'm gonna need it."

Mark glanced up. "Mel, would you mind if I…" He nodded at Julie. "You know."

"And Johnny thinks I'm a ghoul." Meliana handed Julie her coat. "He won't get in the way, I promise. He just has this thing about dead bodies."

"Yeah." Mark zipped his jacket. "I like to figure out how they got that way."

When they were gone, Meliana flopped down next to Johnny on the sofa. "I'd rather be a surgeon, all things considered. Do you still want to go tonight?"

Johnny slid suggestive eyes over her cleavage. "Unless you have a better idea."

She moved on the cushions until her breasts were pressed against his arm and her mouth was practically on his. "I have lots of ideas, Johnny." She gave him a teasing kiss and murmured, "But do you really think any of them will solve our problems?"

He smiled against her lips. "Dangerous ground here. If I didn't know you so well, I'd call your bluff and see exactly where we'd wind up."

Because it had been a bluff—more or less—Meliana kissed him again, then backed off. "Charlie's only going to this party because we are. It wouldn't be fair for us not to show, especially since there's a better-than-even chance that Nick's grandfather, who's eaten dinner with no fewer than three presidents, will put in an appearance."

"Lightfoot can handle a pompous old windbag."

Meliana's brows went up. "You know Dr. Hohlman?"

"No, but I've heard you and Charlie talking about him, although in Charlie's case slagging might be a more appropriate word. I take it Lightfoot doesn't appreciate the old man's psychiatric genius."

"Oh, he appreciates it—he just doesn't like being denigrated in front of his peers. Dr. Hohlman deals in facts, in the black, white and obvious gray matter of things. Charlie tends to throw out curveballs that Hohlman can't quite catch." She grinned. "Still, it's fun watching him try."

"You have a nasty streak, Mel."

"I know." She beamed at him as she tossed him his jacket. "My mother'd be proud of me."

I CAN'T SIT HERE ALONE in the dark all night. I want to, but I can't. I keep picturing Meliana with him. They're together, and I'm afraid of what that means. I'm more afraid of what I'll do.

I'm shaking again, badly this time. I see blood in my mind, and yet I know not a single drop has been spilled.

I'm using Meliana's scalpel to shred her white silk bra. I can't seem to stop myself. I just keep shredding the bra.

Please, God, don't let me do the same thing to her....

Chapter Seven

"White rose for white wine, red rose for red wine." Nick pushed one of each into Meliana's hand. "That's for the women. It's red and white carnations for the men. It's a fun symbolism thing," he said with a grin.

A sensation of cold that didn't come from the huge copper-encased cellar swept over Meliana's skin. She wouldn't freak out. Not yet.

"Novel idea," Johnny remarked in an easy tone. "What made you think of it?"

"My dad came up with it. He met my mom at a wine-tasting party. She was romanced by the roses he gave her, so he thought it would make their get-togethers distinctive if he kept doing it. Thirty years later, it's a family tradition." Uncertain, likely because of the tension that had suddenly sprung up, Nick looked from Meliana to Johnny and back again. "Are you allergic?"

"No, we're fine," Meliana assured him. "It fits the mood, Nick."

"My dad thinks so." Nick's voice dropped. "My

grandfather doesn't." He handed Johnny a pair of carnations. "Glad you could come, Mr. Maynard."

"Grand," Meliana corrected.

"Right. Sorry." Nick glanced at the cellar door, straightened his shirt collar and smiled. "Excuse me. Head surgical nurse at twelve o'clock."

Meliana watched him go. "Don't say it, Johnny."

"No way is this a coincidence, Mel."

"It could be."

"No, it couldn't. Which means either Nurse Hohlman's lying about the origin of his so-called family tradition and he's trying to rattle you, or…"

Meliana knew Johnny's thought processes well enough to follow along. "Or," she repeated, making a quick visual circle of the room, "someone stole a portion of the tradition and put it to a different use." She studied the roses as she reconsidered Nick's story. "Still, sometimes a coincidence is simply that. A coincidence."

"Who at the hospital knows about the roses?"

"No one."

"Not even head of surgery?"

"Not even him." She released a breath. "Well, okay, I'll take back the 'no one' and say no one that I know of, because word could have leaked out. You know how workplaces operate. Gossip's better than a sugar fix for a lot of people."

"Think I'll have a chat with Nurse Nick before this party gets rolling."

As far as Meliana could see, it was already rolling, although no one had a drink in their hand yet.

She thought about stopping Johnny, then decided against it. He wouldn't use full force on Nick. She hoped.

"Hey, Mel. You're looking both pretty and bothered." Charlie dropped a comforting arm across her shoulders. "What's the problem—as if I didn't know?"

She held up the white rose. "Any thoughts on this?"

"Ah." She saw the twinkle, usually present in his dark eyes, fade. "I bumped into Nick in the hospital yesterday afternoon. Literally knocked into his arm. I got a quick flash of a white rose. It could have been connected to this family-custom thing, but the problem is I only saw a white rose, not a red one."

"That isn't reassuring, Charlie."

"I know. Well, maybe this will help. Nick's had similar parties before."

"And used the roses to denote wine color?"

"Yes."

A small amount of Meliana's tension slipped away. "So it is a coincidence."

"Assuming Nick isn't the sender, yes. His previous parties were smaller in scale than this one. This—" he made a sweeping motion "—is Nick's grandfather's cellar, his wine, his house. The other half dozen or so affairs Nick's hosted took place at his midcity condo."

"With or without roses?"

"Relax. With. Tonight he has some rather impressive guests. That wasn't the case in the past. I made the rounds today, talked to some of the hospital workers—orderlies, maintenance people, other nurses. They confirmed the rose deal."

"That's good, then. It means Nick's roses came on the scene before mine did. Unless, as you said, Nick's also the rose giver."

"And lingerie thief. And message sender."

Meliana sighed. "Do you have anything to say here that's going to make me feel better?"

"Probably not. Take a peek in the illustrious Dr. Hohlman's garden greenhouses sometime, Mel. They're brimming with flowers. All kinds of flowers, including an abundance of white roses."

"WHAT DID LIGHTFOOT WANT?" Johnny rejoined her as one of the physicians in attendance drew Charlie aside. "Did he telepathize something?"

Meliana handed him her roses. "Answer's yes. I'm going home."

Johnny stopped her. "It's a thirty-year-old tradition in the Hohlman family, Mel. Nick showed me pictures of some of his parents' parties. They're framed and hanging at the far end of the room if you want to see them."

"I want to leave. Charlie got a similar confirmation about them from several hospital sources. But guess what else he discovered? Grandpa Hohlman grows white roses in his greenhouse."

"Lots of people do, including Andy, who lives next door to you, Julie's mother, Liz, and Eileen Crawford."

"I know—Sam lives with Liz, and Zack would have easy access through Eileen. All sounds good and muddles the picture nicely, but I'm still creeped out and..." She regarded him with sudden skepticism.

"Wasn't it you who just told me you don't believe in coincidence?"

"I don't. I'm trying to make you feel better. Plus, in my line of work, not to mention my present state of mind, cookie-baking grandmothers tend to have ulterior motives when viewed through my eyes."

"So do you believe Nick or not?"

"I believe the idea of red and white roses used to denote wine color at parties such as this is real, yes. Do I think he stole a page from his father's book and altered the lines to serve his own perverted purpose? Possibly. Has he heard about the roses you've been receiving? Unless he's an excellent actor, no."

That mollified her. Meliana's gaze roamed the crowded cellar. "You know, if it was only the flowers and not the other things, I'd be flattered. But finding a rose in my lingerie drawer was so invasive. And now the guy's threatening to hurt you, erasing you from a photograph...." She shook her head. "He was unstable to start with. It feels like he's sliding toward insanity at this point."

"He's definitely obsessed." Johnny's lips twitched as he glanced past her. "Is that the infamous Dr. Elliot Hohlman?"

"The one and only." Meliana smiled. "He'll make a beeline for Charlie as soon as he spots him."

"This night shows promise, after all."

Charlie made no attempt to hide. Instead, he gave his headband a stroke and strolled over.

"Dr. Hohlman."

"Lightfoot." Elliot Hohlman slapped a pair of leather

gloves in his palm. He hadn't bothered to shed his overcoat and likely wouldn't. "I see my grandson has arranged some entertainment for tonight's affair. Are we reading minds this evening, or extracting vibrations from the wine itself? I'm told every bottle tells a story."

Unruffled, Charlie rested a shoulder on one of the tall racks. "Actions tell better stories, Doctor. Yours speak loud and clear to everyone present."

"Oh, come now, is that the best you can do? Stand there and fling insults at an old man? Give something a touch. Tell us where it was born, the sights it's seen, what its ultimate fate might be. Use my gloves, if you like. They're as well traveled as I am."

The murmur of voices around them died off completely. Everyone in the cellar watched the exchange between the two men. Many of them looked embarrassed, but none more so than Nick, whose face had gone from deep pink to a mortified shade of white.

Charlie caught Meliana's eye and signaled for her to hand him her white rose. She hesitated, then relinquished it.

"Very pretty," he said, sniffing the petals. "No scent." He held it up, twirled it. "From your greenhouse, Doctor?"

Elliot Hohlman's eyes glinted. "You tell me. It's your dime, Lightfoot."

Charlie ran his fingers along the stem. "Thorns," he murmured.

"Yes, we can see those," Hohlman said. "Think deeper—Doctor."

If he was trying to annoy his grandson's guest, he failed miserably. Charlie merely winked at Meliana and continued to finger the stem. "Soil could use more nitrogen. The petals are flimsy. The leaves..." He halted, raised the flower. "Someone's right index finger is cut. I see blood, just a dot. It's very warm, humid, almost musty. I sense...strong emotions."

Nick shook off his embarrassment, made a sign of negation with his hands and hastened over to Charlie. "This is wrong." He took the rose. "Dr. Lightfoot is my guest, Grandfather. This is a wine-tasting party, not a battle of wills or a forum for exhibitionism. I think we should move on to the tasting before things get out of hand."

The old man's eyes locked on Charlie's face. "There's nothing of substance in what you do, Lightfoot, nothing of science or fact. If a rose has thorns, fingers will be pricked. It hardly requires a psychic episode to draw such a mundane conclusion."

"Grandfather," Nick pleaded through his teeth.

With a final slap of his gloves and a lingering glare, Elliot Hohlman executed a smart right turn and strode out of the cellar.

It seemed to Meliana that the guests heaved a collective sigh of relief. But there'd be stories told tomorrow in the hospital corridors.

She kept her eyes on Nick, who still struck her as rather shaky. He straightened his shoulders, summoned a smile and motioned everyone to the tables.

"You're with me, Dr. Mel," he said. "Both of you,"

he added to Johnny. "I'm sorry for that thing with Grandfather. I wish I could say his behavior tonight was atypical, but I can't. He's been a drama queen all my life."

"Drama king," Charlie corrected from behind. "I believe your grandfather's been married for close to sixty years, hasn't he, Nick?"

"Sixty-one, actually. My grandmother's a saint."

"They always are," Johnny put in.

"I really am sorry he did that, Dr. Lightfoot. I hope you're not upset."

"I don't get upset, son." Charlie clapped Nick on the shoulder. "I go home and belt out a few hot licks on my guitar. Upset only gets you an ulcer."

"I'm going to adopt that philosophy." Meliana pried his hand off Nick's shoulder and hooked both of hers through his arm.

Charlie had sensed something from that rose—she could tell by his expression. Whatever it had been, it had involved Nick, and she suspected it hadn't been good.

THEY WENT to a sixties-style lounge near Charlie's place after the party. The room had paneled walls, dark carpets and low-back chairs. The music was Nat King Cole, the lighting subdued, the tabletop covered with lacquered 1960s newspaper articles. The nostalgic atmosphere soothed Meliana's nerves, if not her mind.

"So what's the deal with the rose?" Johnny asked once they'd ordered. "What did you sense that you've spent the last three hours not telling us?"

Charlie tapped a pretzel on the table. "Tell me this first, Mel. How well do you know Nick?"

"We work together, but don't really socialize. He used to work in short-term patient care, but early this year he took the extra courses needed to move into the operating room. He's bright, he's efficient and he has the kind of personality people like."

"Have you ever gone out with him, even in a platonic way?"

"With Nick?" The question amused more than surprised her. "Not at all." She picked up a pretzel of her own and bit off the end. "He's too young, Charlie. Not in years, but in attitude."

"He was watching you tonight."

She sat back and thought about it. "He watches a lot of people, actually. Nick's an observer. That's probably why he's such a good surgical nurse. He picks up on the details an overworked surgeon might occasionally miss."

Johnny brought his head around. 'Surgeons miss details?"

She refused to smile. "The operative word was 'occasionally,' Johnny."

"Didn't you say you were overworked and exhausted when you operated on me?"

"I'm the exception. Go on, Charlie. What's the correlation between Nick and the rose?"

Charlie ran a finger over one of the old headlines. "I sensed lust, Mel, deep, almost painful feelings of lust."

"From Nick?"

"He gave you the rose, didn't he? And he had a

small bandage on his right index finger. Thorns draw blood, Mel."

"Well, yes, they do, but—Nick? I don't believe it. I mean, I believe you, but—Nick?"

Johnny lounged in his chair, set his arm on the back of hers and caught a strand of her hair. "You remember that thing we talked about last night? How mothers don't tend to see their children as they really are?"

"Nick's not my son."

"No, but you still don't see him the way someone like Charlie might."

"Why?

"Because you're a beautiful woman," Charlie said. "You're used to being looked at as such." He grinned. "Believe it or not, my baby sister's rather beautiful herself. Yet, growing up, any time I'd tell her some guy wanted to hit on her, she'd say I was crazy. Then the guy would ask her out and she'd wonder why I could see something that totally eluded her. From the time she was a kid, men and women raved about how pretty she was. After a while, she stopped hearing the words and just came to expect a certain reaction. Eventually she stopped noticing even that reaction."

Meliana glanced at Johnny. "Makes us sound like the shallowest creatures on the planet, doesn't it?"

"We're human, Mel." Charlie came forward on his elbows. "Beautiful women, beautiful flowers, beautiful feelings. Your rose giver's created a perfect world, a lovely cocoon where he wants the two of you to live. I'm not saying Nick's that person, but I am telling you

I got a very strong vibe from that rose he gave you tonight. I felt lust and sexual fantasy and possibly even a form of love all tangled together in one highly confused ball."

Johnny eyed Charlie with equal parts doubt and curiosity. "Did you sense anything underneath those feelings?"

"Such as anger, resentment and hatred?" Charlie played with his pretzel. "Sorry to disappoint you, but the only sense of hostility I received came from Elliot Hohlman."

"Dr. Black and White," Meliana said, then shrugged. "I heard he started his career in the military. Personally, I like delving into more colorful areas."

"And yet white's your favorite color." Johnny twined her hair around his index finger. "Interesting anomaly."

"There's nothing anomalous about my preferences, Johnny. And don't you start psychoanalyzing," she warned Charlie. "Julie said the last time she talked to you about her problems, you tried linking them to her mother's need for control coupled with her father's premature second adolescence."

"They were valid conclusions."

"For her maybe, but I don't have issues with my parents."

"We all have parental issues. Some are just more extreme than others. Why did you decide to work your butt off in medical school? You could have chosen an easier career, still medicine related, married a rich doctor and been set for life."

"I wanted to *be* a doctor, Charlie, not marry one. Look at my mother."

"My point exactly."

"I'm making a positive comparison here, not laying blame. My mother's beautiful, she's a commander in the navy and yet she married a man who's now a felon."

"She means the women in her family are stronger than the men," Johnny translated.

"Not stronger, merely strong. Now, if you two Neanderthals are finished dissecting my family life, can we please get back to the rose guy, because any way you look at it, he really does have serious issues."

"Unfortunately—" Charlie scratched his chin "—he has a lot more of them than I can begin to address at this point. Obsession's a tricky thing. Anyone who develops a fixation often has a volatile personality. They frequently appear sound, fit into society when and where they choose, but they can also detach themselves from reality when it suits their purpose."

"In other words, they're chameleons," Johnny said. "Like me."

"Like you became," Meliana corrected, "because your job demanded it."

"It's easy to get lost, Mel." He ran a hand over his mouth. "It can happen to anyone."

"Johnny, there's nothing to compare between you and whoever's behind the flowers, the stealing and the threats." She glimpsed a head over the partition and strained for a better view. "Mark? What're you doing here?"

"Looking for Johnny." Her brother spotted an empty chair, dragged it to their table and asked point-blank, "Are you drunk?"

"Not yet."

"Modesta Perrine."

Johnny stopped breathing for a moment. "What?"

"Do you remember her?"

"She was my contact in Miami."

Meliana's blood chilled. She glanced at Charlie, who was frowning.

"When was the last time you saw her?" Mark demanded.

"Eight months ago."

"So she didn't come to Chicago looking for you?"

"She's in Chicago?"

"Until yesterday. Her body was discovered in a downtown alley, Johnny. Someone slit her throat and tossed her behind a bunch of trash cans. The medical examiner figures she was murdered in another location, probably late last night or early this morning, and dumped there today."

Johnny swore. He looked as if he wanted to bolt but knew he couldn't. He reached for Meliana's hand instead.

She linked her fingers with his as she asked, "How closely were you and Modesta connected—business-wise?"

"She worked with us, for us." He swore again as he concentrated. "She had an aunt here, and a couple of cousins. She could have been visiting them. She never contacted me."

"People in common," Mark pressed. "Do you have names?"

"A few." Johnny caught and held Meliana's gaze. "Top of the list is a man she called Ricky the Lip. The rest of us knew him as Enrique Jago."

IT WAS COMPLICATED and terrifying. If Meliana had been prone to migraines, this night's events would have triggered a massive one. Thankfully, three aspirin tablets and thirty minutes of yoga took her from superstressed down to a dull tension headache.

Off the clock since midnight, Julie did the yoga exercises with her. Johnny and Mark went downtown to talk with Johnny's FBI superiors. Chris's lights were out—Johnny had made sure of that before he'd left—and Charlie was back at his apartment with a promise to share any further revelations he might have in connection with Nick's party.

"It was a brutal homicide," Julie told Meliana in the kitchen. "You didn't know her, did you?"

"I didn't even know of her, although I knew Johnny had contacts in various cities." Meliana ran water into the teakettle. "Do you want to hear something awful?"

"You're feeling just the tiniest bit jealous of a dead woman."

"More than a tiny bit, and what's worse, I can't get rid of it. I keep picturing some redheaded bombshell in a Miami hotel room with Johnny, both of them under orders to do what it takes to get the job done."

Julie found two mugs in the cupboard. "She was a

brunette, Mel, short hair, petite. About forty-five. At the proper weight she'd have been a stunner, but what I saw was an emaciated shell. I'm guessing she'd relapsed and started doing drugs again."

"I really do feel bad that she's dead, Jules. I'm also not sure if her drug use is a good sign or a bad one in terms of Johnny's theory about her murder." She tipped her head from side to side to relieve the tightness in her muscles. "Am I a bad person?"

Julie abandoned her search for cookies to pinch her cheek. "Come on, Mel, you're being bombarded from a hundred different directions. You're entitled to a moment of uncertainty, even if it doesn't seem like the most appropriate moment."

Meliana laughed. "I'll hang on to that thought until the next thing happens." She leaned against the refrigerator. "God, I hope Johnny's cover wasn't blown, that his contact's murder is unrelated to his time undercover."

"His bosses will know more about that than the police do. If Modesta was using, she might also have been dealing. She worked with the FBI for a time, but once usefulness wanes, cash flow stops. She'd have needed a monetary boost, and she knew all the so-called best suppliers."

The kettle began to whistle. Pressing her fingers to her temples, Meliana switched off the burner. "I wish I knew more about what happened to Johnny during that two-year period."

"Why don't you ask him for details? He'd give them to you."

"I'm sure he would, and he did to a point when he first came back. But rehashing it seemed to upset him, so I backed off, gave him space. I figured when he was ready, he'd tell me. Instead, we veered off into some weird realm where we did more fencing than talking. It was like we both carried shields and we'd whip them up even before we knew why we were doing it. It got to be a bad habit."

"I felt the tension between you."

"Everyone did. It was omnipresent in the end."

"Did he threaten you?"

"No, but I saw violence in him, and anger. Frustration. He had his moods before the assignment, but he wasn't moody. He was never dark."

"Just a little shadowy."

"Well, yeah." Meliana smiled. "I like a certain amount of mystery in a man."

Julie added honey to her tea and blew on it. "Were you scared of him?"

"In small doses, for short periods of time. It was more that he didn't seem like Johnny anymore." Meliana rested her elbows on the center island. "Even though he went through the motions, I knew he wasn't the person he'd been before the wedding."

"So you split up, and he headed north for some R and R. Now he's back, you're getting roses, he's getting threatened and the pair of you seem to be getting close again. So what's the game plan?"

"No game, no plan. Oatmeal or chocolate chip cookies?"

"Chocolate chip." Julie squinted at the window as

raindrops began to strike it. "It sounds like someone's shooting pellets out there. Come on, Mel, are you and Johnny going to stay split up or try again?"

Meliana dunked her cookie. "No idea, Jules. I love him—I never stopped doing that. The question is, can I live with him again, or will it be as hellish as it was before we separated?"

"Sleeping dogs, huh?"

"Not quite that simple. It's better between us now than it was even two months ago. I kind of like that, but…" She moved a shoulder. "Right now we're taking things day by day." And that, she decided, was enough of that. She drank her tea. "What about you? How's your love life these days?"

Julie tried to sneak a piece of cookie to a hopeful Lokie, but Meliana gave her wrist a kick with her bare foot. "Chocolate's bad for dogs. She can have a Scooby snack later. Go find Shannon, Lokie. Love life," she repeated to Julie.

"Post Blackburn, kind of dull. Not that I'd date fedman again if you paid me. Zack's a maybe, and I'd take Mark in a heartbeat."

"You and most of the female population of Hawaii." Meliana glanced at the swinging door. "Was that a knock or rain hitting the window?"

"Probably rain. It's pouring."

Leaving the counter, Meliana pushed through to the living room. Lokie was crouched in a playful position in front of the TV with her front paws resting on a leather DVD case.

"She likes to chew the handle," Meliana said. "She pulls it out of the cabinet every night."

"How does she get into the cabinet?"

"Oh, she figured that out six weeks after I got her. I'm hoping—" she took Lokie's head in her hands and gave her a kiss between the ears "—that she'll pick up some manners from Shannon, but so far, no luck."

"Blackburn's home." At the large front window Julie indicated his house, visible around the crescent. "I only see the attic light burning. What does he do, hang with the bats in the rafters, mooning over the one that got away?"

"Knock it off, Julie."

Shannon appeared at the living-room door and barked.

"You've already been out three times today," Meliana reminded her. "This isn't Blue Lake, and I've done enough running in the rain lately."

The dog barked again.

"So much for reasoning." Julie stage-whispered, "Why don't you try a firm no?"

"Because I'm a sucker for big dark eyes. It's wet, Shannon. And cold. We'll run tomorrow."

For an answer, the Irish setter trotted in, caught the hem of her T-shirt in her teeth and tugged.

"What is it, girl? Is someone out there? Julie?"

"Coming. I swear that dog's psychic. Did Charlie give her to you and Johnny as a wedding gift?"

"No. Shannon, we're not going out, if that's where this is heading."

But she sensed it wasn't.

The dog pulled her to the front door, released her T-shirt, then barked twice.

Puzzled and a little uneasy, Meliana used the viewer. She saw no one. She twisted the dead bolt and opened the door.

"Anything?" Julie peered over her shoulder. "Is there a—whoa, rose?"

Meliana stared at the box on the mat. A white box wrapped with a white ribbon.

"Use gloves," Julie cautioned as Meliana bent to inspect it. "I'll get us both a pair." She rummaged in the closet. "Here. Now, be careful. Let me feel. Is it heavy?"

"Not at all. Are bombs heavy?"

"Don't be cute. This rose guy's a freak. Anything's possible."

With Julie holding the box, Meliana gave the ribbon a pull. Her heart, already racing, began to thump. No more pictures, she prayed.

She removed the lid, drew back, then did a double take.

"Is that a bra?" Julie asked.

Feelings of dread and revulsion twisted together in Meliana's stomach. "I think it's *my* bra." Her fingers trembled only a little as she hooked one of the straps and lifted out the shredded silk. "Or it used to be."

Chapter Eight

He'd slashed her bra—with a sharp knife, by the look of it. He was watching her, judging her, beginning to doubt her.

Johnny didn't know what to make of it, and he was lost as far as Modesta Perrine's death was concerned. Connected to him or not? His superiors couldn't give him answers. They wanted him to disappear. They offered to help him do it, and Meliana, as well, if she wanted to go.

He'd spent over thirty hours talking to people—agents, police officers, specialty-trained psychologists. No one knew what Modesta had been doing in Chicago, and in the end he'd walked out.

Meliana had left for the hospital by the time he reached the town house. His cell phone rang while he was being mauled by the dogs. He made an impatient sound when he spied Eileen Crawford's name on the screen. It wasn't the one he wanted to see.

"That ridiculous pipe's burst again," she told him. "Zack's helping me mop up, but he can't stay much longer, and all Eddy the plumber says is he'll come when he comes."

He wanted to sleep, Johnny thought, leaning against the fridge, sleep and not wake up until all his nightmares were over. He pushed his hair back and asked, "Is the shut-off valve working?"

"That's where the pipe burst. Tim Carrick's got a pump. If you want, I can send Zack over to borrow it."

"Yeah, thanks." He found a bag of fresh fruit and a container of yogurt, took both and headed for the door. "I'm on my way, Eileen. If you can get hold of Eddy, tell him I'll pay double if he'll just fix the damn thing."

"We'll try to keep the flood level down in the meantime," Eileen promised.

Johnny ended the call, then punched Julie's number. She answered on the first ring.

"It's Johnny. Where are you?"

"Sitting at my computer, filling out reports and having daymares about slashed bras. You?"

"En route to Blue Lake. Another water pipe emergency. I should be back before Mel stitches up her final patient, but I wanted to update you on Modesta Perrine."

"Was she dealing?"

"Apparently."

"Any suspects?"

"We're tracking Jago down. If he made me, he might have had her killed, but my feeling is he'd have come after me instead. Or Mel." He heard a beep, glanced at the screen and said, "She's trying to reach me. Keep an ear open about Perrine, okay?"

"No problem. Your wife's off at seven. Make sure you're back in Chicago by then."

He switched to Meliana's call as he climbed into the ancient pickup he'd borrowed from Andy. His own SUV was still in the shop. "I'm here, Mel. Are you okay?"

She sounded rushed. "Between surgeries. Any news?"

"On Modesta's death, no. But another pipe's blown in Blue Lake. Eileen and Zack are dealing with the overflow until I get there." He opened the fruit container and searched for a chunk of pineapple. "Wanna come?"

She laughed, and the sound of it loosened the knots in his stomach. "Love to. But you'll have to break it to my next patient. She's got a cyst the size of a kumquat on her liver."

"Sounds nasty."

"It will be if it's malignant, but I prefer to be optimistic. I'll be fine here, Johnny."

"I might not be back by the time you're off."

"We could have a late dinner," she suggested. "If I get lucky and finish before midnight, I'll meet you."

"Mel…"

"I'm not going to stop doing things, Johnny. I'll park at the entrance."

"The entrance to where?"

"Nino's."

"The restaurant in Evanston?"

"I like the atmosphere and the food."

"I don't like the obscure location."

"Obscurity is what makes it so perfect. Eight o'clock?"

He checked the dusty watch Andy had taped to the

dashboard. "I can do that. If the plumber doesn't show, I'll jam something into the pipe myself."

"Yeah, well, if Eddy gets cantankerous, remind him about the time the snake bit him and I was the only one working at the clinic." She softened her tone, "I'm really sorry about Modesta Perrine."

"Yeah, me, too. For a lot of reasons. Do me a favor and double-park in front of the restaurant if you have to. It's worth the ticket."

"Eight o'clock," she repeated. "And, Johnny, that slashed bra he sent wasn't your fault."

"Yes, it was." His fingers tightened on the wheel. "In a way it was. Given his state of mind, if he hasn't already, it's only a matter of time before he goes from slashing bras to slashing people." He had to steady his breathing before he added a grim "To slashing you."

MELIANA DIDN'T FIND THE ROSE until she arrived at Nino's. She'd tossed her jacket on the passenger seat, apparently right on top of it.

"Not going to overreact," she said out loud. But she stood on the street and stared for almost a full minute without moving.

It wasn't damaged as her bra had been, and the thorns were gone. What did that mean?

Preoccupied, she reached into her shoulder bag for her cell. She felt a whisper of air behind her. Her head shot up as a man's hand clamped onto her shoulder. His voice flowed into her ear.

"Whatcha doing all the way out here?"

She breathed out, spun and checked her annoyance. "That was a really stupid thing to do, Chris, considering all the defensive maneuvers I've picked up from Johnny, Mark and Julie."

He merely grinned. "Uh-huh. But then I've picked up a few of my own along the way."

Meliana used the heel of her boot to nudge the car door closed. "Did you follow me here?"

His grin widened. "Would you believe me if I said no?" He made a show of looking around. "I notice you're minus your watchdogs tonight."

"Canine or human?"

"Both." He tapped her nose. "Let me guess. Julie's working, and your ex-hubby flipped out and had to return to the sanctuary of his lakeside cave."

"We're not divorced, Chris."

His expression faltered; the glint in his eyes deepened. "But it's only a matter of time, right? Because you can't seriously believe that hiding out in no-man's-land has helped him cope with whatever it was that sent him over the edge in the first place. If anything, it's probably added to the damage."

Meliana turned away. "I'm not going to do this with you, Chris." She started for the front entrance. "I've had a hard day. I want a relaxing evening."

"With Johnny?"

She swung to face him. "With whomever I choose. If that happens to be Johnny, it's my business and I'm sorry, but none of yours."

He hadn't moved. His voice reached her from the curb. "I care about you, Mel. I wouldn't want to see you get hurt."

She took a moment to study him. Something in his face caused her skin to prickle, like a thousand tiny ant feet scurrying over her. What could she say to him? Why did she feel so uncomfortable all of a sudden?

She put the sensation down to rattled nerves and softened her tone. "Look, I know you want more from me than I'm giving you, but it's not there, Chris. We're friends. We can't be anything else."

He breathed out, forced a smile. "You're not telling me anything I don't already know, but, hey, a guy can try, right? FYI, I spent most of the afternoon here in Evanston. We're working on a kidnapping, an eight-year-old girl, likely stolen by her maternal grandparents because mommy and daddy have been using her as a rope in their nonamicable postdivorce tug-of-war."

It sounded plausible enough—and very sad. "Did you find her?"

"Not yet. The grandmother has family here, but it's a long haul from Texas when you're driving a twenty-year-old Fiat with a history of mechanical problems. We've tracked them as far as St. Louis through repair charges on various credit cards." With his good humor restored and a slight swagger in his step, Chris approached her. "That said, can I buy you a drink while you wait?"

"A drink." She'd scanned the street for Andy's truck and hadn't spotted it.

"Scout's honor," he promised, and pushed on the door.

She checked her watch. It was eight-forty. Not so late, but late enough that Johnny should have called her by now.

A waiter took their orders. The room was crowded.

The hands of the clock crawled toward eight forty-five. By the time their drinks arrived it was eight-fifty and Meliana was getting worried.

She removed her cell phone from her purse and punched Johnny's Blue Lake number.

Chris watched as the call went unanswered.

"He's probably sleeping."

"And can't hear the phone beside the bed?"

"On the sofa, then."

She sent him a dry look, waited through five more rings, then aborted the call.

"We could order dinner," Chris suggested.

Meliana propped her elbows on the table and cupped her chin. "I planned to meet Johnny for dinner, Chris, not you."

Another five minutes passed. She tried Johnny's other number. As she waited, she caught the quick smile on Chris's lips.

"No luck?" he asked.

Meliana's gaze roamed the crowded room. "Not so far, but I'm a very persistent person."

"Big surprise." Chris spread his fingers in a concil-iatory gesture. "Look, Mel, I don't like the strain that's developed between us. We've been friends for almost six years. That's worth a lot to me. I'm not going to lie and tell you I wouldn't like Johnny out of the picture, but since he's not there yet, let me at least help you find him." He leaned forward with a humorous expression. "I can give you the number of the local FBI office."

She poised a finger over the keypad. "Go on."

He reeled off the number, and she made the call. But no one there had seen Johnny since late morning.

Meliana gave up. "What do you know about Enrique Jago?" she asked Chris.

"He's nasty, vindictive and powerful in limited circles. He wants to be a lot nastier, a lot more vindictive and a whole lot more powerful before this decade runs out."

"Not what I wanted to hear. Where does he live?"

"He has homes in New York, Miami and Cartagena."

"Do you think he murdered Modesta Perrine?"

"Odds are good. Why her and not Johnny, I can't tell you. Unless she scammed him in some way—one not related to Johnny's undercover work."

Meliana kept an eye on the door and the other on her watch. "I wondered about that. I assume the possibility's being investigated."

"From the back alleys of Chicago outward. Now, relax and lighten up. He'll get here when he gets here."

"You sound like Eddy the plumber." Meliana decided to try one more person, and this time got an answer on the third ring.

"Crawford."

"Hi, Zack, it's Mel."

"Well, hello, stranger. What's up? If it's that pipe again, it'll take more skill than I've got to replace it. And borrowing Tim Carrick's pump only made me question his sanity as well as his lifestyle. His place smells like a science lab—like formaldehyde or something—the furniture's wrapped in plastic and I think I saw a pair of ducks hanging from a wire through the kitchen door."

"Thanks for that, Zack."

"Hey, I got the pump. Now, what can I do for you?"

"I'm looking for Johnny. Do you know if he's left Blue Lake yet?"

"He took off about three hours ago. Last I saw, he was headed south, toward Route 90."

"That's his usual route." She gnawed on her bottom lip. "Okay, thanks. I might come up there later this week. Depends on my schedule."

"Bring your cop friend," Zack said, "and good luck finding Johnny."

She ended the call with a vexed "I wouldn't need luck to find him if he'd keep his phone charged."

Chris finished his beer. "If he did that, Mel, he wouldn't be Johnny. I'll help you look." At the mild suspicion in her eyes, he caught and squeezed her fingers. "Call it a peace offering, okay? We'll take your car."

Except that her car had a white rose on the passenger seat. "I'll drive," she told him. "I know Johnny's shortcuts."

They left the crowd noise behind at the door. The street was dark and virtually silent. Until Chris peered into her car and spied the rose. "Not a word." Meliana said. "I don't need you to spook me. I'm doing that just fine by myself."

Chris glanced from the rose to her face, then nodded and made a zipping motion across his mouth with his thumb and forefinger.

His easy response was a relief to Meliana—until she pulled away from the curb and saw him dangling the rose between his legs and yanking the petals off one by one.

HEADLIGHTS SWEPT OVER the pickup every few seconds. So far, no one had stopped for the raised hood.

Unfortunately for Johnny, ninety minutes of searching for the source of the breakdown had produced nothing except a number of inventive curses, a cut hand and two belts that looked older than the truck. His cell was dead—not unusual—he'd gotten grease in the cut and banged his head twice on the sagging hood. The moral, he decided, was never borrow a vehicle from a person over eighty.

He gave the dented fender a whack and yanked open the door. His eyes narrowed when they landed on the dash. The gas gauge read half full, but hadn't it read that when he'd started out this morning?

He made a sound of disgust—at himself this time— hunted up a piece of hose from the box and dipped it into the tank. It came up bone-dry. Figured.

"I hate you," he said to the vehicle, then blew out a gusty breath and reviewed his options.

There weren't many. He could sit here and hope a Samaritan would stop, or hike back two miles to the last filling station he'd passed. Neither prospect appealed, but the second one made the most sense.

His gaze drifted toward Chicago. He needed to get hold of Meliana before she did something he'd regret, like…

"Hell." He recognized her car instantly. With the recognition came two opposing desires, one to kiss her and another to punch Chris Blackburn's lights out. What were they doing together?

Jumping out of the car, she ran to him. She threw her arms around him, grease and all, then pulled away, grabbed him by the hair and yanked.

"You knot head, why didn't you call me?"

"Dead cell," she answered in perfect sync with him. She tugged again, this time not so hard. "I'm going to buy you six more phones so you'll have one for every day of the week."

"He'll still forget to charge them," Chris put in.

His sour tone saved him. Otherwise, Johnny was thinking about shoving a fist down his throat simply for being there.

"Why?" he asked Meliana instead.

"I ran into him outside Nino's. He was in the area. Is that blood on your shirt?"

"Probably. I have a three-inch gouge on my hand courtesy of Andy's rusty distributor cap. No stitches," he said before she could speak. "And I'm just out of gas." He raised his voice and his eyes. "What were you doing at Nino's, Blackburn?"

Chris's lip curled. "Thinking about going in. I needed a break. I'm not like you, Grand—I have to work for a living. You know, the boring kind of work you could never be bothered with."

Meliana pressed a hand to Johnny's chest. "Just don't," she warned.

Johnny pushed against her. "That's real rewarding work you do, Blackburn. Tracking the grandparents of a little girl whose mother's a lush and whose father sleeps with a carousel of women barely out of high school."

"The kid's grandparents broke the law, pal. They want custody, they need to go through legal channels, not act like fugitives in a bad movie."

Johnny regarded him with contempt. He looked down and away for a moment, then gave a humorless laugh. "You're right," he said. "It's not their place to make that decision."

Meliana kept her hand on his chest. "So are we all friends again?"

At Johnny's slitted eyes and Chris's thundercloud expression, she sighed. "Guess not. Oh, well." Sliding her fingers upward, she brushed the hair from Johnny's face. "I'm glad you're okay, Grand."

"Me, too," he said, and drew her into a deep, heart-stopping kiss.

MELIANA'S BRAIN DIDN'T RESTART until after Chris roared off in her car. When she realized he'd gone and why, she rammed a fist into Johnny's stomach. "You're a snake."

"And Blackburn isn't?"

Because she felt like it, she kissed him again, then

stepped out of reach. "That's it, no more. You're broken down, and I was frantic."

"I'm out of gas, and you're never frantic. Blackburn's gone for fuel, and the moon's up. We could make out in Andy's cab and be done long before your sulking champion returns."

"*If* he returns. You keep goading him, and one day he might…"

"What?"

"I don't know. Challenge you to a duel, I suppose."

"That's illegal, Mel."

"It's always been illegal. Didn't stop people from doing it in the past." She moved closer again, ran a finger along his jaw until he looked at her. "What's the real deal between you two? It can't be all me. I sensed antagonism the day you came to the hospital with a gunshot wound to the shoulder. He seemed angry at you for getting hurt."

Johnny said nothing, then finally raised his hands, fingers spread, in what she suspected was a bid for self-patience. "It's complicated."

Meliana caught his chin. "Translation—it involves a woman."

"It does, yeah, but not in the way you're thinking. Do you remember Maxine?"

"Your cousin from Indianapolis?"

"She came to Chicago with a couple of friends about a year before you and I met. Chris liked what he saw, so he talked her into bed."

"Typical."

"You think that's okay?"

"No, but most men would—with anyone other than their wives, sisters or cousins. Go on."

"We'd just met, so I didn't know much about him. I discovered later that he had a fiancée in Atlanta."

"Ah."

"What does that mean?"

"Nothing, just ah. I'm not a great believer in long-distance relationships. I know some of them work, but obviously this one didn't. I assume Chris didn't mention her to Maxine."

"No, but he mentioned Maxine to a lot of other agents. They were guys I worked with, Mel, and she was my cousin."

Meliana frowned in the direction of the filling station. "Did you do something?"

"I punched him out, then went looking for Maxine."

Judging from the expression on his face, finding her hadn't been a pleasant experience. Meliana risked a canny "She was with someone else, right?"

"You could say that. His name was Ken Magister." Johnny's brows went up. "Ring any bells?"

More than she cared to hear. "He's a state court judge." She met his stare. "And a self-proclaimed family man. His wife owns seventeen boutiques in the Great Lakes area. His son's been scouted by a number of NFL teams. I'm really sorry, Johnny. And you're right, it is complicated."

"She's a call girl, or was back then."

"Are you saying Chris paid to have sex with her?"

"She says he did. He says he didn't. That wasn't the

point. She was still my cousin, and he was bragging about how great she was in bed to a bunch of other guys I knew and worked with."

She dropped her head back, looked up at the stars. "You men are so touchy in some ways and so oblivious in others. I see why you have a problem with Chris, Johnny, but I'm not Maxine, and I'm not interested. Okay?"

The smile that curved his lips was reluctant, but at least it was a smile. "Okay. End of story."

"You're a good cousin, Johnny." Meliana rested her hands on his shoulders as he drew her up against him. "You're also really dirty."

"So are you. Look down at your sweater."

It had been cream cashmere once. Now it was a grease-streaked mess. She hid a smile. "You're an expensive bad habit, Johnny Grand. I don't like bad habits."

"In that case," he said, "you'll have to try and break me." With a move too swift for her to counter, he switched their positions. Bracing his hands against the cab on either side of her head, he murmured a soft "Or try," and covered her amused mouth with his.

SHE KISSED HIM! Got all excited when she saw him on the road and rushed right over to him. You can't do that, Meliana. You're not his anymore. You're mine. Why can't you see that?

You're too smart to be so stupid. I sent you a warning, a blatant one. A fool might misinterpret it, but you're no fool. You don't belong to Johnny. You're not his wife!

That whole horrible scene has made me shake all over. I've pulled off to the side of the road. There's blood in my head, Meliana, Johnny's blood. Your blood, too, if you don't start behaving the way you're supposed to. The way you did when Johnny first came back.

I have dreams about you all the time, even when I'm awake. I spun them out of nothing—a touch—wove them into a tapestry of love. *I love you, Meliana.* I love you, and I'm going to have you. One way or another.

I have a pretty white slip folded up in my pocket. It still smells like your perfume. If I hold it up to my face, I can see you wearing it for me. Or—no, it can't be. Is that Johnny I see in my place?

The shaking's so bad now I can't control it. I can't control the dreams, or myself. The knife I'm using to shred your slip has gone too deep and cut my leg. There's blood on the white lace, blood on the silk, my blood on your slip.

I want to cry. I want to kill. I want you to listen.

Because next time, Meliana, the blood will not be mine.

Chapter Nine

Meliana walked into Julie's ground-floor condo. "Here's the key to my house, Julie—hi, Sam," she said to Julie's stepbrother. "I'll only be in Blue Lake for four days, but the two big plants in my living room need water every morning."

"You gonna fish?" Sam asked. He offered Meliana a cheerful smile. "I caught three trout last time I went up there."

"You can come again this weekend if you want to," Meliana told him. "Both of you."

Julie set the key on a shelf. "Offer accepted, for me anyway. Andy can take over watering duty. Any more news on Modesta Perrine?"

"Only that Enrique Jago's in Miami and talking strictly through his lawyers."

"What a surprise. She was high when she died, we know that much, but probably not high enough to have overdosed."

"The shredded bra?"

"No prints on it or the box. No hair, stray threads or animal fur. The guy must live in a bubble."

"Why would someone cut up your bra?" Sam asked Meliana. "It doesn't make sense."

"A lot more things don't make sense than do, Sam. How are the headaches?"

"I haven't had any lately. I stopped reading, like you said. Well, except I had to go through the phone book last night online."

"He means the New York City phone book," Julie revealed. "Took him five whole minutes to locate a certain person with the first name Alfred and a last name that starts with a *P*, a *D* or a *G*, currently living on Albacore Avenue. He was doing a favor for a colleague who suspects her ex-hubby's gone into hiding with one of his old college buddies in order to avoid making support payments."

"Sounds complicated."

"Not really," Sam said. "When's a good time to come to Blue Lake?"

"Friday afternoon. It's supposed to rain until then."

"Tell Zack to watch your back," Julie warned, "and be careful."

Meliana smiled. "Yes, Mommy." She gave Sam's hair a tug. "See you Friday."

"Don't catch all the fish before I get there, and don't…" Sam blinked, trailed off. His eyes seemed to glaze over.

Meliana glanced at Julie, then back. "Sam?"

He snapped his head up, zeroed in on her face. Before

she could move, he clamped a hand on her wrist. A muscle ticked in his jaw.

"Are you all right?" When he didn't answer, Meliana trapped his chin and peered into his eyes. "Sam, what's wrong?"

Julie bumped her shoulder from behind. "Is he sick? Are you sick?" she repeated to her stepbrother.

"What is it, Sam?" Meliana tried again.

"Don't," he said. "Don't…"

"Don't what?" She noticed that his pupils were dilated and wondered briefly about drugs. "Are you on medication?"

He tightened his grip. "Don't eat…"

"Don't eat what?" Julie demanded, white-faced.

He turned his head, gazed northward. "Don't eat the fruit!"

"THERE'S NO FRUIT in the house, Mel—trust me."

On her knees in front of the vegetable crisper, Meliana sent Johnny an exasperated look. "How can you not have at least apples or oranges?"

"You're lucky I've got milk."

"Yeah, a whole quart, three days past the sell-by date. You know, it's a miracle you're not malnourished—which, come to think of it, you probably are and just don't realize it." She pushed aside a bag of stale bread, three cans of soda and a jar of pickle water. "This is pathetic, Johnny. We need to go shopping."

He crouched beside her. "Tell me, if we buy fruit at the store, can we eat it?"

She sat back on her heels. "It was weird. It's like Sam went into a trance for a moment, and when he came out of it—after he told me not to eat the fruit—he gave me a big smile and said he'd be here Friday, and you should get the fishing poles ready."

Johnny ran a hand over his mouth. "If it was anyone but Sam, I'd think it was an act, but he's too childlike to be yanking your chain."

"He seems childlike, Johnny, but he has an IQ of 185, and he's an organizing whiz. Food Services has never been in better shape." Standing, she brushed dust from her jeans, then her palms. "When's Eileen coming back?"

"Tomorrow. She was too busy with the broken pipe to get much done last time she was here."

"Not good news."

"This is a lakeside retreat, Mel. You're being overly picky."

She poked through the cupboards. "In other words, you want to let the dogs in from the sunporch."

"Eileen doesn't mind mopping up a little mud."

"Eileen's paid by the hour. I'm not." Amused, Meliana removed a box from the second shelf. "Prunes?"

Johnny shrugged. "My mother came to visit three months ago."

"Yeah, well, they're rock hard and they're also fruit, so they can go." She retucked the cardboard lid. "I wonder where Sam's mini-epiphany came from? I talked to Julie afterward. Except for this and that thing at the hospital when he knew I was going to be paged, he's never had any extraordinary episodes."

"Maybe he's been taking lessons from Charlie."

She shot him a humorous look over her shoulder. "You nonbelievers are so dull." Her gaze circled the large room, eventually coming to rest on the wedding picture he had sitting on the mantel. It was the only item there, and it appeared dust free. "Feels like a long time ago, doesn't it?"

She felt his eyes on her when he said, "In some ways it was."

"I only saw you six times in two years. By the end, I was starting to feel awkward when you showed up, like some long-lost best friend I should know, but didn't anymore."

"I thought about you all the time, Mel, day and night. You were never out of my mind."

She rubbed her arms. "Was I out of John Garcia's mind?"

She could tell by his expression that he understood her meaning. He opened his mouth, spread his fingers, then closed his mouth and dropped his hands. "I was John Garcia in public. I had to be. I flirted and teased and played the game. Sometimes I got rough."

"How rough, Johnny?"

An edge crept into his voice. "Look, don't judge me, okay? You weren't there. Hell, I was barely there. It was one big acting job, with a single overriding objective."

"To shut down a major drug cartel."

"Yes."

"No matter what the cost." She could have said more, but she stopped herself there. This was Johnny, not John. And the time was now, not then. She took a deep breath. "I'm sorry. I'm being unfair. I knew what your work entailed from the night I met you." Her lips curved at the memory. "The first words out of Chris's mouth were that you'd been shot by a hooker."

"Who was an integral part of a very large smuggling op. Weapons, drugs, people. I crossed the wrong person on the wrong night. I still haven't figured out how she knew I was in that alley."

Meliana could almost see his mind working. Because he seemed adrift in the large room, she strolled toward him. "You better not be thinking what I think you're thinking."

He held her gaze. "I was the one out there, Mel. Chris was inside the club."

"He didn't tip her off, you know that. He risked his own life to save yours." Or so Chris had claimed in the E.R. "You might see him as a rat, and he might be one in some ways, but not in the slimy turncoat way." Halting in front of him, she slid her hands around his waist and tilted her head to regard him from a seductive angle. "Know what we're gonna do now?"

She loved the artful grin that stole across his mouth. "Make up for lost time?"

She pressed her lips to his. "No cigar today, I'm afraid. Find a pen and paper, Grand. I'm hungry for food that isn't three months old." She gave his nose a quick kiss. "We're going into town."

THEY BOUGHT TEN BAGS of groceries and a carton of other supplies. It took the cashier twenty minutes to ring in their order because, as she demonstrated several times, her arthritis had flared up last week and no one at the clinic could give her anything for it.

"Tim, he offered me pills last time he came in, but I said no thanks to that. Sounded illegal to me, taking drugs without a doctor's say-so. Besides which, I heard he's turned his place into a nudist camp these days."

"Mrs. Wilmot at the post office shared that information," Johnny explained to Meliana. "The rest of us are just running with it."

The cashier gave her glasses a poke. "You work for the government. Isn't it illegal to walk around in public with your clothes off?"

"Probably, but I'm not the person to enforce that law. Did you get candy bars, Mel?"

"Three four-packs. What kind of pills did Tim offer you, Agnes?"

"I didn't ask—just said no." She rearranged the knit cap she used to cover her thinning gray hair. "You gonna be at the clinic tomorrow, Doc?"

"Bright and early. Do you want me to take a look at your hands?"

"Better you than Nurse Hooper." She plopped a bag on the scale. "These organic or regular apples?"

"Organic," Meliana said. "Gala."

"You bought fruit?" Johnny picked through the rest of the order. "Four different kinds?"

"There's nothing wrong with this fruit, Johnny. I'm not sure what Sam meant, but he can't have been referring to anything fresh from the produce section."

"Got a twinge or two in my knees, as well," Agnes said.

"I'll be at the clinic by nine," Meliana promised. "Pay the nice woman, Johnny. I'll start loading the car."

She left him with Agnes, whose eyes gleamed with curiosity.

"What?" he said when she didn't speak.

"Nothing at all. That's $182.90."

"We're not back together."

She showed her false teeth. "Course not. Who'd ever think that?"

With a sigh, Johnny reached into his jeans for his wallet. When he came up short cashwise, he checked his jacket pockets. He found a stick of gum, a twenty and a small white card. He gave Agnes the twenty, read the card—and found himself grinding his teeth.

"Something wrong, Mr. Grand?"

Johnny stared at the printing. "Nothing important, Agnes."

He turned the card over, thought back, tried to remember where he'd worn this jacket lately.

"You feeling poorly? You've gone all white."

He summoned a quick smile. "Yeah, thanks. What's that?"

"Your change."

He took it and started for the door.

"Don't you want your groceries?" Agnes called after him.

"I'll be right back." He caught Meliana's arm as she was returning, and eased her away from the storefront.

"Not enough money?"

He handed her the card. "I found this in my jacket pocket."

He gave her credit for steady nerves. She didn't tremble at all when she read the malevolent message.

I'M GOING TO KILL YOU.
BOTH.

"WHO EXACTLY did you phone, Mel?"

The lake house was overflowing with people. It had taken Johnny ten minutes of searching to locate Meliana in the kitchen.

She counted burger patties and matched them with the buns Eileen had brought. "The only person I talked to was Mark. I couldn't get hold of Julie."

Johnny dropped his eyes as something crash-landed on the porch. "So it was Mark who gathered the troops and brought them over?"

"I guess." Meliana used her thumb and forefinger to tip his mouth up at the corners. "Be happy. At least we can't be killed in a crowd."

"Don't count on it." But he relaxed slightly and began tearing the lettuce she set out.

The past two nights had been pure hell. He'd lain awake with his gun on the nightstand in the guest bedroom and thought about the kind of lunatic they were dealing with. What sort of mind went from flowers to slashed bras to death threats in the space of a few days? A mind with absolutely no balance, he'd concluded, no grasp on reality, no sanity.

He'd spent Thursday talking on the phone with his FBI cronies, people who'd dealt with similar situations and might be able to help. They hadn't, because as one agent put it, no two minds ever went crazy in exactly the same way.

But there were frequently common factors. Adoration turned to disappointment, disappointment to rage, rage to acts of violence and destruction.

He'd worried about Meliana at the lakeside clinic. He'd gone there twice to check on her. In each case she'd been busy, and there'd been a backlog of patients in the waiting room. In retrospect, it seemed as safe a place as any for her to be.

That brought them to today, Friday. He'd been talking to a federal agent in New York when people began arriving. Julie and Sam had come first, followed by Mark and Charlie, two female physicians on staff at the hospital, a male surgeon, Nick Hohlman and five minutes behind the main group, Chris Blackburn and Andy McRae. Zack showed up with Sheriff Frank. Eileen and Agnes from the grocery store brought up the rear.

Everyone brought food except Mark, who unloaded several flats of beer from his rental car while he chuckled at Johnny's blank expression.

"I only made one little call after I talked to Mel," he'd said. "It's all down to strategic maneuvers, my friend. You got any coolers?"

In the kitchen, with voices buzzing and someone— likely Charlie—playing his guitar on the sunporch,

Johnny reached above the cupboard for a large platter. "I don't even know half these people, Mel."

"Me either. They seem to be multiplying from the original group. Who's the old man sitting next to Agnes?"

"I don't know, but the hearing aid he's wearing doesn't work. I asked him if he wanted a drink, and he just smiled and said the rain stopped sooner than expected."

Her eyes twinkled as she took the platter from him. "Well, it did, didn't it? Go with it for now, Johnny. A party's better than sitting around wondering if we're being watched by a psychopath."

Zack brought a handful of empty glasses in from the living room. "Did someone mention Tim's name?"

"Tim's unusual," Meliana agreed. "He's not psychotic."

Eileen came in with more glasses. "Refills all around, Johnny. I won't clean for Tim. I heard he's into taxidermy. Started out stuffing birds in his barn, then moved the operation into his house when his wife left him."

"Nice avocation," Zack remarked. "I can't imagine why Vivianne took off."

"If she took off."

Johnny let his head fall back at the sound of Chris's voice. He didn't turn but said, "Plenty of beer on the porch, Blackburn."

"More interesting conversation in here," Chris countered. His slurred words told Johnny he'd been into the beer already.

Julie worked her way through the crowd. "Sam's got the barbecue going, Johnny, if you want to start the burgers—which you probably should because more than a few of your guests are wobbling badly."

It was also getting dark, which meant it was getting late. "Are you drunk?" Johnny asked Chris.

"Working on it."

"I'll cook the burgers," Zack offered. "I'm on duty as of midnight. Can't drink," he said to Meliana.

She grinned and patted his cheek. "Think how much better you'll feel in the morning. Just do the whole platter and shout 'Food' when it's full."

"One of your physician friends is draped all over your brother," Julie informed her above a burst of background laughter.

"Redhead or blonde?"

"Blonde."

"That's Laura. She's married. Johnny?"

"I'll break it up." He snagged a beer from the fridge on the way outside. Might as well be in the majority.

Across the room, Agnes caught his eye and pointed to her cheeks. "Not looking so pale today, Mr. Grand."

He nodded, dredged up a smile. The noise and general chaos was giving him a headache, though Meliana probably had a point. There was a certain measure of safety in numbers.

"I brought wine," Nick called out. "I gave it to Meliana."

A redhead bumped into his arm. "Hey, Johnny. Long time, no see. You and Mel sure split up funny."

"We like to keep people guessing. Have you seen Mark?"

"He came through here a few minutes ago—" she raised her voice "—didn't he, Charlie?"

Charlie nodded. "He was making a halfhearted attempt to disengage himself from Laura Whelen last I saw."

"I'm supposed to help him disengage," Johnny said.

Charlie propped his guitar against the sofa back. "I'll keep you company. It's getting awfully hot in here."

They made their way through the throng of bodies on the sunporch. "Who are these people?" Johnny wondered out loud. "I only recognize about a third of them."

"I'll be generous and say a number of them are crashers from town."

Johnny spotted Nurse Hooper, who more or less ran the Blue Lake Clinic. She had her hair down, her pants rolled up and she was showing off her cleavage in a tight green top. Not bad for fifty-five plus.

"I don't see Mark or Laura," he said when they reached the yard.

Charlie chuckled. "Would you seduce a man in the great wide open?"

"I like to think I wouldn't seduce a man anywhere. The woods?"

"That'd be my guess, since your shed's barely standing. Did you lose much in the fire?"

"Nothing that matters."

"Was it arson?"

"Fifty-fifty chance, according to the local fire chief. But he's leaning strongly toward the possibility. There's been a lot of mischief and vandalism in the area lately."

"They call it mischief when vehicles get rolled into bogs and lakes, huh?"

"I imagine they think it was kids who did it. Me, I'm still looking for a guy in a plaid jacket who might or might not be a neighbor." He raised his voice. "Mark?"

Because he hadn't expected an answer, Mark's voice from the woods to his left surprised him.

"You want to give me a hand here, Johnny?"

Humor kindled in Charlie's expression. "This could be interesting."

Johnny doubted that, but headed toward the path anyway.

They found Mark on one knee beside a bed of leaves under a large maple tree. A woman in smudged white jeans with a blanket wrapped around her shoulders half sat, half sprawled against the trunk.

"Come on, Laura." Mark tugged on her hand. "You have to get up now. We need to go back to the house."

She snickered and let her head loll. "Don't wanna go. Too tired."

"Laura?" Johnny crouched down. "Mel wants you to come back, okay?"

She had a pretty smile even if her eyes were beginning to roll back in her head. "Really bad—" Her head bumped against the bark. She squinted her eyes. "Where are we? S'at you, Charlie?"

"The one and only. What say we head back to the house?"

"Okay." She beamed at Mark. "You can carry me."

"Why did you come out here?" Johnny asked,

pulling her forward so Mark could hike her up and onto his shoulder.

"She said she needed air."

"Sure she did." Charlie folded the blanket over his arm. "Is there a bottle somewhere we should be bringing back with us?"

"Knock it off," Mark said with a grunt. "You okay, Laura?"

Her words came out muffled and indignant. "I meant carry me in your arms."

Johnny checked the ground for extras. "Mark prefers the caveman technique."

"Man, you're funny." Mark shifted his load. "How about I make the jokes and you carry her?"

Johnny smiled a little, backed off and let Charlie lead the way. When Mark staggered, he grabbed Laura's legs and gave a quick boost.

"You're getting soft, Maynard. Put her down on the step away from the barbecue smoke. I'll find Mel."

She was already halfway out the door with a tray of buns when Johnny caught her eye and motioned her over.

She seemed surprised to discover her friend more or less passed out against the railing. "What happened?" she asked the three men.

Mark shrugged. "No idea. She was okay when we started out."

"She's married, you know."

"Update, sis—she's separated."

"Really?" Meliana sounded disappointed. She knelt

and raised Laura's eyelid. "Pinpoint pupils, and her breathing's shallow." She glanced at Mark again. "Was she doing drugs?"

"Not that I saw. She was fine at first, not slurring her words or stumbling or making stupid jokes."

"Any alcohol?"

"No."

"Why did you leave?"

"She wanted to talk. I thought she seemed sad."

Johnny crouched. "Is something wrong?"

"I don't like her breathing. Her lips and fingertips have a bluish tinge, and her pulse is weak. She's also unresponsive." She felt the pulse in Laura's neck again. "We need to get her to the clinic. Someone find Ronnie—the redhead—inside. She's an internist."

"I'll do it," Charlie offered.

While Meliana attempted to wake Laura, Johnny motioned to Julie to keep the others back and say nothing. He didn't know Sam was there until he heard his voice behind them. At that, only a choked sound emerged.

"It's okay, Sam," Johnny promised. "Go back inside."

But Sam's eyes were locked on Laura's face. When he raked the hair from his forehead in agitation, Johnny stood and caught his arms. "What?"

"I said don't to Meliana." His breath hitched, his voice rose. "I didn't think about anyone else."

A film of ice coated Johnny's skin. He gave Sam a small shake. "Not now, okay?"

"Yeah." Sam brought his hands down, lowered his

voice. "Sure." He stared woodenly at the woman on the stairs, then in a tone devoid of emotion, whispered, "She shouldn't have eaten the fruit."

Chapter Ten

They treated Laura at the Blue Lake Clinic. They gave her a gastric lavage, administered activated charcoal with a narcotic antagonist, then started an IV.

Ronnie Lord, an internist at the party, oversaw the procedure with Meliana. They agreed the drug in Laura's system was heroin, amount unknown, but based on her symptoms a definite overdose.

She was transferred by ambulance to Chicago for further treatment. She'd recover, of that Meliana felt certain. The question was, how had the heroin entered her system?

"I assume she's not a user," Johnny remarked as they waded through the remnants of the party and into the house.

Meliana gazed around at the mess. She could smell the scorched burgers Zack had abandoned in the chaos. "Laura's not into drugs or alcohol. I knew that anyway, but she confirmed it at the clinic." She spied a bowl of grapes on the coffee table and plucked one from the bunch. "We need to get all the fruit in here analyzed."

Mark, who'd come in behind them with Julie, looked up from his perusal of the kitchen counters. "Why fruit specifically?"

Meliana explained. Julie rubbed her forehead. Johnny paced.

Mark glanced toward the woods. "Laura was eating an apple when we left."

"Apples." Meliana thought back. "I bought apples at the Blue Lake Market. Johnny?"

But he was already counting the ones in the crisper. "There's five here, Mel. How many did you buy?"

"Six, but I ate one on the way home from town."

"Other people brought food." Julie went to the window to peer out. "Sam's throwing sticks for the dogs. Do you want me to get him in here?"

"He says he doesn't know anything other than the fact that words jumped into his head telling him to tell me not to eat the fruit in Blue Lake. What kind of apple did Laura have?" Meliana asked Mark.

"I'm not sure. It was red, and she said it was mealy in the center." He tapped a finger on the door frame. "She didn't eat it all. She threw half of it into the trees while we were walking."

"It could have been a red Delicious."

Meliana looked at Johnny, whose lips curved into a faint smile. "Let me guess—you want me to find it."

"You'll have a better chance tonight than tomorrow. Mark can help you."

"Peachy."

Julie removed a burned burger from the platter and

dangled it. "You can chow down on one of these while you search."

"I'd prefer it to the local apples." Mark zipped his jacket. "Has anyone seen Charlie? Mel?"

"He's outside with Sam, probably lighting up one of the cigarettes he insists he doesn't smoke."

"Tell you what," Julie offered. "I'm wired anyway. Why don't I go with Mark, and you and Johnny can gather up the apples in here. Find all the fruit. Pile it on the counter. We'll bag and tag it later. Are Zack and the sheriff coming back?"

Meliana checked her watch. "It's after midnight, and there was a big racket coming out of the Lakeside Bar as we drove past. Zack'll have his hands full there for a while."

"And the sheriff's where?"

"Home in bed, snoring," Johnny told her. "Off duty's off duty to Sheriff Frank."

"It's never like that in Chicago," Julie muttered. "Fruit, Mel," she instructed, and let the screen door slam behind her.

Meliana felt a scream rising. Not because she was angry, but because she needed an outlet for the tension coiled up inside her. And because—stupid, stupid—she hadn't monitored the food coming in, even after Sam's warning. And maybe, just a little, because the house was a mess, and she hated disorder.

"Laura will be fine, Mel." Johnny was standing directly behind her. Meliana felt the warmth of his body. She inhaled his scent and longed to dissolve into him.

He solved her dilemma by wrapping his arms loosely around her neck and kissing the side of her head. "She's young and strong, and you and Ronnie worked fast."

"All sounds good, Johnny, but I'm still responsible. Not directly, but in a roundabout way. People brought food, and I didn't look to see what it was. Even if I doubted Sam's premonition, I should have checked."

"*We* should have checked. We didn't. Not smart, I agree, but—"

"Uh-uh." She cut him off. "It was our party. It should have been safe for people to come here. Still…" She sighed and bumped her head against his chin. "Moaning about mistakes won't remedy them. We need to find all the fruit, like Julie said, and take it in to a lab."

"You want to go on a fruit hunt, huh?"

What she wanted to do was make love to her husband, and… Her mind stuttered. Like an old record, it skipped back over the same words again and again.

She wanted to make love to Johnny, she really did. She had for some time now. She would, given half a chance.

But she couldn't, she knew that. She shouldn't. She wouldn't.

She needed air.

To her frustration, Johnny's arms held fast when she tried to pull them from her throat.

"No one can find a half-eaten apple in the dark that fast." He nuzzled her ear. "We can do all kinds of kinky things before they get back."

She couldn't stop the laugh that threatened to spill out. "You can't possibly know what I was thinking. Everyone can't be turning into a mind reader."

Johnny's breath stirred her hair. "You think Sam reads minds?"

"I don't know what Sam's deal is." But she knew her knees felt weak. "Charlie picks up vibes. Sam's more of a mystery…. Johnny, I really don't think you should be doing that."

"Doing what?"

"Kissing my neck."

He ran his tongue along the vein that throbbed on the side. "You have beautiful skin, Mel."

"So does a nectarine. Speaking of which, we're supposed to be…"

He nipped her earlobe. "What?"

She had no idea. Every thought in her head scattered, and for the life of her, she wasn't interested in retrieving them.

"Sex won't solve our problems, Johnny."

"It won't add to them, either."

"It might."

"I've missed you, Mel. I want to make love to you."

Bad timing, she thought. But the words were a distant murmur, hardly worth straining to hear.

She let her eyelids close halfway, focused on nothing except the feel of Johnny's mouth as he pushed aside her top and explored her neck and shoulder.

She'd missed this, she really had. She was a tactile person, and no one, not any man she'd ever known, could awaken as many sensations in her as Johnny Grand did. As he was doing at this minute.

His hands cupped her breasts. She hissed in a breath of reaction and pressed herself into him.

Really bad timing, her mind cautioned again. They weren't alone.

But she wanted him.

She saw it, first with her mind, then with her eyes. Her head jerked up. "Johnny?"

"Mmm."

"No—wait. You have to…" She eased away so she could capture his chin. "Look." She directed his gaze to a small table under the stairwell.

He squinted into the shadows. "Are those apples?"

"A whole big bowl of red Delicious." Arranged, she noted, in a spiral. Anybody choosing would automatically take the one on the top.

She approached the table with Johnny. To an outsider, she imagined their actions might appear rather comical. Who'd sneak up on a bowl of apples?

Meliana doubted there'd be fingerprints on the skins, but they might get lucky. Assuming Laura had been poisoned with this particular fruit. For all anyone knew, she might have eaten a banana or a peach or grapes before she left with Mark.

Johnny gave Meliana's neck a light squeeze. "Let's leave these for now and concentrate on collecting the rest of the fruit. Man—" he shook his head "—who brings fruit to a party?"

"People who are into healthy living." Meliana regarded the bowl and shivered. "And others who aren't."

As they worked, she tried to figure out which person had arrived with what food item. Julie had brought bags of potato chips and two big jars of peanuts. Charlie had been carrying a tray of meats and cheeses. Sam had brought soda pop—and something in a bag. Meliana hadn't asked what it was and didn't plan to. Sam's name wasn't going on any loony list she drew up.

"What did Zack bring?" she asked Johnny.

"Doughnut holes. Four dozen of them."

"Really?" Meliana balanced the oranges in her arms. "I never saw those."

"She who hesitates... They were delicious. I saw your surgeon friend come in with a big tub of potato salad and a veggie platter."

"His name's Lawrence, and it was a pasta salad. Eileen brought hamburger buns and some of her special barbecue sauce. Sheriff Frank—I have no idea. But there must have been more stuff. I remember seeing a lot of grocery bags in the kitchen."

"From Chicago stores?"

"Mostly. Is it important?"

"It could be." Johnny worked the muscles in the back of his neck. "I keep thinking about the card I found in my pocket at the market. I've worn that jacket into the city a few times lately."

Meliana separated oranges, apples, bananas, grapes and a box of garlic bulbs she'd discovered near the front door. They weren't fruit, but she hadn't purchased them in town.

Her head swam with names and faces. When had Chris showed up? Had he come empty-handed? Nick's wine sat next to the fridge. Did wine qualify as fruit? Because they'd opened three bottles.

But only Laura had been poisoned.

Exhausted, Meliana sank onto the sofa. When Johnny dropped down beside her, she laid her head on his shoulder. "How did everything get to be such a mess?"

"I was wearing it the last time I talked to Chris."

It had to be the strain that made her laugh. And once she started, she simply couldn't stop. Tears rolled down her cheeks. She had to sit up and bend over to keep her sides from hurting.

"I'm sorry," she gasped, and wiped her eyes with her fingers. "It's just all so absurd. Poison apples, covert notes, blatant threats, pretty roses, missing lingerie, rocks flying through windows, naked neighbors—I know that's irrelevant, but it's so bizarre when you toss it in with everything else." She sucked in a deep breath and glanced at Johnny. He was lounging in the corner of the sofa, the side of one finger resting on his lips as he contemplated her. Was he wondering about her sanity? Then she caught his smile and knew he was simply amused by her reaction.

She sobered, or tried to. Because nothing about this situation was remotely funny. Certainly her friend being poisoned was nothing to laugh about. Neither were the threats on Johnny's life.

"I need to eat," she decided, and toppled facedown onto his chest.

He stroked her hair. "We need answers."

"One answer." She hiccupped. "I knew that was going to happen. We either have to catch this guy in the act or put the pieces we have together and figure out who he is."

A smile stole across Johnny's lips. "Sounds simple, doesn't it, when reduced to its basic form, but he's got us looking in every conceivable direction, at everyone and at no one. Whatever else he might be, Mel, this guy's clever."

"And dangerous." She rolled over, pictured Laura's labored breathing before they'd administered the counter drug and pressed her fingertips to her temples. "She could have died, Johnny. Probably would have if she'd eaten the whole apple." She paused, bit her lip. "He must have meant it for me. A poisoned apple. It's like *Snow White and the Seven Dwarfs.*"

"So now we're looking for a wicked queen?" He fluffed her hair. "You do need food, darling."

She pushed herself upright. What she needed was to splash cold water on her face. "Back in a minute." She gave his knee a smack. "Check the sunporch for fruit while I'm gone."

She heard Sam outside, whistling at the dogs. She imagined Charlie would be meditating close by. She wished one of them would simply visualize the stalker and end all of this right now.

With her fingers she combed the hair from her face and twisted it into a knot. Johnny had his laptop open on the upstairs desk. She glanced at it, saw an envelope float across the screen and backtracked. If the FBI was sending uncoded messages about Modesta Perrine's death, she wanted to read them.

She brought up the new e-mail, but dismissed it when she realized it was from one of Johnny's long-winded cohorts in New York. Let him sift through the man's ramblings. She turned for the bedroom.

Her cell phone rang in tandem with the house phone. She let Johnny pick up downstairs and answered her cell.

"Meliana..."

She didn't recognize the man's voice. "Yes." She paused. "Can I help you?"

A prickle of unease crawled down her spine when he didn't respond. "Is something wrong?" she asked.

"You're still with him."

The prickle became a set of very sharp claws. She searched the desktop, found a pen and tossed it over the railing at the sunporch window to attract Johnny's attention. "Who are you?"

"He's there with you, I know he is." He sounded angry now, and agitated. "You told him to go away six months ago, but then you let him come back. Why?"

Meliana threw another pen, and this time Johnny came to the door. She motioned him to the staircase, started for it herself. "We're not together the way you think."

"I've seen you kissing him."

Her heart thumped so hard in her chest, she thought he'd hear her terror. "We're friends." She mouthed the words *It's him* to Johnny at the bottom of the stairs.

From the waistband of his jeans he pulled a gun she hadn't realized he was carrying and scanned the lower windows. "Are you here in Blue Lake?" she asked.

"I'm always with you, Meliana." The voice became a purr. It was still unrecognizable but not quite so distraught. "You're the woman I've always wanted, the perfect female. At least, I thought you were."

She had to set her teeth to keep them from chattering. "What are you going to do?"

"I've already done it."

"You poisoned an apple at the party."

"I poisoned," he whispered, "as I've been poisoned. You were everything, Meliana—my dream, my ultimate woman. We were going to be together, you and me. I would have treated you like a queen, put you on a pedestal."

"But I don't want..." She watched Johnny slip outside, ordered herself not to overreact. "Why me?"

"I told you why." The rough edge returned. "And now I'll tell you something else. I poisoned more than an apple tonight."

She pictured the burger Julie had been dangling in front of Mark and spun toward the woods. "What else?" she demanded. "Please—" She lowered her voice to a calmer level. "Please tell me."

"I'll say what I choose to say." The poison flowed from his mouth now. "You listen to me, Meliana. Someone's going to die very, very soon. You won't know how or when or where, but know this. It won't be fast. It won't be merciful. And it won't be pretty."

MELIANA DIDN'T WANT to recall his threats, let alone repeat them to Julie. Thankfully, Julie relayed the conversation to Zack and her captain in Chicago.

"Look at it this way," her friend consoled. "At least the police are on board with you now."

"Right. And exactly what are they planning to do?"

"Okay, fine, there's not a lot anyone can do, unless the FBI decides to pitch in, but we're aware, Mel. You're aware, and so's Johnny."

Meliana held her cell phone with both hands and stared at it. "I'm not sure awareness will help us here. He's got some kind of plan."

"He says he does."

"Whether it's formed or he makes one up on the fly, chances are he'll execute it."

"Do you think he'll go after Johnny?"

"Yes. Well—yes and no." Meliana considered. "Actually, I'm not sure he will. He wants to, I know that, but I think he might be afraid."

"Of Johnny?"

"He's FBI. Not only is he good at his job, but he's also got friends at the agency, and they take care of their own. This guy knows enough about Johnny to realize that. He might feel intimidated."

"You hope."

"Fervently." She regarded her watch. "My God, is it only 1:00 a.m.?"

"It is, and I'm spending the rest of the night with you. I'll go back to Chicago tomorrow, see how much room my captain'll give me to move. It'll help that Mark found the apple Laura was eating. He and Charlie are taking it into the city, right?"

"They're en route as we speak." Meliana dredged up a smile. "Thanks for everything, Jules. You're always there. I appreciate it."

They flopped back on the sofa, shoulder to shoulder. "Do you remember how we met?" Julie asked.

"Vividly. You gave me a speeding ticket. I put an old Hawaiian curse on your hotshot rookie butt, and you immediately threw your back out when you bent to pick up my driver's license, which my curse caused you to drop. You're lucky I know a thing or two about chiropractic. You were able to straighten up just enough for me to help you into your car."

"Hey, I tore up the ticket, didn't I?"

"Only after I threatened you with another curse."

"I also called and invited you to Carlson's for ribs and beer."

It felt good to laugh. "You called me," Meliana corrected, "because you misplaced the name of the extremely hot chiropractor whose name I wrote for you on my torn-up ticket."

"I didn't misplace it. I couldn't read it, and neither could the three pharmacists I took it to. He was hot, though," she agreed. "Unfortunately, he was also married."

"Well, hey, I was in med school. I didn't get personal with the people I met there."

Julie popped the seal on a fresh bag of pretzels. "How many vacations have we taken together?"

"Not counting Mindanao, five."

"I'm definitely not counting that. I still have nightmares about those jail cells." She glanced at the door. "Is there any beer left, and where are Johnny and Sam?"

"Plenty on the sunporch, and they've gone into town to talk to Zack. Sheriff Frank, too, if anyone can rouse him."

"Sam feels guilty." Julie headed for the porch. "He thinks maybe if he hadn't said it, the poisoning wouldn't have happened. You know, he totally baffles me, Mel. He's not—what's the term—mentally challenged, and God knows, he was never slow in school, but he can't eat his morning cereal without dribbling milk down his chin, and nine times out of ten he confuses left and right. Give him a stack of mathematical problems, though, or a set of books to balance, and it's done before you can blink. Go figure, huh?"

"He's gifted." Meliana picked up the pretzels, toyed with the bag. "I heard Thomas Edison couldn't tie his own shoelaces." She ran her finger around the dimpled rim. "I've also heard there's a fine line between genius and insanity."

Julie returned with a cold lager. "I hope you're not referring to your freaky rose guy, because there's no trace of genius in him."

"Only insanity." Meliana studied the pretzels. "No, don't," she said when Julie reached for one.

"What is it?" her friend demanded.

Meliana indicated the seam where the seal had been broken. "Do you see that?"

"Mel, it's after one and I'm beat. All I see is junk food."

"There are two seams here, Julie. One was made by the factory, the other was made by someone else." She set the pretzels on the coffee table in front of them. "This bag's been opened and resealed."

"—and I can't be sure it's from all that rigmarole, of course, but things are just so..."

She thinks you're some kind of miracle-worker, right? Or set the process in motion—when it comes to these things—I can at least try to help.

Chapter Eleven

Meliana and Julie had the cupboards cleared out, and they were working on the fridge when Johnny and Sam returned.

Meliana saw the leashed fury in Johnny's expression. She read it in his body language. That he didn't verbalize it was undoubtedly due to Sam's white-cheeked presence and the fact that Julie's stepbrother continued to blame himself for the poison Meliana's friend had ingested.

"I should have seen it was an apple," he said over and over again. "I don't mean for things to go wrong like this."

They worked until dawn, collecting every scrap of food in the house and loading it into garbage bags.

"I'll call in a favor," Johnny told her, "and have everything checked out."

Meliana fell into bed and slept until two o'clock Saturday afternoon. She grabbed a quick shower, rushed to the clinic and spent the next four hours listening to a blend of symptoms and sympathy.

Agnes and her arthritic hands were among the last

patients to leave. "You and your husband need to join forces, Doc. It's all over town how someone's been giving you roses and sending you lingerie and chocolates. Alicia, my granddaughter, had something just like this happen to her in high school right here in Blue Lake, except for every gift she got, something else was stolen. Someone'd send her a pretty scarf, then her nightgown'd go missing. A book of poems would appear and, poof, her favorite shoes disappeared. She got so rattled, her mom and me called Sheriff Frank and told him he'd better do something or we'd take matters into our own hands. We meant we'd hire a private detective, but I think he thought we were going to set out leghold traps, because he got his slow-as-molasses deputy to sleep outside my daughter's home for five nights in a row."

Meliana wrote a prescription to ease Agnes's stiffness and asked, "Did they catch the guy?"

"Someone snuck into the backyard, but he got away. Clumsy deputy had size-fifteen feet and stickpin legs. He tripped over his big shoes and plowed headfirst into a hedge. Still, there was no more trouble after that. I guess almost caught was as good as got."

Meliana tore the sheet from the pad and handed it to Agnes. "One tablet, once a day, okay?"

"You're a sweetheart, Dr. Mel. I hope they catch whoever's been pestering you."

"Me, too, Agnes."

Johnny passed the old woman in the doorway. She drilled a finger into his chest and said, "You watch her close, you hear? I fixed up a big hamper of food from my own kitchen. It'll do the pair of you till Monday." Her expression softened, and she gave his cheek a pat. "You're still looking a little off-color. Eat some of my horseradish. It'll have smoke shooting out your ears."

"Sounds great." Johnny waited until the door closed between them and added a wry "Like being stretched on a rack until your bones snap."

Meliana smiled at his testy tone. He looked good today, she thought. Not put together—his jeans were torn at the knees, his khaki T-shirt was torn at the shoulder and his ancient hikers probably had holes in them. But long hair suited the planes and angles of his face, and a three-day growth of stubble gave him a vaguely piratical air. Or was sinister a better word? Either way, Johnny Grand wore moodiness and danger better than any man she knew.

She began locking cabinets. "What do you think he'll do next?"

"Crawl back under a rock if he's smart. But his kind never are, so I'm guessing he'll find a way to vent his anger."

"On you or me?"

"Take your pick. Unless he decides to do us both at the same time."

"Thanks for the reassurance." She eyed Agnes's hamper. "Not wanting to sound ungrateful, but let's go out for dinner, okay?"

"Here in Blue Lake?"

"Well, yeah, unless for some twisted reason you want to drive to Chicago and back tonight. I promised to open the clinic for a few hours tomorrow, since I slept most of today away."

"You're all heart, Mel."

"It's guilt, and you haven't answered my question. Mama Mia's?"

"Best pasta in town."

"Only pasta in town. Give me five minutes."

Johnny was on the phone when she returned. The scowl he wore didn't improve her appetite. She wished she could board a plane for Hawaii and lose herself on one of the lesser-known islands until sometime next year. Maybe by then the stalker would have given up and moved on.

Except that moving on wasn't what she wanted him to do. And a sick mind wasn't going to be cured by magic. They needed to find a way to expose him before he hurt anyone else.

Johnny ended his call, stuffed the cell phone into his jeans pocket. "That was a friend of mine in Chicago, same one who called last night while your stalker was talking to you. Our insider grapevine says Enrique Jago's got some nasty Colombians after him right now. They're offing his people one by one trying to locate him."

"I thought he was in Miami."

"His lawyers are. Apparently Enrique's in hiding. My guess would be Brazil."

"What, in a native hut on an Amazon tributary?"

"More likely in a high-tech bunker in Rio. Either way, he's on the run and unlikely to have ordered a hit on Modesta Perrine."

"Good. I mean—" She waved a hand. "You know

what I mean. He didn't have her killed, ergo, he's not looking for you."

"And therefore not behind the roses."

"Did you really think he was?"

"No, but the first rule of law enforcement is never discount any possibility without proof. If Jago's on the run—and his status is being ascertained as we speak— then that's close enough to proof for me. For now."

Meliana removed her lab coat and swung a slim black jacket over her shoulders. "So, what's next?"

"We wait for details on the food, particularly Laura's apple and the double-sealed pretzels."

She removed the keys from her purse, shoved him ahead of her and locked the clinic door. "Sort of puts you off eating, doesn't it? Do you have Agnes's basket?"

"All fifty pounds of it." He peered under the snow-y-white cloth. "What's in here besides horseradish?"

"She didn't say. I didn't ask. It was kind of her, but I'm in the mood for spaghetti and bad Italian music." She nodded at the intersection. "Is that Tim Carrick's truck?"

The vehicle rolled past, its headlights cocked at different angles. The back was piled with old steamer trunks. Inside the cab, Tim's open coat and shirt indicated he had the heater running full blast.

"Does anyone really know where Vivianne is these days?" Meliana asked.

He blew out a breath. "You're not helping my nerves here, Mel."

Meliana grinned. "She left him, Johnny. There aren't any body parts buried on his property or hidden inside those old trunks. Mrs. Wilmot probably saw Tim naked because he decided to go skinny-dipping, and the path from his house to the lake is visible from Shoreline Road, which she's on all the time coming and going from Agnes's place."

"What about the crates and trunks he's forever loading into his truck?"

"That's easy. He bought his place from a ninety-three-year-old pack rat whose ninety-two-year-old wife had had a stroke. You must remember them. They moved to Chicago, and only took the bare essentials. They left a barn, a cellar, two big sheds and two attics full of a lifetime's worth of collectibles. Or junk, as Vivianne preferred to call it."

"Was there a plaid jacket in with this junk?"

Meliana laughed. "Probably."

Johnny eyed her with suspicion. "Are you making this stuff up?"

Her smile widened. "I might be, but if it helps you relax, why not go with it? I don't think Tim's a stalker."

"He wasn't at the party."

"That we know of."

"Thanks for helping me relax."

She kissed his cheek. "Okay, not at the party. Better?"

"No, but we can work on that later tonight."

Not if she was smart, they wouldn't.

Johnny shoved the basket into his newly repaired SUV, locked it and made sure their table at Mama Mia's overlooked the street.

It was terrible, Meliana reflected, to feel so paranoid.

Every bite of food became a question. Had the spaghetti sauce been poisoned, or the cheese, or the pepper flakes? What about the wine? Could someone have broken into the restaurant's cellar and tampered with the cork?

She managed to eat all the food on her plate, and drank two glasses of wine besides. Then she spotted Eileen Crawford sitting in a booth with Sheriff Frank and choked.

"What?" Johnny paused midbite.

"Is that—" she craned her neck for a better view "—a romantic dinner?"

Johnny looked over, made a sound of displeasure. "Eileen's the same age as my mother, and Frank's a lumbering ox. My mind doesn't want to go there."

"Wuss," she accused. "I think it's…" She hesitated, tipped her head. "Well, it's interesting anyway. Eileen's very pretty."

"Frank isn't."

"It's not about appearance, Johnny. Oh—did he kiss her?"

"Stop staring, Mel. No wonder Zack wants to leave Blue Lake."

She leaned forward on her elbows. "Paramedic's probably a good career move for Zack. Julie thinks he's sexy."

"What do you think?"

"Not my type."

"I don't know, Mel. His mother grows roses in her greenhouse."

"So does Nick's grandfather and Sam's mother.

Anyway, Julie likes him, and she has good instincts where men are concerned."

"Yeah? Then why did she go out with Chris?"

"Hey, anyone's radar can be off. The chemistry was wrong. I dated a few creeps in college myself."

Johnny arched a humorous brow. "Are you calling Blackburn a creep?"

She hadn't meant to. "Come on, Johnny, Chris is a nice guy. So are Zack and Charlie and Sam and Nick. I wouldn't vouch for Nick's grandfather, but he's probably fine in his own way."

"If you like vipers." Johnny swirled his wine. "Do you know why Zack wants to be a paramedic?"

"I'd guess it's a way out of Blue Lake. Small towns are nice, but they can be a little stifling. Did you know he dated Alicia Ross for a while?"

"Agnes's granddaughter?"

"Apparently."

"Is that significant for some reason?"

"Alicia only dated bad boys."

"Yeah, you told me about that. Did I mention that Alicia had a stalker in high school?"

"It was after she graduated, and it wasn't Zack."

Johnny's lips quirked. "Did I say it was?"

"Everyone's a suspect to you right now. Anyway, Agnes said they caught a glimpse of Alicia's stalker. He was short and fat, and he ran flat-footed. Sounds a bit like Tim Carrick, actually."

"They had a description like that here in Blue Lake, and they didn't catch the guy?"

"Problems are handled differently in remote communities. For all you know, Sheriff Frank identified the guy and had a quiet chat with his parents."

"What happened to Alicia?"

"She had a fight with her mother and moved to Decatur. I think she lives in Chicago now." Amused, Meliana straightened his T-shirt. "Tell me, do you communicate with anyone in town, Johnny?"

"I say hello, smile at people."

"That's not the same as engaging in conversation. You're supposed to chat, show an interest, ask questions."

"I question people for a living. I don't want to do it on my off time."

She sighed. "I give up. How about a walk around the lake? It's a nice fall evening. The moon's out, and so are the stars. We can make impossible wishes, drink too much wine and not worry about driving home."

"Sounds like a plan. Mel." He touched his thumb to her lips, slid his fingers under her chin. "Just so you know, I didn't have sex…"

She set her own hand over his mouth, stopping him. "It's never been a question. I'll admit, I'm normal. I had a few gruesome visions of what you might be forced to do, but deep down, I always figured you'd find a way out of it."

He smiled a little. "It required some tricky maneuvering in a few cases, but I did."

"Why don't you re-create a scene for me." She leaned in until her mouth was almost on his. "Let's say we're at this point exactly. You're undercover, and I'm a reluctant informant. I want you, Johnny. You're a very sexy man. You have a great mouth, and if I'm lucky, even better hands. What could you possibly do to turn me off?"

"Not do." He gave her the lightest of kisses. "Say. Whenever things got sticky, I'd pull out my trump card."

"Which was?"

He kissed her again, and summoned a sly smile. "I'd hint that I was a carrier—of more than a few unpleasant diseases."

THE ONLY DISEASE on Meliana's mind was the fatal one she'd contracted the night she'd met Johnny. He'd been shot, but it wasn't fear she'd glimpsed in his charcoal-gray eyes—it was a warning. If she hurt him more than he was already hurting, he'd find a way to inflict his own brand of pain on her.

She must have hurt him more than she realized, because the six months after his undercover assignment ended had been the most painful of her life.

They left the restaurant and drove back to the lakeside house. Restless for many reasons, Meliana wandered onto the sunporch and stared out over the blackened expanse of water.

She preferred lakes to oceans, even the warm Pacific where she'd been born. Lake water smelled better. In her opinion, it sailed better, too, although it had been years since she'd been aboard a boat without a motor.

She heard a loon and saw wispy tendrils of fog near the shoreline. She and Johnny had swum naked here when they'd first bought this place. That was before Tim Carrick moved in and long after their elderly neighbors had gone to bed.

They'd made love on a small patch of sand, sheltered by trees and two lovely large boulders. Johnny had called the spot Mel's Cove. She wondered if he still thought of it that way or if he even went there anymore.

She heard music behind her and smiled when Johnny came to the door.

"Setting the mood, huh?" He played Beatles ballads whenever he wanted to settle, soothe or soften her up.

He leaned a shoulder on the door frame. "I didn't think you'd feel like doing a hula."

But she did feel like swaying to the slow, rather sensual beat. She ran exploring fingers over her midriff. "The woman at the body shop in Tahiti was playing retro rock the day I got my navel pierced. I'm not sure why I let her do it. She was burning sandalwood incense—always a tip-off—smoking cigarettes and singing along to 'Maggie May.' She sounded just like Rod Stewart."

"You sure she was a woman?"

"Well, she wore a sarong, and she didn't have hairy arms. Her tools were sanitized—that was my main concern. She gave me tea in ninety-degree heat. After we talked about the health risks of a two-pack-a-day habit, she told me her brother'd been killed in Vietnam. I think she meant there are all kinds of ways to die. She intended to choose hers. Anyway, I let her pierce me, and I'm still alive." Her gaze moved through the yard to the lake again as she added a subdued "So far."

"He's not going to kill you, Mel."

Johnny pushed off as he spoke. She felt the floorboards give at his approach. Her skin tingled when he stopped.

He threaded his fingers through her hair and, giving up, she leaned back into him. "You're a disease I'm not sure I want to catch again, Johnny. It's been—" she searched for the right word and finally settled for "—easy between us lately. No fights, no anger, not even any potentially explosive buildups."

She heard the amusement in his voice as he pulled her lower body against his fly and murmured. "Two out of three."

The need for this, for him, had been simmering in her for a very, very long time. But what if it backfired? Would they be able to clean up the mess and restore the relatively peaceful stasis between them? Did she want a stasis between them?

She shoved the thought away, pivoted and caught the front of his shirt in her fists. "You better be ready, Johnny."

Her warning brought a cocky smile to his lips. "I've been ready since the day I got back." And catching her mouth, he stripped her mind, stole her breath and swallowed any protest she might have made.

SHE WOULDN'T EXPECT TOO MUCH, Meliana promised herself. To be with Johnny again, to have him inside her, would be enough. She wasn't so greedy that she needed to feel the same raging fire she'd felt before he'd left.

Then he kissed her again, spun her head in circles and destroyed her resolve. To hell with low expectations. She took his face in her hands and ravished his mouth.

His throaty growl excited her. She wanted to tear off his clothes and jump him right there on the floor of the sunporch. But the shadowy niggle in her mind cut through her hunger and put a hitch in her kiss.

She drew away just far enough to murmur, "He'll see, Johnny. I don't want him watching us."

"If he's watching us now, he's already in a rage."

But he kissed her again, hot and hard, then scooped her into his arms and headed for the door.

Since his T-shirt was already torn, she used the tear line to rip it right off. She left the pieces in their wake as he carried her toward the stairs.

Halfway there, she sank her teeth into the smooth skin of his shoulder. She heard the hiss of his breath and felt herself tumbling onto the sofa.

He flicked off the light as they fell—or maybe he knocked the lamp from the table. The drumbeat of blood in her head drowned out all other sounds. Only Johnny's breathing remained.

Nothing mattered except the feel of his skin under her hands, the taste and scent and texture of him. The heat that throbbed between them.

He could ignite desire in her from nothing—scraps of memory she called up only when she was alone. She'd gotten good at not remembering how it used to be. It kept her sane and focused on what she did have— her friends, her family, her career. With little more than a kiss, Johnny crumbled that restraint, allowing need and hunger to crash through.

She let her head fall back as he stripped off her sleeveless top and ran his hands lightly over the swell of her breasts.

"Black's definitely good on you, Mel." His eyes glittered in the muted half-light. "Black lace is even better."

He loved black lace. He'd bought her a lot of it during their marriage. Wearing lace made Meliana feel sexy, and the sight of it drove Johnny mad.

She loved to drive Johnny mad.

He used his tongue on her hardened nipple, dampening the silk and drawing it into his mouth. The flimsy barrier created friction, but she wanted even that gone. There wouldn't be any barriers between them tonight, not even sensual ones.

She thought she wanted him to go slowly, but realized the instant he covered her body with his that it had been too long for that. Something wild and urgent broke free inside her. The fingernails of one hand bit into his shoulder, while the other moved along his chest to his waistband and the insistent bulge inside his jeans.

"You're breathless, darling." He smiled and nuzzled her throat. "I thought you wanted to draw this out."

"Slow buildup, Johnny." She nipped his ear. "But a fast burn."

The stubborn zipper of his jeans gave at last. Meliana drew it down and him out. Oh, she'd been waiting for this since he'd come home. Nothing tentative, no sense of strangeness. Just eagerness and anticipation and the ever-growing need for more.

He filled her up, even before he was inside her. He used his clever tongue, his skilled mouth, his deft hands. He knew where to touch her to elicit a gasp. He knew just how far to push before he eased off.

He slid his fingers inside her first. It was barely begun, and her head arched on the cushion. Her hips rose to meet him. She wanted their rhythm to match the pounding in her brain. She wanted her orgasm to go on forever.

Perspiration beaded on her brow. He wasn't unaffected by any means, but so far she'd let him have all the control. Where his mouth touched, her skin burned her—under her breast, across her belly, along her inner thigh.

His tongue circled her navel. He played with the tiny gold ring she wore there. When her hands closed around him this time, it was Johnny who gasped, Johnny whose breath was torn from his lungs. It was Johnny whose eyes went black and opaque.

He covered her again with his body. He crushed her breasts with his chest until she cried out and bucked up into him.

Time became a blur. Sensation took over. It consumed and fueled her. She wanted him inside her, all the way inside.

Colors and shapes swirled and blended in her mind. There was only Johnny now, drawing her up to a peak, letting her slide, then taking her even higher. She'd tumbled over the edge once already. She wanted to go there again, from a higher place, where her fall wouldn't be broken by anything.

The hand between her legs shifted to her hips. She felt him slide into her and, for a moment, couldn't breathe. Then she did, and the air was like fire in her lungs.

No thought registered, but instinct had her rolling over. She wanted to ride him, to do to him what he'd done to her. She needed to have him under her. She needed to see his face when he fell.

She slowed the rhythm, saw him gnash his teeth at the delay.

"Mel…"

"I know, don't tease." Despite the storm inside her, she took her time, bending to kiss him. Her eyes sparkled, her lips curved, her hands slid over his sweat-slick ribs. "I just don't want to break you."

She was on her back before the last word left her mouth. She didn't object, merely wrapped her arms around his neck and pulled him down.

"Be anything," she whispered in his ear, "but don't be gentle." Then she set her palms on his shoulders and pushed him upright as he drove himself hard and fast into her.

IF THE HOUSE FELL DOWN around them, Johnny thought he wouldn't care. He couldn't move if he tried. And he had, three times, because he was thirsty and the room had grown cold.

He couldn't remember how many times they'd made love. Four, maybe five. Whatever the number, they'd been animals, or he had. Female to the core, Meliana had been more gracefully elemental—primitive, passionate and seductive. Wanton, too. And so arousing he'd thought at one point he might blow apart from touching her.

Two years was too long to be away from her. Oh, they'd had sex whenever he'd come home, mindless, jungle sex, but the emotional connection had faltered. You couldn't simply walk in, say you had forty-eight hours and expect to pick up where you'd left off with your marriage. They'd been strangers, picking their way over ground that felt familiar yet foreign. Even their words had been stilted toward the end.

He'd been trapped in a persona he'd grown to hate, living a life that was a lie. But, as he'd learned, if you lived a lie long enough, the line between reality and fantasy blurred. John Garcia had been a ruthless individual, pleasant enough to deal with, but cross him and he became a dangerous man, in one case, a deadly man.

That single bad memory sliced through the haze in his mind and had him disentangling himself from Meliana's lovely limbs. God, but he loved her. Not even bad memories could tarnish that emotion. He pressed a kiss to her forehead, covered her with a cotton blanket and headed for the kitchen.

He drank from the tap, then filled the sink, dunked his head and let the cold water clear the last of the cobwebs. He needed to think, and he couldn't do that properly in a fog.

When he felt revived, he toweled off, shook the damp

hair from his face. For the first time in months he felt in control of his life. He'd meet the lunatic who was tormenting his wife head-on and beat the bastard at his own game. No one was going to threaten Meliana and not pay the price.

Johnny shifted his determined gaze southward. The first order of business was to get back to Chicago. Or, well… He glanced at Meliana, still asleep on the sofa, and was amused by his body's instant reaction. Maybe getting to Chicago would be the second order of business.

IT'S ALMOST DAWN, and I'm still here. I feel weak and drained, no energy left. I had plenty to start with, but the more my anger crumbled, the less strength I had to finish the job.

I'll go home now and sleep. That'll help. I'll wash away the blood and watch the news. I won't play Hawaiian music. I won't think about her. She'll be gone soon. It'll be done. I'll burn everything, and that'll be an end to all my shattered dreams. Dreams I spun so lovingly, dreams I wove so carefully through the threads of my own life. They're gone, and I'm here, standing in the ashes.

I'm shaking, but that's normal these days. I have her garter belt in my pocket. It's so pretty, like she is—was. Like she *was*.

I'm confused. This substitute exercise hasn't helped. Why not? Did I do it wrong?

It's not fair. I didn't ask for this. It's her fault. She only had to notice me. I never wanted her friendship—

can't she see that? Well, no, she can't, because he blinded her. And she let him do it. Make no mistake, Meliana is as guilty as him.

There's a horrible pain in my head, like knives being stuck into my brain. Hitting myself isn't taking away the pain. But pain or not, at least I can move.

My energy's coming back, maybe because I feel angry again. This was a cheat. Substitution, hah! I knew it wouldn't work. Doesn't matter—I'll use it to send a message.

When I smile, the pain's not so bad. I can move and smile. That's more than can be said for someone else in this alley.

The blood on my hands is sticky, but I can clench and unclench my fingers just fine. It feels good to squeeze them together.

I wonder how it'll feel when they're wrapped around Meliana's throat?

Chapter Twelve

Meliana had two surgeries scheduled for Tuesday. Julie suggested she cancel them, but then Julie hadn't spent most of her life wanting to be a surgeon. Absolutely nothing got in the way of procedure when Meliana entered the O.R. Not even having Nick dart out partway through the removal of an esophageal tumor.

Another nurse handed Meliana a swab. "He's either got a major problem with Granddad, or he's caught the nasty bug that's going around. You know, the one where you don't dare get out of range of a bathroom."

"Suction." Meliana kept her eye on the monitors. "How's the BP, Gary?"

"Steady. One-ten over seventy. I heard about your wild weekend, Mel."

"Nightmare at Blue Lake. I'm glad Laura's out of danger."

The technician shook his head. "She won't be chowing down on apples for a while. Must be bad karma that the half she ate contained the bulk of the drug."

Which meant, Meliana hoped, that her stalker hadn't

actually been trying to kill anyone. "Done," she said. "A little more suction, and we're ready for sutures."

It had been a lengthy procedure, she reflected thirty minutes later. The tumor had wrapped itself around the patient's esophagus. The biopsy revealed it was benign, but the size of the thing had surprised her. No matter how many surgeries she performed, the human body never failed to amaze.

"I'm going to my office," she told the head nurse. "I'll check on the patient in Recovery before I leave. Hey, Nick." She spotted him on a hard chair halfway down the hall. "Are you all right?"

He rubbed his hands over his flushed face. "I think maybe I've caught that virus flu. I'm sorry I ditched. I just wasn't sure if I'd—you know."

She tugged on a spiky lock of his hair. "You should go home."

"I'd love to." He gave her a weak smile. "But Grandfather's being honored at a banquet tonight, and unless I'm E.R. material, I have to be there." He looked up into her eyes. "I'm really sorry about the party, Mel. We were all having a good time until Laura ate that apple."

"Does everyone in the hospital know the story?"

"Pretty much." He drew a small cross over his heart. "I didn't tell. Ronnie said a few things, then the head of surgery got curious and started asking questions. I think it was Doc Lawrence who spilled."

"At least he wasn't there for the pretzels."

"What?"

"Nothing." She patted his cheek. "Have fun at the banquet. Sit near a bathroom."

He buried his face in his fists and moaned.

Up on seven, Meliana checked her office chair for roses. When she saw it was empty, she released the breath she hadn't realized she'd been holding.

So far so good. Until...

She glimpsed the white envelope as she bent to tap her computer keyboard. The printing on it said simply "Open Me."

She stared at the words for a full thirty seconds. The pretzels in the resealed bag had been sprinkled with arsenic. A grapefruit had been injected with eucalyptus oil, and the FBI lab had discovered traces of cyanide in the sugar.

But this wasn't a food item. It might even be a prank, though she doubted it.

There wouldn't be any fingerprints. There never were. Regardless, she used medical tweezers to open the flap and draw the contents out.

Meliana spent the better part of her life looking at the inner workings of the human body. She'd seen blood and organs, tumors and polyps. She'd never seen anything as grisly as the photograph in front of her.

She forgot to swallow, almost forgot to breathe. But she couldn't make herself look away, and the scream in her throat was growing larger every second.

The subject was a woman, or she had been once. Now she was a puppet, propped up cockeyed against a dirty brick wall, with her legs bent and her arms hanging limply at her sides. Her blood-smeared mouth had been tilted up at the corners in a hideous parody of a grin. Her eyes, rimmed with black, were open and staring. Her hair appeared to be matted with blood. It hung over her shoulders in lank black strings. Her fingers clutched something white.

Meliana backed away. All that horror, and she still hadn't gotten to the worst part—the manner of death. The woman's throat had been slit from side to side. The incision was deep, so deep that more than blood spilled from it.

Icy hands closed around Meliana's windpipe. She managed a choked sound before her knees gave out and she dropped onto her chair.

The woman in the picture was dead. She was holding something white in her hand.

She looked like Meliana.

JOHNNY ARRIVED FIRST. He'd been on his way in any case. When Meliana called him, he'd doubled his speed and quadrupled the risk factor. He figured it saved him ten minutes and put him well ahead of the police.

She was sitting on the wide windowsill when he entered her office. She still wore her scrubs, but her hair was down around her shoulders, and although she'd untied her mask, she hadn't completely removed it.

"It's me," she said in a tone so flat that his eyes went to her face instead of the photo. "It's a symbolic reference, but it's me. He killed a woman, probably a stranger, because he wants to kill me."

"Mel." Johnny took her by the arms and forced her to meet his gaze. "You didn't do this. It's not your fault."

"Look at her and tell me that."

He didn't want to look at anything until he was sure she was all right. "Come on, Mel. Talk to me. Make me believe you're okay."

"If I was going to fall apart, I'd have done it fifteen minutes ago when I opened the envelope." She took a deep breath, let her head fall back and regarded the ceiling. "No matter where I look, I see her face. It rained where he killed her—you can tell, because her makeup ran and her hair's flat. He propped her up like a doll, Johnny. He made her smile. He took her picture. He's not a stalker. He's not even a murderer. He's a monster."

Johnny watched her face as she spoke. When he felt sure she was dealing, he turned to the photo.

Although he couldn't argue with her, he'd actually seen worse. What made this particular death so gruesome was the way the killer had arranged his victim at the scene.

Still studying the photo, he punched Julie's cell number. "Where are you?" he demanded when she answered.

"Coming through Mel's office door in five seconds. Hang up." She strode across the threshold. A young, fresh-faced officer followed. "Mel?"

"I'm fine. The photo's on my desk. I didn't touch anything."

Julie shook her head. "What a mess. I checked on the

way over. This isn't on the daily report sheet, so if she's out there, no one's spotted her yet."

"*If* she's out there?" Meliana untied her surgical mask completely. "Are you saying the picture could be a fake?"

"Don't get your hopes up," Johnny advised.

Julie studied the background details. "Why does that wall look familiar to me?"

Meliana slid from the sill and reluctantly joined her friend at the desk. She pointed to the graffiti above the dead woman's head. "I recognize that. It's the left side of a spray-painted peace sign."

Julie frowned. "Those signs are everywhere, aren't they?"

"Maybe." Meliana's hand dropped. "But this one's been drawn on a dirty brick wall. Brown brick with black scorch marks. There was a fire six or seven years ago, a bunch of old crates in the alley, I think. They had some kind of chemical coating that caused them to burn at a very high temperature."

Julie frowned, but Johnny made a comprehending sound. "Charlie's apartment building?"

"The wall's part of an old brewery warehouse. It's used for storage these days. If you look, you can see the scorch marks behind the woman's head."

Julie turned to the young officer. "Call it in," she ordered. Then to Meliana. "How did this photo get here?"

"Not through the nurses' station or any of the other normal channels. He must have planted it himself."

"When?"

"Sometime after 10:00 a.m. I had back-to-back

operations, both long. I haven't been in here since this morning."

"Okay, we'll make the rounds." She aimed a quick look at the elevator bank. Johnny knew what she was thinking. Apparently so did Meliana.

"Don't go there, Julie," she warned. "Charlie wouldn't commit a murder in his own backyard. He wouldn't commit a murder at all, but if he did, he'd do it far from home. We all would."

"We would if we were sane. You have to admit, Mel, this guy's only got a few functioning marbles."

"Charlie's not a killer."

"I know. Knee-jerk reaction. Someone's done this on purpose."

Meliana moved away from the photo. Johnny watched her work a kink from her lower back as she skirted the desk. He slid his gaze to Julie and murmured, "She looks like Mel."

"Still in the room, Johnny," Meliana said over her shoulder. "Shock hasn't affected my excellent hearing."

"Just trying not to worry you, darling."

"I'm not worried." She pushed her fingers into her hair, held it off her face while she regarded the floor. "I'm freaked. Damn." She continued to stare downward. "He left me more than a photo."

Johnny came up behind her—and spied it instantly. How could he not? There was only one thing in the aluminum wastebasket. A single white rose coupled with a sprig of baby's breath and tied with a white ribbon. Except the stem of this rose was broken in three places, and the petals had been plucked off and crushed.

"MAN, THIS IS FARTHER OUT than I've ever been." Charlie sounded as dazed as Meliana felt. "How could this happen right outside my home without me noticing it? The coroner estimates she's been here since one or two in the morning. I left at eight."

"Other cars in the lot," Julie said. "Three of them are still here. Look around, Charlie. Vehicles make good screens."

Meliana touched his hand. "Don't forget, you also stumble into the hospital with your eyes tightly closed. It was raining. You park on the far side of the lot. It's more than possible you wouldn't have noticed."

"I'll go with that because—well, because it helps." He removed his bandanna, gave his head a brisk shake. "Is Johnny ready to be involved in this?"

"He seems to be handling it." Meliana rubbed her chilled arms. "Do you think she looks like me?"

"From here, no, but your brother showed me the picture. On closer inspection, the answer's yes."

Johnny came toward them. He was wiping something from his hands. Mud, blood, some other body fluid—did it matter what? A woman was dead, a stranger who bore an uncanny resemblance to her.

"Your brother should enter the FBI's training program, Mel. He picked up on details the police totally overlooked."

"Such as?"

"The bra she's wearing is the wrong size for her."

"Not hers?"

He regarded her through steady eyes. "It was muddy and bloody, but underneath the stains, it was white."

She kept her voice calm. "Anything else?"

"She's wearing a garter belt."

Meliana's mind skipped back. "My white garter belt was stolen." She closed her eyes. "And he put it on her. This is so depraved. Any chance it's hers?"

"Unlikely." He brushed damp strands of hair from her cheek. "The stockings she's wearing have elasticized tops."

"What was in her hand?"

"A white slip."

"Muddy, bloody and also mine, right?"

Reaching out, he pulled her close and buried his face in her hair. "I'm really sorry, Mel. You shouldn't have to go through this."

Meliana stared past him to the crowd of people surrounding the woman's body. "I'm better off than her. Does she have a name?"

"Not yet."

She pulled back to look at him. "Did he leave any clues this time?"

Johnny breathed in, held it, then exhaled in a rush. She knew what that meant.

"Another picture?" she surmised.

"A note."

"Just in case we missed the connection, right?"

She wanted to scream, but settled for asking. "What did it say?"

He kept his hands on her arms, his eyes on hers. "Two words, Mel. *'You're Next.'*"

MELIANA DREAMED ABOUT big white roses that sprouted legs and chased her through the hospital corridors. She ran into the O.R., backed away from the door and bumped into the operating table. When she turned, she saw the dead woman lying there, eyes open and grinning as she had been at the murder scene.

She heard breathing. It seemed to come from the walls. She covered her ears, but it got louder. When the dead woman sat up, Meliana ran from the O.R. into Recovery.

Everything there seemed peaceful—until the lights came on and she realized each of the beds was occupied by a human-sized white rose.

She caught a sound behind her and spun, or would have if someone hadn't slapped a surgical mask over her mouth. She clawed at it while she struggled to scream. She glimpsed—someone. But the person holding the mask was strong, and he was saying her name.

"Mel. Wake up. It's me. It's only me."

Her eyes flew open, and she spied a silhouette. It looked like the one in her dream, except she knew this man wouldn't hurt her. He certainly wouldn't try to suffocate her.

So why couldn't she breathe?

She pushed his hand from her mouth and gulped air. "Are you crazy?" she hissed.

"Shh." Johnny raised his head as if listening. "There's someone downstairs."

Meliana stopped struggling and listened with him. When no sound reached her, she tapped Johnny's wrist to get his attention. "Maybe it was the dogs."

"Shannon's awake now, but they were sleeping under the window on my side. Stay," he ordered the Irish setter. "Could it be Mark?"

She gave her head a shake. "His captain asked him to spend at least three days in New York with a sharpshooting team. He left late this afternoon, after the thing in the alley. He'd have called if the session had been canceled."

Ten seconds passed, then fifteen. Meliana heard a low thud and brought her head around.

"Front door?"

Johnny nodded, set a finger on her lips and slipped from the bed to find his jeans.

Meliana's mind worked in time with the frantic beat of her heart. She heard Johnny checking his gun, eased open her dresser drawer, grabbed a fresh pair of jeans and a top and dressed quickly.

"Stay behind me," Johnny told her. "If I tell you to duck, duck fast."

She hooked two fingers through his belt loop and hoped her eyes would adjust to the dark. Rain pelted the windows, which meant there'd be no moon to guide them. No night-lights, either. The bulbs had burned out, and because she'd bought them in Europe, they needed specially ordered replacements.

In the hall, Meliana prevented Johnny from ramming

into a long ebony table. As they passed it, she picked up a lava egg her brother had discovered on the big island. It would throw like a rock. As a kid, Mark had taught her how to throw rocks to within half an inch of a distant target.

She had no idea what had caused the earlier thud, because the front door was being eased closed when they reached the top of the stairs.

The alarm hadn't gone off, Meliana noted. Had she set it? She'd been so hungry for Johnny she might have forgotten. But Johnny wouldn't have.

The stalker had gotten in here once before; however, whether he'd tripped the alarm deliberately or by accident was still a question. Chris thought it had been deliberate. Julie said he'd just messed up. Johnny hadn't said a thing. Yet.

She spotted an outline below them and poked Johnny's back. He unhooked her fingers from his belt loop and handed her a gun. Not the one he was carrying, but a second weapon he'd stuffed into his waistband.

Meliana's heart wanted to hammer right through her ribs. She took the gun, halted at Johnny's motion and pointed the barrel over the rail.

Then she waited. She'd lost sight of the outline, and Johnny was gone, as soundless a shadow as the intruder. The air felt damp and chilly. Goose bumps crawled up her arms. Every breath she released moved the strands of hair that hung around her face.

She still had the lava egg in her palm. If it came down to a choice, she was better with rocks than bullets.

"Do something," she whispered to Johnny under her breath. "Jump him or hit him or knock him into a wall."

She detected a quick swish of fabric, like a windbreaker, a split second before the darkness erupted with motion. She heard grunts and scuffling and an odd strangled sound.

Meliana knew where Johnny and the intruder were, but she couldn't tell who was who. She glanced at the light switch ten feet away, then looked over the rail as someone, likely Johnny, landed a fist.

Why was he using his fists?

Comprehension dawned. She released an irritated breath and went for the switch. When she looked down, she was tempted to bounce the rock off both their heads.

"What are you doing here, Chris?"

He was on his back on the floor, with Johnny on his knees straddling him and a forearm shoved under his chin. Chris choked and tried to buck his attacker off, but all that earned him was a knee jammed up hard into his groin.

"Okay, I give." He coughed. "Mel, tell this jackass husband of yours to get off me."

Meliana rested her arms on the banister. "Johnny."

He kept his eyes on Chris's face and a firm forearm under his chin. "Answers first, Blackburn."

"I can't talk without air."

"Johnny," Meliana said again.

He eased off, but only a little.

"That's as good as it's going to get for now, Chris." She let the gun dangle. "Why are you here?"

"I saw someone outside."

"I knew you were going to say that." Johnny's arm tightened. "Do better."

"I saw someone," Chris repeated, coughing again. "Outside. I thought you were over at Andy's. Your SUV is."

"Old habits." Johnny's smile glittered.

"And maybe he was thinking about outwitting a stalker," Meliana added.

Chris endeavored to counter Johnny's hold. "I didn't come here to hurt you, Mel. Stop playing he-man, Grand, and let me up."

"Do you believe him?" Johnny asked.

"I guess so." But she kept a firm grip on the lava egg. "What did the guy look like, Chris?"

"I saw a shape." Chris darted Johnny an ominous look as he climbed to his feet. "You know, a shadow. In the bushes outside your front porch."

Johnny remained in a crouch on the floor. "Did he step in the dirt?"

"How should I know? I saw him, I came out to investigate. I didn't look in the dirt."

"Are you always up and dressed at two in the morning?"

Was it that late? Meliana glanced at her wrist, then realized her watch was on the nightstand. "Redundant question, Johnny. You know he's a night owl."

"I know he's here when he shouldn't be."

The phone near the kitchen door rang. The sound was so unexpected that Meliana simply stared at the doorway until she heard it again. At two in the morning? This couldn't be good.

She picked up a split second ahead of the machine. "Meliana."

She had to cover her ear to hear the woman on the other end. Free and cocky once again, Chris had launched into a sarcastic verbal assault on Johnny.

A minute later, Meliana jogged past them. She snatched her keys from the bowl by the door and her raincoat and boots from the closet.

"What is it?" Johnny demanded.

She needed socks and her purse from upstairs. "Emergency at the hospital. It's one of the nurses—Emily. She's seven months pregnant and hemorrhaging for the second time. Placenta's pulled away from the wall of the uterus. We have to do a C-section."

Johnny's brows went up. "And you're the only one who's available?"

"She asked for me." She had socks in her locker at the hospital. Hopping, she tugged on her right boot and at the same time tossed him her keys. "You drive. My license is upstairs in my purse."

"So's my shirt."

"Emily's blood pressure's dropping, and the baby's in distress. She's forty-six years old, Johnny. This is her first and probably only shot at a viable pregnancy."

"Right." Johnny removed his jacket from the closet. "Lock up," he told Chris in a dark tone. "And don't forget to reset the alarm." He flipped up his collar. "We don't need any more intruders tonight."

At least he hadn't called Chris a stalker. Meliana took that as a positive sign and concentrated on her friend's medical problem.

She didn't do C-sections as a rule, but she'd done many of them in the past. The older the patient, the higher the risk, both to the mother and to the child. To complicate matters, Emily hadn't been in the best of health for the past three months of her pregnancy.

Traffic was light at two in the morning. Maybe that was why Meliana noticed the headlight behind them. A single headlight, which followed them from the town house to the hospital.

She looked back twice, then said, "Johnny?"

"I see it. I'll get you inside, then see what I can do."

A surgical nurse met her in the lobby. "Johnny, get Security," Meliana began, but broke off when she realized she was talking to air.

"Maternity ward, Doctor," the nurse urged.

She had to shut it out, or at least put it away for now. Johnny knew how to do his job.

It was time for her to do hers.

Chapter Thirteen

The baby was two months and ten days premature. The mother lost a great deal of blood. The baby's oxygen supply had been compromised. Meliana had no idea what to say to Emily's distraught family, so she simply told them the truth. Both mother and child were in critical condition.

She hated that part of her job.

Another C-section came in right behind Emily's. Since she was already there, Meliana performed that one, too. This baby was full-term and screaming its tiny lungs out when she left the O.R. The father cried happily on her shoulder.

She checked on Emily and discovered there'd been some improvement in her condition. The baby, a little girl, continued to hold her own in an incubator.

"What do you think?" the ward nurse asked. "Fifty-fifty?"

Meliana watched the baby's chest rise and fall as oxygen was pumped into her lungs. "Her chances get better with every hour that passes."

The nurse smiled. "I've said that to the family seven times already." But Meliana was already halfway out the door. Preemie wards were especially hard for her.

"I'm supposed to tell you, your husband's on six," the nurse at the station informed her. "The message is 'I lost him.' Make sense?"

"Unfortunately." Meliana removed her cap and headed for the elevator.

More shadows than people inhabited the corridors at this time of morning. Predawn, prechaos. She would have found the silence restful if she hadn't kept expecting a lunatic to pop up every time she turned a corner.

She found Johnny, as expected, in the lounge. He was eating chips and watching TV with two other male patients. One had gray hair and wrinkles, the other had acne.

Arms folded, Meliana rested a shoulder on the door frame and regarded them. Her earlier amusement rekindled when she realized they were absorbed in a very old cartoon show.

"So this is what the intelligent American male watches at five-thirty in the morning, is it?" she asked from the doorway.

"It's a classic, Mel." Johnny ate another chip. Then he handed the kid the bag, dropped his feet from the chair he'd been using as an ottoman and gave the older man the remote. "You watch the rest. My wife's not into cartoons."

His easy humor faded when they left the lounge. "The car followed us into the lot, but not as far as the main entrance. He had too big a head start for me to catch him."

"If he was even worth catching."

"Anyone's worth catching at this point, Mel." Johnny stopped in front of a vending machine. "Do you want a soda?"

"No, I'll have some of yours—save you from a junk food overdose."

"Don't go all healthy on me now. Remember whose idea it was to have pineapple pancakes for breakfast on our honeymoon."

"Pineapples are healthy."

"With whipped cream and maple syrup?"

"That doesn't count on honeymoons." She glanced down as the soda can dropped. "It's so quiet right now that sounded like a bomb."

"What time do hospitals come to life?"

"The E.R.'s always up. Everything else, pretty soon. Patients need to be fed and bathed, probed and medicated. Not my job, thankfully."

"How's your friend?"

Her heart gave a hard thump. "The baby's holding on."

"Any damage?"

"It's too early to tell. I hope not." She pressed the elevator call button. "Johnny…"

The doors swished open, surprising her. The elevator was never where she wanted it to be.

"I hate these things." Johnny looked around the sterile space. "They're slow and creaky and big enough for what—three corpses?"

"We tend not to think in those terms, but in a pinch it could probably accommodate four." The image that popped into her head had Meliana's fingers curling. "Why did he prop her up like that, and make her smile?"

"Because he's sick, and he knew it would get to you."

"Why kill her in the first place? Why not just come after me?"

"His mind's doing a slow turn right now."

"From obsession to disillusionment?"

"Exactly. Where are we going?"

"Push seven. I need to stop by my office. Listen, Johnny, there's something I have to tell you."

"About the rose guy?"

"No, before him. A year ago, in fact. I was really busy, and I hadn't seen you for almost three months…." The lights flickered, and she paused. "Did you hear a clunk?"

"I hear every clunk, grind and rattle when I get into these elevators."

"Why? You're not claustrophobic."

"No, I just hate hospital elevators. Especially—" he pressed the button for seven again "—when they don't move."

But they had moved, at least for a few seconds. "Try kicking the wall," Meliana suggested.

"I don't abuse mechanical devices when I'm inside them and at their mercy."

The lights flicked off, then on, and for the first time a sliver of apprehension slid down Meliana's spine. Reaching out, she pressed six. The elevator lurched, then gave a metallic groan and began to stutter downward.

"You know what?" She raised her eyes to the

ceiling. "This isn't good. These elevators are rigorously maintained."

"That's reassuring, but I'd suggest a bit more rigorousness during the next overhaul."

The elevator shuddered. One of the overhead gears ground in protest, and then suddenly they were moving smoothly.

"Back to four." Meliana eyed the light panel. "I suppose it's just as well this happened while it was us in here as opposed to a cardiac patient."

"No comment."

She smiled, grabbed his soda and took a drink. "Relax and enjoy the ride. I'm guessing it'll be your last for the day."

"Stairs are healthier anyway, right?"

"You wouldn't say that if you had to stand in the O.R. for four hours straight."

He raised the can to his lips, but stopped as the elevator continued its whirring descent. "Why are we still moving?"

She'd noticed that. The overhead indicator showed they were approaching the third floor. "It'll stop on one," she promised.

He expelled a deep breath. "I have nightmares about situations like this. I'm stuck in a hospital elevator gone amuck."

Determined not to be concerned, she teased, "Naked or dressed?"

"Always dressed, always wondering if I'm stepping into a faulty piece of machinery. I always am. They either shoot up or down, but whichever way they go, they do it at top speed."

"What happens when they stop?"

"I tend to wake up before that happens."

"Okay, then maybe you want to wake up now, because we just passed the main floor."

He stared at the panel. "There's something below main?"

She tried the buttons again without effect. "Where do you think we take the people who die?"

"Not to the boiler room, huh?"

"We have one of those, too, but this elevator can't access that level. Ah…" The cage hit bottom with a disquieting thunk. "Looks like we're here."

The doors slid open on cue. They remained open despite Johnny's repeated attempts to close them.

"It's not that bad," Meliana assured him, although she had to admit this wasn't her favorite area of the hospital.

Johnny sent her a disgusted look. "Medically speaking, this is as bad as it gets, Mel." He pulled his gun and blocked her with his body as he glanced down the poorly lit corridor. "We're in the morgue."

She wanted to tell him it was nothing, a glitch, no cause for alarm, but how could she, with a band of fear wrapped tightly around her throat?

This was silly. She was overreacting. They both were. She'd been here before, several times. Of course, on those occasions the decision to come had been hers….

"We're being paranoid, Johnny." She maintained a calm tone. "We're not trapped. There are three stairwells down here. And people. Live people—attendants and technicians."

"How many live people do you see right now?"

"It's five forty-five in the morning. This is the night shift."

"And the technicians you mentioned are where?"

She sighed. "Stop trying to spook me. Okay, they're home in bed, but there are still attendants."

Although neither of them wore hard shoes, their feet made squelching noises on the vinyl composite tiles. Johnny led the way along the corridor toward the nearest stairwell.

Meliana's mind dredged up ghastly pictures of the dead woman in the alley. The woman who'd been wearing her bra and garter belt and whose stiff fingers had been clutching her slip.

He was here somewhere. Probably watching. Almost certainly waiting. Did he plan to ambush them, or just let them scare themselves to death? Because her heart was jumping and the muscles in her legs felt tight enough to snap.

Had he rigged the elevator to malfunction? Was that even possible anymore?

They kept walking. Johnny's eyes never stopped moving. He nodded toward the exit sign twenty feet farther along the corridor.

Meliana wouldn't have believed she'd be afraid in a hospital, not even in the morgue. Death was a natural part of the life cycle.

But murder wasn't.

She heard a noise to her left and pivoted. A door opened, and a man stepped out. He wore a white lab jacket, had straight dark hair and was about the same height as Johnny. His brows went up when he spied them. He started to speak, then seemed to freeze.

Johnny swore, shoved Meliana to the left and caught the man in his free arm as he pitched forward.

"Get inside," he shouted, and fired into the shadows near the exit sign.

Meliana caught a fleeting glimpse of blood as Johnny lowered the attendant to the floor. She grabbed the man, checked the pulse in his neck and dragged him inside with her.

He wasn't dead. She held on to that thought. Then she looked around. Where had Johnny gone?

A silenced bullet zinged off one of the metal door-jambs. Another shattered glass. Meliana tore the attendant's jacket and grimaced when she saw how much blood was already on her hands.

It took her only a few seconds to locate the entry wound. The man's mouth moved, but no words emerged. There was nothing she could do except be there as he rattled out his final breath.

Another bullet, this one more distant, ricocheted off a beam. She closed the dead man's eyes, eased his legs through the doorway and breathed in and out three times.

She made no sound, just crouched on the threshold and listened. She spied a movement to her right and strained for a better view.

Two more silenced bullets zinged off the walls.

Johnny fired back once. She heard a clang, then saw Johnny running toward her. "He's in the elevator. Are you all right?"

"I am." She gestured to the man behind her. "He's not."

He barely spared the man a glance. "Come on. We'll take the stairs."

She looked back once at the dead man, then let the door close and ran with Johnny to the stairwell.

There must have been some kind of logical flow from that point on, but for the life of her, Meliana couldn't follow it. Even twenty minutes later, out of breath and facing an empty elevator on seven, she wasn't sure what had happened.

They hadn't reached the main floor in time. No one they questioned in passing had noticed anyone getting on or off the elevator. But then, they hadn't been watching.

He wasn't anywhere between two and seven and he wasn't, thank God, in her office. With Johnny combing the increasingly trafficked corridors, Meliana summoned the duty nurse. "Call Security," she said, and told him what had transpired in the morgue. She used a second phone to contact Julie.

Her friend answered on the third ring. "There's a dead man at the hospital?" she repeated in a thick voice. "Look, I just woke up here. I take it you mean dead as in not in the hospital way."

"He was shot, Julie." Meliana didn't want to examine the blood on her hands. "In the morgue. I sent Security down to make sure nothing was disturbed. I think he was firing at Johnny, and the attendant simply got in the way."

"Yeah, okay." She could tell Julie was struggling to clear her head. "Look, stay put. I'll call it in and be there in fifteen."

It took her closer to thirty, and when finally she did arrive, she had seven uniformed officers in tow. She greeted Sam, who'd been hovering around Meliana like a nervous rabbit since the start of his shift fifteen minutes earlier, then drew her friend aside.

"I had to stop downtown for an update from my captain. The lab results are in on Jane—on the dead woman."

"You can say Jane Doe, Julie. We get several of them in the E.R."

"I know. This case is really messing with my head. Anyway, we typed her blood. It was everywhere, on almost every piece of clothing she was wearing. It was also on your slip, the one in her hand."

Meliana regarded her, expecting more. "And?"

"It wasn't the only blood we found."

"You mean…" Meliana hated to think what she meant. "Another victim's blood? Or—no, maybe the stalker's blood." It helped to imagine that. "She cut him, or he cut himself."

"Possibly, but the second blood sample we took was older—by several days, apparently."

"This isn't making me feel a whole lot better. You're telling me he could have killed someone else earlier?"

"We're cross matching any and all possibles, Mel. It could take awhile to get the results."

Meliana pushed on her temple. "Is there some reason

you feel compelled to tell me this? Because the last thing I need right now is more unanswered questions in my life."

"I'm simply keeping you apprised. It could very well be the stalker's blood. The thing is—" she lowered her voice "—there were holes in the slip when we found it. Those holes read like blade marks. When the slip's held, you can see the small slits all over the place, same with the blood. It's all patchy and disjointed. Which leads us to believe that the slip was folded when the blade cut through it and drew the blood."

"So either he stabbed his victim through the folded slip or—hmm." Meliana's mind stalled. "That is a puzzle, isn't it?"

"What's the matter, Sam?"

Meliana turned as Julie looked past her. Sam stood there with his curly brown hair disheveled and his clothes askew.

"What is it?" Julie asked again.

For a moment, Meliana thought he was going to cry, then his cheeks blotched with anger. "One of the security guards knocked into my cart and spilled everything on it."

"When?"

"Right now, outside Meliana's office. I got mad when he shoved me."

Meliana stared in surprise. "You got mad?"

"He said it was my fault. No!" He jerked back when Julie touched his arm. "I'm not a kid, Julie. I'm tired of everyone treating me like I am. Even Audrey in Food Services acts like I'm stupid and backward, and I'm not." He slapped his sister's hand away. "The big bull bumped into my cart, and he can clean up the mess."

"Hey, who dumped coffee, milk and oatmeal all over the floor?" Charlie came around the corner, halted, observed the situation and stuck his tongue in his cheek. "Problem?" he asked, all innocence.

"Too many to count." Meliana glanced past him at one of the orderlies. "Call maintenance," she said. "Sam?"

He stared at the floor, refused to look up.

"No one thinks you're stupid, Sam, Julie and Charlie and me least of all. You knew about the apple Laura ate, and it takes you what, five minutes to do your taxes every year?"

He glanced up from under his hair. "More like thirty."

"Well, it takes me hours, and I was good at math in college."

Sam's fingers twitched. He still struck her as agitated, though he appeared to be fighting it. "I guess he didn't mean to push me." He looked at Julie first, then Meliana. "Should I apologize?"

"For being pushed?" Meliana smiled. "Other way around, I think."

"Yeah, but I kind of—you know, fought back."

Julie masked her astonishment. "You shoved him back?"

"Not exactly." Now Sam's shoulder twitched. "I punched him in the nose."

"SAM PUNCHED A SECURITY GUARD?" Johnny was impressed. "Good for him. Wish I'd seen it."

Meliana tossed a pen at him across her desk. "It's not good, and it's not like Sam."

"Sure it is. He's finally coming out of his shell." Johnny tossed the pen back. "You doctors overanalyze people. We don't all fit into tidy little molds."

"Julie's worried."

"Julie lives to worry. It's her job and her hobby."

The laugh rose so quickly, she couldn't keep it in. "What time is it?"

"Two-thirty. I'm beat, and so are you."

"Thanks for reminding me."

"Just stating the obvious."

"Again, thanks. Any other part of my ego you'd like to stroke?"

"Any and all parts." His lips quirked. "You look great, Mel. You always do, but you've put in a twelve-hour shift on two hours of sleep. I saw you in the E.R. You stitched a gunshot wound, sent another up to surgery—though you'd rather have done it yourself—dealt with a case of d.t.'s, removed a knife from a man's shoulder and God only knows what else. I was only passing through."

Meliana stared at her computer screen. "The attendant's name was Ron Lockwood. He worked in the morgue for six years."

Johnny's forced humor faded. He knew that expression on her face too well.

"He was thirty-two," she went on. "He had a wife named Jess. She's a nurse's aid. I talked to her. She was still crying when I left." Meliana closed her eyes. "It was awful, Johnny."

He took her in his arms and stroked her hair. "You can't soften a blow like that, Mel. And you can't turn back the clock. You said it yourself—there's a monster out there. Human life means nothing to him, and that makes him the most dangerous kind of monster."

"Did you see anything, notice anything?"

"I smelled disinfectant, but other than that, I was tracking a ghost."

"So he knows how to evade pursuit."

"Or he got lucky."

She raised her head to look at him. "I have to tell you something."

A tendril of fear curled in his stomach. "Is this the same something you mentioned as we got in the elevator, the thing that happened a year ago after you hadn't seen me for three months?"

Her lips took on a faint curve. "I didn't think you were listening."

"I didn't want to hear. It's not the same thing."

She drew away, regarded him through her lashes. "You think I had an affair, don't you?"

"No, but I'm afraid you met someone you wanted to have an affair with. And if you did, I still don't want to hear about it."

He saw the spark of amusement in her eyes and felt absurdly relieved. "So where do you think this guy is now? And you better not say living two doors away from me, because I've never had those kinds of feelings for Chris Blackburn."

The knot in Johnny's stomach untangled. "You didn't meet someone. What then?"

She ran tired fingers under her eye. "I was pregnant, Johnny. With our baby. I lost it—miscarried, less than three months after you left again."

Johnny didn't react. Didn't move. Couldn't think. He felt paralyzed, mind and body.

"I think it would have been a girl. I don't know why. I called her Mikala—that's Michelle in Hawaiian. Everything was fine at first, then suddenly it wasn't. When I lost her, I didn't know where you were, and I didn't want to go to your boss, so I—dealt with it. But I didn't really—I just buried it and carried on as before. Right before your assignment ended, I started thinking about it again. I wanted to tell you, but everything felt wrong between us, so I didn't. I told myself the right moment would come, eventually. Instead, things got worse. After we split up, there didn't seem to be any point in telling you."

He found his voice, but he still couldn't move. "No point telling me, Mel? About our baby?"

"I didn't want your sympathy, Johnny, or your anger. I didn't want you to feel bad, and I was tired of feeling that way myself. I wanted you to be Johnny Grand again. If you ever were, I promised myself, I'd tell you then."

He realized his mouth had dropped open, so he closed it. "You think I'm Johnny Grand again?"

"Aren't you?"

He searched his thoughts, his emotions. "I feel like I've swallowed a medicine ball."

"Charlie would call that the bombshell syndrome."

Johnny blinked, regrouped. "Does Charlie know?"

"No one except Julie knows. I had to tell someone, and she's a really good friend."

Johnny wanted to approach her, to touch her, to tell her he was sorry. Another, smaller part of him wanted to resent her for not telling him about this sooner. Or should he have sensed it? In all the thirty-five years of his life, he had never felt so completely out of his depth.

When the phone rang, he ignored it. Meliana picked up.

"Dr. Maynard." She relaxed visibly. "Hi, Julie."

She said nothing for several seconds, then glanced at him. "Yeah, okay. No, I'm—we're leaving. Johnny's here. Yes, we'll be careful." She paused and relaxed enough to smile briefly. "No, I haven't seen Sam since this morning. Thanks, Jules. Later."

Johnny arched inquiring brows. "Anther bombshell?"

She rested her backside on the windowsill. "The dead woman's been identified. Her mother came to the police looking for her. Her name's Elena Torrence. She was a dental hygienist, born and raised in Chicago." Meliana's eyes held steady on his. "Her father's from Peoria. Her mother was born in Wahiawa—in Hawaii."

Chapter Fourteen

With everything that had happened, Meliana completely forgot about the hospital fund-raising dinner being held on Friday evening. After the morgue attendant's death and the revelation of the dead woman's identity, one day melted into the next. The mood in the hospital was guarded, and understandably grim. The police had no answers. Neither did the FBI—except that no one there believed Enrique Jago was behind any of this.

That was good news to Meliana. A lunatic flying solo was bad enough. A lunatic drug lord would have been, if possible, worse.

"I'm bringing Zack, wearing green and expecting to meet you and Johnny outside the hotel at eight." Julie spoke from inside Meliana's closet. "This is a five-hundred-dollar-a-plate dinner. It's to benefit sick kids, and you're not weaseling out no matter how big a pariah you imagine yourself to be." A red gown with three spaghetti straps on each shoulder came flying out. "The temperature's perfect for velvet, and this has a side slit that'll have men's eyes popping out of their sockets and their tongues lolling on the floor. While they're busy rerolling those tongues, you can hit them up for a generous donation."

"I don't want to look sexy." But Meliana smoothed the front of the dress. "I told Johnny about the baby."

Julie's head emerged. "Good. That's a huge monkey off your back."

"Did they teach you that compassionate attitude at the academy?"

"Miscarriages happen, Mel. Something wasn't right about the pregnancy."

"Something wasn't right about Emily's pregnancy, and I'm happy to say her baby's improving."

"That's because mommy and baby had an excellent surgeon to perform the C-section. You didn't do anything wrong, Mel. I know—I was there. Wear silver shoes and accessories. I'm borrowing your black wrap. Where's Johnny?"

"He had an errand to run."

"He wants to take you up to Blue Lake, doesn't he?"

"He thinks I'll be safer up there, but I don't know. Zack said a man got shot two nights ago trying to rob a filling station on Route 90, right near the edge of town."

"Eileen wants me to come for dinner next week," Julie confided. "She thinks I should consider running for sheriff when Owen Frank retires. I've given it more than a passing thought."

"Sheriff, huh? What does she envision for Zack?"

Julie chuckled. "Mayor, with a sideline in boat charters. Zack says she has an active imagination."

"I thought she might have the hots for Sheriff Frank."

"Zack'd probably like it if she did. She's a bit—well—pushy."

"She's nurturing, Julie, and I'm glad she's that way. She helped Johnny when he went up there six months ago."

"Like a surrogate mom?"

"He already has a mom. Eileen's more like a surrogate aunt."

"She thinks that neighbor of yours is totally strange."

"The pharmaceutical pill pusher." Meliana experimented with her hair. "Tim's a bit off the map, that's for sure." She grinned. "His wife found a blow-up doll in the barn one day. He said it wasn't his, but we figured it had to be. The previous owners were elderly and frail. No way does a ninety-two-year-old man own the latest sex toys, let alone store them in a hayloft he couldn't possibly climb into."

"If I was feeling ornery, I'd push Zack to watch Carrick. If he pushes pills here in Chicago, who's to say he's not doing the same thing in Blue Lake?"

Meliana let her hair fall. "Up or down?"

"Halfway between. You have gorgeous shoulders. And speaking of which, does Johnny own a tux?"

"Other closet, still in dry cleaner's plastic."

"This is going to be a fun event."

Julie's tone was so emphatic that Meliana laughed. "Did I mention that Chris is going? Nick Hohlman and his grandfather, too. And Charlie."

"Better and better. I love a good fireworks display." Meliana picked up her medical bag and started for the closet. When she slid it onto the shelf, she noticed something caught in the zipper.

It was as if a giant hand slowly closed around her windpipe. She couldn't speak, so she didn't try. She set the bag on a lower shelf and opened it.

Her eyes fixed on the scrap of lingerie inside. It was another bra, hers, of course, one that was more silk than lace. He'd laid it out across her instruments, and it hadn't moved. Neither did she for several seconds.

"What are you doing, Mel?" Julie returned with the borrowed black wrap slung over her shoulder. "I'm a little short on jewelry, so if it's—"

She broke off when she spied the bra. "Holy sh—hah. No, don't touch it."

"I wasn't going to."

It amazed Meliana that she could sound reasonably normal. She felt very hazy and strange. Her hand found the dimmer switch and turned it up.

"He got into my bag, Julie. How did he do that? I lock it up in my office."

"There's always a way, Mel." Julie bent closer. "My God, that's a bullet hole. He's put a bullet through the left cup."

"The heart's on the left side."

Yet as jarring as that was, the bullet hole felt less ominous than the words he'd written in descending order on the right cup. LOVE, HURT, HATE…DIE!

JOHNNY FIGURED HE HAD enough time to do this. Didn't want to, couldn't have explained why he was bothering, knew he shouldn't, but here he was, knocking on Charlie Lightfoot's apartment door with a six-pack of cold beer in his hand.

Charlie answered before the third rap. "Right on time. Come in. Don't mind the parrot. I'm birdsitting for a friend."

Johnny set the beer on the counter. "The cops are getting nowhere with this, Charlie. Maybe they will in time, but I'm beginning to think we're running out of that."

Charlie nodded. "I'll have one of those cans you brought. Grab a seat. This could take a while."

Johnny cracked a beer as he dropped onto the sofa. "I must be out of my mind," he muttered.

"Or desperate." Charlie removed the bloodstained white slip from the bag and ran the fabric through his fingers. "There's a fair bit of blood here. How much of it is the victim's?" He shrugged at Johnny's expression. "Sam overheard Julie talking to Mel at the hospital. He told me about the older blood. Julie thinks Sam's having emotional problems."

Johnny took a long drink and settled back. "Is he?"

"He's moodier than usual…. I sense fear."

"That'll be the victim's. I need more, Charlie."

"This is nothing like the first slip Mel brought to me. This one has a malevolent aura."

"I could have told you that from the blood."

"Hey, I'm working on it, Johnny. I care about Mel, too." He rubbed one of the slits. "Everything's muddled. I see Mel at a ceremony. Something related to sailors."

"Her mother's in the navy."

"I hear shouting."

Now, that intrigued him. "No one in Mel's family shouts. What else?"

"There's movement, but it's dark. I'm really not getting much."

"Try the old blood."

"I am. That's where the muddle is. It's like I'm pulling images out of a big tub of molasses. Everything's sticky and black. I know there's something to see—I just can't get past the layers to see it."

"Would more incense help?"

Charlie offered him a lazy grin. "Don't be sarcastic. Magic's not my thing. It's all vibes, and I promise you, this slip's loaded with them. The trick's in the separation—which I'm not having much luck at doing right now. Mel took this with her on a trip. I smell slow water. Could be Italy."

"She went to Venice six years ago, Lightfoot."

Charlie fingered the silky strap. "Slip's held up well. Meliana buys quality."

"Meliana is quality." It was getting late. Johnny finished his beer and checked the clock. "If the guy touched the thing, why can't you see him somewhere in the muddle?"

"Maybe I will, but my gift, if you want to call it that, doesn't work on a timer. I can be late for the benefit if you need to leave."

"You're not supposed to have that slip."

"I could have figured that. Did you call in a favor to get it?"

"Julie's not my only friend on the force. The slip's been misplaced for a day or two."

"Captain Walker'll pitch a fit."

Johnny lounged back on the sofa. "Unlikely." His lips curved into a vague smile. "He's the one who misplaced it."

IT WAS PURE LUXURY. The hotel on North Michigan Avenue catered to events like this. Crystal sparkled, china gleamed, flowers speared from silver urns to a height of fifteen feet. Champagne flowed like water and the food had been prepared by some of the best chefs in Chicago. The theme, if indeed there was one, felt late forties. A sense of glamour prevailed, yet the cause remained clear: raise money for Chicago's Children's Hospital.

Meliana estimated there were close to five hundred people in the ballroom. Linen-covered tables had been set up. However, at the request of the organizers, seating was to be by choice—with the exception of a few dozen VIPs and local celebrities.

It should have been an enjoyable affair. Meliana loved good causes. She also loved dressing up, especially when she didn't have to make a speech. Her friends were here, and several of her coworkers. She'd come with Johnny—and she couldn't remember the last formal party they'd attended together. She wished her brother had agreed to come, but learning new cop techniques intrigued him more than five-hundred-dollar-a-plate dinners, so he was undoubtedly happier where he was.

"I thought he came to Chicago to watch out for you," Julie grumbled when Mark's name came up.

Meliana sipped her champagne. "Trust me, he's watching. He calls, he e-mails, he calls again. He also feels confident that Johnny's back on track enough to do what needs to be done. He's always had faith in you, and if he doesn't know by now that I can take care of myself, then he's not really my brother."

Julie sampled one of the more colorful canapés. "Blackburn brought a date." She used the canapé to point.

Meliana waited until a group of media people moved. "She looks familiar. Do I know her?"

Julie patted her cheek. "Pick up a mirror, Mel. She looks like you."

A chill swept over Meliana's skin. "She's got dark hair. It's a superficial resemblance."

"She's got light-colored eyes—close enough to your gray. She's tall and svelte, not as pretty, but, hey, I'm a little biased, right? She also looks snotty."

Meliana laughed. "You can't tell that from here."

"Her upper lip's curled, like she's sniffing boiled cabbage. I'd guess she's FBI, low level—maybe in Administration, on the hunt for a sugar daddy. This event's high profile, and Chris got her in the door."

"But then you're a little biased, right?"

Julie raised her glass. "Touché, Dr. M." She finished both her drink and her canapé. "Where's Johnny?"

"Scoping the room. Zack?"

"He got sidetracked by some guy he knows. I kept walking. Memory lane bores me."

"Mel." Chris caught her attention. He drew his date forward. "This is Bianca Foley. She organizes current data at one of our branch offices, but she's done some field work, as well."

The woman's smile looked more like a grimace. Her accent, when she spoke, contained a hint of Spanish.

"Chris has told me all about you, Dr. Maynard. Is your husband here tonight?"

Meliana glanced at Chris, noted his smug expression and arched a humorous brow. "Oh, he's around somewhere. He's an elusive man, my Johnny. Short fused on occasion, but he's working on that. Hates being set up."

Chris looked down at his shoes. Bianca smoothed her hair. Julie murmured, "Idiot" into her glass.

On cue, Johnny came up alongside Meliana. "Room seems fine."

"Hello, Johnny." Bianca's smile widened. "It's been several months."

"You know each other?" Meliana offered Johnny a smile of her own. "What a coincidence."

"He was John Garcia when we met." Bianca spaced her thumb and index finger an inch apart. "We only worked together for a very short time."

"She played a hooker."

"Well, now there's a surprise," Julie muttered. "Has anyone seen Zack?"

"Right behind you, Officer Denton." Handsome in his tux, Zack handed Julie a full glass of champagne and took her empty one. "Have I missed anything?"

Julie shrugged. "Nothing important. Chris introduced us to his hooker, and Johnny was just about to ask Mel to dance."

"Sounds like a plan." Johnny sent Chris a level look and took Meliana's hand.

She went with him, but pinched his arm. "That was rude."

"Leaving a hornet's nest isn't rude. It's smart."

"I'm not upset."

"I didn't think you were. I also didn't think you'd want me to start an argument with Chris."

She glanced over her shoulder. "He's disappointed."

"Good. That gives me the advantage."

Meliana let him ease her closer. "God, you two are a pair." She tipped her head back. "So what's the deal with Bianca?"

"She's an unhappy Miss Universe wannabe whose father works for the FBI in Missouri. He got her a job here in Chicago because, in spite of the fact that she's not happy, she's a good daughter who loves her parents and knows you can't have everything you want. The fact that she's here with Chris tells me she has really bad taste in men, and no, I didn't have to pretend to have sex with her while I was undercover."

Meliana refused to laugh. "Did I ask?"

"You were wondering. I read it in your eyes."

"You need to work on your comprehension, Johnny.

What you're reading is concern. Do you think she looks like me?"

"Maybe a little."

"Do you think my stalker's here tonight?"

His arm tightened around her waist. "I'd say there's a strong possibility."

"Two and two together, Johnny."

He silenced her with a kiss. "One thing doesn't preclude another. Chris brought Bianca either to trigger me or to make you wonder. Assuming he's not the stalker—and that's a big assumption on my part—then her being here isn't part of any murder plot."

"It could turn into one."

He rested his cheek against her hair. "Crowd's too large, Mel. And she doesn't look as much like you as Elena Torrence did. It's nothing, okay? Just a barb on Blackburn's part."

Meliana ordered herself to relax. It wasn't difficult. Dancing with Johnny always felt wonderful. He smelled like soap and warm skin and sex, and if Zack looked handsome in his tux, Johnny looked positively wicked. For a moment she wished the glittering crowd would disappear. They could dance to Benny Goodman and make love on the ballroom floor. Or maybe on the grand piano.

"Cutting in." Charlie tapped both their shoulders, then began to push. "We need to talk. Not here. Don't be obvious."

"Ouch." Julie gave Charlie a swat from behind. "That's my toe you're stepping on, Lightfoot." She and Zack stopped dancing. "What aren't we being obvious about?"

"Very little, it seems. Back door," he said to Meliana and Johnny.

"Maybe they don't want company," Zack suggested.

"Tough, they're having it anyway."

Meliana avoided a couple who'd begun to jive. "Let's at least try not to look like we've formed a conga line."

Charlie led the way to an offshoot rear corner comprised of secondary washrooms and utility closets. Music drifted in, but it was muffled. It wasn't until they stopped that Meliana noticed his clothes.

"You got through the door in jeans?" She was amazed. "How?"

"I started bickering with Elliot Hohlman. He and his entourage were just arriving when my cab peeled up to the entrance." He caught her arms. "I got into your slip, Mel. The one with the double bloodstains and blade marks."

"Not going to ask," Julie muttered and sank onto a bench.

"He didn't have to wear my slip to feel the vibes," Meliana remarked to the group. "How he obtained it—" she raised a brow in Johnny's direction "—is a whole other story."

Charlie waved her off. "Unimportant."

"What did you see?" Johnny demanded. For a self-proclaimed nonbeliever his attitude was intense.

Charlie removed his headband and paced. "There was a room," he began. "It could have been an attic. It felt stuffy. I smelled perfume—the kind you wear, Mel. He uses candles to light the room. Six of them, I think.

That was part of the reason for the blackness, Johnny. I got my vibes from the old blood, which tells me the guy cut himself, several times. Could be he stabbed himself in a fit of rage."

"I'm getting really nervous here." Still seated, Julie took Meliana's hand.

Charlie started to speak, but stopped when a spiky blond head appeared around the corner.

"Is this a private party?" Nick asked. "I saw you leave, thought something might be up."

Zack straightened his black tie. "Tell you what, Nick—it is Nick, right? Why don't you and I grab the closest thing to a beer and give these people some space."

Nick's smooth brow furrowed as Zack endeavored to propel him away. "Did someone else get poisoned? Are you okay, Mel?"

"No, and I'm fine. We all are. This is old business, Nick, nothing to worry about." She wished.

"Your friend Chris from the FBI's looking for you."

"Tell him we left," Johnny said.

"But he's…okay, okay, I'm going." Nick gave in to Zack's repeated attempts to steer him away, made an impatient sound and finally vanished around the corner.

"Chris, minus date, is closing in." Julie observed. "Get to the meat, Charlie."

"I sensed six candles, all white, and dozens and dozens of pictures, all black-and-white. Every shot involved you, Mel. Walking, running, swimming, posing. Some of the prints were close to life-size."

"I'm flattered." And feeling decidedly sick. When

Johnny ran his hand up under her hair, she realized her teeth were close to chattering. "Were any of the photos—damaged?"

Charlie nodded. "Oh, yeah. Ten or more at least. Remember, though, this came to me in fragments, so what I sensed could span a period of days or even weeks, depending on how long the time frame is between when he cut himself and when the murder of Elena Torrence occurred. I sensed other things," he continued. "Poison, weapons, a long strand of hair."

Meliana curled her fingers around her hair. "Mine or Elena's?"

"I couldn't tell. Snatches only, Mel."

They heard a small noise in the shadows. Johnny checked, but shook his head. "What else, Charlie?"

"There was a bullet."

Johnny's eyes met his. "What?"

"I saw a bullet, on a table. There was a tiny red heart drawn on it, except the heart was fragmented—as if it had been struck by a bolt of lightning. Mel, it was sitting on a picture of you. There was a red circle on your chest where your heart is. The marked bullet was inside that circle. Unless the vibes I'm sensing are way off, your stalker's more than ready to make his final move."

Chapter Fifteen

This was not good. Meliana was shaken and terrified. She understood that her terror was based on nothing more than a vision, and that Elliot Hohlman and his intellectual fellowship would heckle Charlie out of the room, maybe even out of Chicago, if they heard about it, but she believed in her friend and colleague.

The rest of the night was a bad dream where her feet were weighted with lead and time was completely distorted.

Johnny kept her close; he even stood guard when she went to the washroom. Julie switched from champagne to soda water. If she hadn't believed so strongly in the cause, Meliana would have left right after Charlie's revelations.

"Chris has been circling the room like a vulture," Johnny noted at one point. "Bianca looks bored enough to fall asleep."

Meliana knew Julie was watching her closely, but she actually saw very little of her friend as the evening wore on. Nick insisted on dancing with her. Charlie mingled and observed and chatted with people he knew, most of whom hadn't expected him to arrive in a tuxedo in any case.

The temperature in the ballroom climbed. Meliana fanned her face with a cocktail napkin. "I think Zack's keeping an eye on Nick," she said to Johnny. She picked up his wrist and regarded his watch. "It's after midnight. I've made my rounds twice. No one'll mind if we leave."

"Before the door prizes?"

Despite Johnny's teasing tone, Meliana knew he was as anxious as she was to be gone. "It's a silent auction, and the only thing I bid on was an abstract painting that doesn't really work in the house. Anyway, the last total I saw topped my salary for a month."

"I bid on the Mickey Mantle autographed baseball."

"I noticed that. Unfortunately, the last bid on your ball topped our combined monthly salaries by a substantial sum. I thought Chicago fans hated the Yankees."

"Man transcends team, or at least his legend does. There's Charlie. And Julie. Let's see if they want to go."

Julie was more than willing. "My feet can't deal with three-inch heels," she moaned. "I'm telling you, as successful as this fund-raiser's been, it's turned into one disappointing evening."

"I'm really sorry, Jules." Meliana adjusted the sleeve of Julie's dress. "I know you wanted to have fun."

"Not your fault at all. Trust me. I'm used to nights that bust like this. You and Johnny go on. Take Charlie with you. I promised your friend Nick a dance, then I'll round up Zack and get out of here. I hope. Last I saw, our Blue Lake deputy was fox-trotting very badly with Chris's date."

Meliana craned her neck. "Where's Chris?"

"Good question. When I have an answer, I'll let you know. Uh, Mel." She caught Meliana's arm. "I know my timing's lousy, but about Sam…"

"More problems?"

"Call it atypical behavior. Now he says he's having trouble sleeping."

"That's called insomnia, Jules."

"Well, the insomniac trimmed my mother's forty-foot-long hedge with hand clippers on Wednesday after dinner, then cleaned out her cyclone-struck three-car garage last night."

"Sounds like—" Meliana hated to say it, but for Julie's sake sighed and finished the sentence "—speed."

"That's what I thought, but he swears he's not doing drugs. Sam's a bad liar, Mel, and I'm trained to spot lies even if he was adept at telling them. The truth is, I don't know what to make of him right now."

"Belated growing pains," Johnny remarked from behind. "Here's your wrap, Mel. I told Charlie we'd drop him by his place."

Meliana smiled. "It'll give you a chance to pick up my slip, which mysteriously found its way into his hands. Smooth maneuvering, Grand."

"It's all in the training. Are you limping?" he asked Julie.

"My size-eight feet are rebelling against size-seven-

and-a-half shoes. Tough luck for my feet. I'll call you tomorrow, Mel. Be careful, both of you."

Charlie was on his cell phone when they reached the front entrance. "Good cause," he said, ending the call. "But not my kind of gig."

"It's the clothes." Meliana arranged her wrap while the valet called for Johnny's SUV. "They make a difference, Charlie. One adopts a different attitude in formal wear."

Johnny leaned in. "She means the tie cuts off your oxygen supply and the cummerbund restricts your mobility. The need to breathe forces you to become a whole new person."

"Take it from an expert in false personas."

Charlie grinned. "You two really have the gloves off these days. How does it feel?"

"Liberating," Meliana said.

"Enlightening," Johnny added. "Car's here. Stay low in your seat, Mel."

"Maybe I should just hunker down on the floor."

"How much did the dress cost?"

"More than you want to hear."

He gave her a hard kiss on the mouth. "Stay low in your seat."

She did, more or less, not so much because he told her to, but because she kept envisioning the bullet Charlie had seen. It had a broken heart and, apparently, her name on it.

"How do you ferret out a crazy person?" she wondered aloud. "It can't be anyone I know."

Both Johnny and Charlie shook their heads, but it

was Johnny who said, "It could easily be someone you know, Mel."

"I mean know know, not a patient I treated who developed an obsession." She gave Johnny's arm a poke. "And stop thinking about Chris."

"I'm not."

"Yes, you are. You get that sulky expression on your face whenever his name crosses your mind. He's not a stalker. The worst I can see him doing is sending me roses, but this has gone way beyond that. Now the guy's killing people, innocent people, and setting aside bullets for me."

Charlie sat back. "I wonder if I misinterpreted that."

"Unlikely," Johnny said. He glanced in the rear-view mirror.

Meliana swiveled her head. "Is someone back there?"

"Reflex action, Mel. I told you before, everyone's a potential stalker right now."

The streets narrowed as they neared Charlie's South Side home. The tires bounced through puddled potholes, one of them so large that water splashed up hard on Meliana's window.

"That sounded like buckshot." She pushed a fist into her breastbone. "If I had my grandfather's weak heart, I'd be in full cardiac arrest by now."

Charlie caught a handful of her hair, kissed it and winked. "You have a strong and beautiful heart, Meliana. No lunatic's going to put a bullet through it."

"I wish I thought you'd foreseen that. Are we going up?" she asked Johnny.

"I need the slip back."

"You can have some of my special tea."

"Not and keep a clear head, we can't." Johnny scanned the lot, then opened his door. "Come out this way, Mel. Your side's too exposed."

"Uh-huh. So why didn't you park with my side against the wall? Have you ever tried to climb over a stick shift in full-length velvet?"

"I'll enjoy watching you try." He slid his hands around her waist, lifted her up and over. "Did I mention I like the slit?"

"At least five times tonight." On her feet in the lot, she smoothed the dress. "Charlie, what are you doing back there?"

"I dropped my cell phone."

Johnny's gaze combed the shadowy area. "I'm surprised you carry one. I thought you hated technology."

"Only harmful technology." He climbed out, adjusted his headband and jingled his keys. "Tea, cookies and one bloody slip upstairs, people. Watch the puddles."

Meliana glanced at the wall where Elena Torrence's body had been propped up like a wooden puppet. Preoccupied, she set her foot in a rut, twisted her ankle and would have fallen flat on her face if Johnny hadn't caught her.

She thought maybe that misstep saved their lives.

Before Johnny could steady her a shot blasted through the air. It hit one of the old bricks and ricocheted sideways.

Johnny dived on top of her. Charlie dropped to the

ground behind the SUV. "I sure as hell didn't foresee that."

"Stay down, both of you," Johnny ordered. He eased up over the hood, his own weapon drawn.

A second shot zinged off the wall above his head. A third shattered the passenger's side window.

Meliana curled her fingers around the leg of Johnny's pants. No way was she going to let him rush the shooter. Not that she expected him to do anything so foolish, but when pushed hard enough, Johnny had a temper, and tempers, no matter how rigorously restrained, could snap.

"Do you see anyone?" Charlie whispered.

"No." Johnny rested his chin on his arm as he squinted into the darkness. He used his gun to point. "I think he's hiding behind those trash cans."

"Use your cell," Meliana said to Charlie.

"What— Oh, yeah—911."

"Try Julie first," she told him.

Charlie punched the number, then gave his head a shake. "She's switched off. I'll do 911."

Two more shots ripped through the air. This time Johnny fired back. Meliana heard a trash can topple. When he fired again, she secured her grip on the leg of his pants.

Her mind worked in frantic spurts. Had the stalker followed them from the banquet, realized where they were going and arrived here first? Why use this lot again? Why involve Charlie?

"The slip. Johnny, is he after the slip?"

Johnny spared a downward glance. "I thought about that. Charlie?"

"I have a safe. I locked it inside."

The silence stretched out for a minute, then two, then three. Meliana raised her eyes to the apartment windows. "Your neighbors don't seem very curious, Charlie."

"We hear gunshots around here from time to time. It's best to mind your own business."

"And keep out of the line of fire." She shivered and raised her head slightly. "We can't stay here all night, Johnny."

"Won't have to. Cops are coming."

The wail of sirens built as the police cars approached. Although she watched, Meliana detected no movement in the shadows. Johnny indicated a narrow passageway between the buildings. "He must have ducked in there and slipped away."

Charlie waited until the police were almost on them, then he tapped Johnny's shoulder. "I'll check my safe."

Johnny covered him while he ran for his apartment. "I don't trust this," he said to Meliana. "Stay behind me."

"You think he's still here? Johnny, I can see the flashing lights. He'd be crazy..."

That was as far as she got before the darkness in the parking lot exploded.

I AM SO ANGRY. No, I'm way beyond angry. I could tear both of you apart with my bare hands and stomp your body parts to a pulp, that's how much I hate you. Not just Johnny, but you, too. Oh yes, Meliana, you, too.

I didn't think tonight—I reacted. You were together, and I couldn't stand it. You've cheated on me, Meliana. You've given yourself back to him.

Well, it won't last. Do you hear me? It's over. Johnny's going to die, and then I'll come for you. You think the substitute suffered? Hah! That was nothing compared to what you're going to feel. In the end, you'll plead with me to use my special bullet. You'll beg me to fire it into your heart.

And I will. I'll shatter your heart and all your dreams, just like you've shattered mine.

Just like you've shattered me!

"IT WAS A NIGHTMARE, and I don't want to relive it. The trash cans exploded, no one was hurt, the shooter got away. He didn't steal my slip, and he didn't leave any clues at the scene." Meliana sidestepped Julie and continued walking down the hospital corridor. But Julie was dogged and followed.

"Any little detail, Mel. The smallest thing could be huge."

Meliana swung around. "Look, I've been through this with your captain, two detectives, some guy from the FBI who scared me almost as much as the shooter, you, my mother, my brother and you again, three times. I told you what I remember, and it jibes to the letter with Johnny's account."

"Charlie's was a bit different."

"Charlie got into the champagne at the banquet. I smelled it on his breath. He's not a good drinker."

Julie took Meliana's hand. "I'm only trying to help."

Meliana stopped, let her head fall back and rolled the tension from her neck muscles. "I know you are, and I appreciate it. Everyone wants to help, and no one can."

"Yet. It'll happen, Mel. He'll screw up. People like him always do. All it takes is…hell."

"Feels like it."

"No, I'm vibrating." She whipped out her cell. "Denton. What? Where? Yeah, I'm on it." She ended the call and punched in another number. "Roney, front entrance, now."

"More trouble?" Meliana asked as Julie disconnected.

"A homicide on Wabash. I wanted to check on Sam before I left."

"I'll do it," Meliana offered. "I have time."

"If he seems weird, I need to know about it."

Meliana nodded. "Stop by the house later. Mark's back—well, temporarily. He's got some mysterious meeting in New York tomorrow or the next day. He's being very evasive about it."

"Sic Johnny on him. You might get more information than you want. Later, Mel."

She was gone before Meliana could ask her about Sam's shift. Not that it mattered. She wasn't going anywhere until she downed some aspirin and did at least fifteen minutes of yoga in her office.

"Mel!"

She halted, didn't turn. "What is it, Nick?"

"I'm thinking about another wine party." He caught up to her. "You like wine, right?"

"To a point. Have you seen Charlie today?"

"He's on three, doing a group therapy thing. About the party..."

"Let me know when it is, okay?" She pivoted and headed toward the elevator before he could object.

Rude, Mel, she told herself. But she wasn't in the mood for small talk right now.

When her own cell rang, she glanced at the screen and, for the first time since Friday, relaxed.

"Yes, Johnny, I'm still alive." She diverted to the solarium and sank onto one of the padded chairs. "Are you downtown?"

"I'm all over the place right now, computerwise. I've been running your extensive patient list all day. So far, no psychos."

"Do the E.R. list. We get a fair number of unstable patients on a daily basis, and I've been covering down there quite a lot lately."

"Already working on it. How's Charlie?"

"He's his usual cool self. I think he was more worried about my slip than his own safety."

"He's lucky he only got nicked by flying metal. The shooter used plastic explosive with a timer to rig the blast. My guess is it was mostly for show—to let us know what he can do."

"I think he's letting us know how angry he is. All wound up, ready to go off."

"He went off a long time ago, Mel. Is Julie with you?"

"She had to leave. Homicide on Wabash."

"Mark?"

"He's giving Administration headaches, going through personnel files. If I've been in contact with a crazy person, one or the other of you will unmask him."

"Yeah, if," Johnny agreed.

She recognized the tone. "You still think it's someone closer, don't you?" She frowned. "Whose phone's beeping?"

"Yours. I'll finish up here and come by in an hour, okay?"

"Dinner and sex?" she teased.

"Thanks for that, Mel. You just blew my concentration to hell."

Good, she thought, switching over. Because sex was better than murder any day, especially with Johnny Grand.

"Hi, Jules, what's up? You can't be at the scene yet."

"I don't have to be. We got an ID on the Wabash homicide. My captain's contacting the FBI as we speak. It's the woman Chris brought to the banquet Friday night, Mel. It's Bianca Foley."

"WHAT THE HELL'S GOING ON?" Johnny grabbed Julie's arm and dragged her aside.

The police station was buzzing. It smelled like old sweat, coffee and vomit. Johnny wanted out, but he wanted answers more.

"Where's Mel?" Julie asked.

"In surgery. Mark's standing guard outside the O.R."

"Okay, good, that helps. Security's been alerted, so she should be safe."

"Bianca, Jules."

"Come to my cubby. I'll fill you in."

If tearing his hair out would have helped, Johnny would have done it. An FBI agent had been killed. Now the feds and the cops had to cooperate, officially. No one ever liked that situation, and Johnny least of all.

"So are you here as an agent or Mel's husband?" Julie poured coffee and handed him a mug. "It's really bad."

"The coffee or the case?"

"Take your pick, and answer the question."

"Screw conflict and animosity, Jules. We're talking about Mel's life. I won't let anything happen to her. We were told Foley was shot."

"Right between the eyes. Dead center. She'd just gotten out of a taxi on Wabash. She was meeting a friend for dinner and a movie."

"Male or female friend?"

"Female. It was drizzling. Her friend was already inside the restaurant—a steak house, nothing fancy. The trajectory of the bullet suggests the shot came from directly in front of her, like the guy was walking toward her when he took aim."

"Witnesses?"

"We have five. One was stoned and out of it. The other four have conflicting stories. The first says Bianca turned before she was hit. He figures the shot came from an office across the street. Number two swears Foley tipped her head back to look up, and the shot came from a second-story window. The third was giving directions to a confused woman. She says Foley got out of the taxi, turned and started walking toward Washington Boulevard, which is the wrong direction if she was headed for the steak house."

"Was there a drugstore nearby?"

"Yeah, why?"

"Bianca smoked. She could have been going for cigarettes."

Julie made a note on her computer. "We'll check it out."

"Did this third witness see anyone?"

"Only the old woman she was helping and the guy I mentioned earlier who was wandering around stoned and mumbling. The last of the four is a retired teacher. He was fighting to get his umbrella up. He saw a man in jogging gear bent over, as if he was getting his second wind. The man had a bag strapped crosswise over his chest and a knit cap on his head. Teacher says the jogger shot Foley while he was straightening to run again."

"Can the teacher describe the jogger?"

"He's with the police artist now. They're doing a composite. Unfortunately, like I said, he was busy with his umbrella when Foley was hit."

Johnny drank some of the godawful cop coffee. "I want to talk to the teacher, the woman giving directions and the stoner."

"No problem." She typed some more, then peered up at him from under her fringe of bangs. "Why the stoner?"

"Covering the bases, Jules. How long does a spleen removal take?"

"Well, gee, let me think. It's been a while since I watched *General Hospital.* Mark'll take care of her, Johnny. Damn," she snarled when the phone rang. "What now?" She picked up and barked, "Denton."

Johnny tuned her out and placed his own call. Mark answered on the first ring, assured him that Meliana was up to her wrists in blood. In other words, she was safe and unharmed.

"I hate days like this," Julie declared, slamming the receiver down. "D-days."

Johnny recalled the term. "Death days?" He risked another mouthful of coffee, grimaced and set the mug aside. "That's slop. Get Mel to give you some Kona."

"I will." Julie rubbed her eyes with the heels of her hands. "We've got a dead guy in the river near Polk."

"Hardly unusual, Jules."

She dropped her hands. "Either I need a vacation or it's time to get out of the city."

"You could consider Sheriff Frank's job."

"I am. Sam'd like it."

As badly as Johnny wanted to be gone, he also cared a great deal about Julie and Sam. "How's he doing? Mel said there was a problem."

"He's acting strange, even for Sam. He's up, then he's down. He's got my mother's house topsy-turvy, re-arranging it. The headaches are gone, but now, suddenly, there's uncharacteristic aggression."

"Cocaine?"

"He says he's not doing drugs. I don't know what to make of it or him right now."

Johnny stood. "Tell you what—when this nightmare's over, bring him up to Blue Lake for a few weeks. I'll go fishing with him. Maybe he'll talk, guy to guy."

"Yeah, maybe." She tapped her computer keys, then started the printer. "I'll get you an address on the third witness. Number four's upstairs. The stoner's in the lockup. He hit a uniform at the scene." She plunked a cap on her head. "Lucky me." She made a face. "I'm off to the river to look at a bloated corpse."

THE CORRIDORS ON the seventh floor were lightly trafficked late at night. He went to Meliana's office door, set his ear against it and listened. No sound. She must be gone.

He reached for the key he'd stolen months ago and slid it into the lock. But when he twisted, nothing happened.

He tried again, jiggled and twisted, then tightened his grip and rattled the door. Still nothing.

He stared at the knob. His fingers curled and uncurled around the key. She'd changed the lock. He couldn't get inside. His eyes came up slowly, turned toward the nurses' station.

And he smiled.

Chapter Sixteen

"Mark's flying back to New York under duress." Meliana pulled a tray of homemade lasagna from the oven, grated fresh Parmesan on the top and returned it to the baking rack. "I had to threaten him with a full physical to get him on the plane, but he's going."

Behind her, Johnny rested his forehead on her hair and slid his arms around her waist. "He loves you, Mel. And don't even think about threatening me with a physical. I'm staying."

"I'd threaten you with an operation." She licked spicy tomato sauce from her thumb. "Or maybe an hour in a hospital elevator." She didn't turn. "Did you talk to the witnesses who saw Bianca Foley die?"

"Three of them. Their stories were all over the place. As it turns out, I think the guy on drugs had the best view of her murder. Unfortunately, his account's not worth much right now, since he's the least coherent."

"What about the teacher?"

"He's fixated on the color of the jogging gear the man he thinks killed her was wearing."

"An out-of-shape jogger carrying a bag sounds like a viable suspect to me."

"Julie's captain and one of our agents are going to question all of them again. I'll sit in, see where it goes." He nuzzled her neck. "Not that I'm complaining, but why are you making such an involved dinner?"

She laughed. "Just because it's not as easy as tearing into a box of Kraft Dinner doesn't make it involved, Johnny. Eileen must love it when you're in Blue Lake. Gives her two men to cook for. Three, if you count Sheriff Frank."

Johnny set his mouth close to her ear. "We could move up there, you know. Both of us."

A haze of longing clouded her mind and had a shiver feathering along her spine. "I'd run the clinic, and you'd do what?"

"Same thing I've always done, but with a longer commute."

"Lead the simple life, huh?"

"Julie's thinking about it."

"No, she isn't. She's fantasizing. There's a difference."

"Yeah?" He smiled against her cheek. "Tell me about fantasies."

Lowering her lashes, Meliana melted back into him. She wanted to purr.

She couldn't remember the last time she hadn't felt all knotted up inside. A night of sex was what she needed. But was a night of sex with Johnny the right thing to do?

She let herself be drawn into him, savored the feel of

his mouth on her skin. It was hot where he touched her and, finally, that tangled ball of tension began to dissolve.

A smile curved her lips. "You know how confused I am, right?"

He moved her hair aside. "Does that mean you want me to stop?"

"If I wanted that, I'd have stopped you long ago." Now she did turn. Hooking her arms around his neck, she looked straight into his eyes. "What I want, Johnny Grand, is to go away from here for a few hours. Far away. I don't want to think or talk or hear about murder."

"Ah, well, in that case..." Reaching past her, he turned the oven to low and scooped her up into his arms. "There's a certain little fantasy I've been waiting to act out."

"Uh-huh. And what exactly have you been waiting for?"

He kissed her, then hit the light switch with his elbow. "The right moment. Nothing more than the right moment. And you."

A THICK BLANKET OF FOG crept over Chicago Harbor the following morning. Lake Michigan was obliterated, and traffic was snarled in all directions. They closed O'Hare before dawn and rerouted incoming flights to Milwaukee. It took Johnny over an hour to drive Meliana to the hospital for a surgery she flatly refused to miss.

"Yesterday it was a damaged spleen, today it's open heart. You're not a cardiac specialist, Mel. Why are you doing this?"

"Because the patient's an eighteen-year-old boy. I've done two other surgeries on his younger sister, and his mother requested that I be there. Anyway, I'm not performing the surgery—I'm assisting. Light's red."

"I see it. Why can't—?"

"I promised I'd be there." Grabbing a handful of his hair, she swung his head to face her. "You wouldn't go back on a promise, would you?"

His lips twitched into a reluctant smile. "Haven't yet. Julie's got a uniform posted outside the O.R., right?"

"From start to finish. I've also got hospital security trailing around after me. I feel like a rock star."

"You have an excellent shower voice."

"That might make for an interesting stage show, but I'll stick to surgery. Green light. Where are you meeting Julie?"

"At her mother's place. She says it's easier than the police station. She made audio copies of the witnesses' statements. I want to hear them."

Meliana squinted into the fog. "There's Charlie at the staff entrance. And Officer Roney."

"I don't know, Mel. A rookie?"

"A two-hundred-and-forty-pound rookie who'd probably have made all-pro linebacker if he hadn't chosen to become a cop. I'm okay with him watching my back."

Braking at the curb, Johnny reached over to cup her neck and give her a hot, hard kiss. "I prefer to watch your back and all other body parts myself. This shouldn't take more than an hour or two. Keep your cell phone with you."

Charlie heard the last thing as he opened the door. "You'll be gray before your time, Johnny. Come on, Mel. Officer Roney and I will walk you to the surgical wing. She'll be fine," he promised when Johnny darted him a quick look. "It'd be crazy for someone to shoot up a crowded hospital. He'd never get out alive."

"I know." Johnny pressed a final kiss to Meliana's forehead. "That's what worries me."

"LOOK, I DON'T HAVE A CLUE what's going on inside this guy's head." Julie met Johnny in the doorway of her mother's Wilmette house. "I'm not even sure what's happening inside mine right now. Everything's all jumbled up. Roses, dead bodies, bloody slips, bras with bullet holes, death threats, poison—you name it, it's there. I'm terrified for Mel and worried about Sam. I've got feds coming at me from all angles and a captain who insists I deal with them." She unlocked the door and called, "Sam?"

"Why are the disks here again?"

"Convenience. I got an officer to drop the copies off on his way to an assignment. Lucky me, I spent the night helping to fish a corpse out of the river. No ID, and the M.E. figures he's been dead since early Saturday morning. What's that, three days now?"

"It's no fun being immersed, is it?"

"I'm amazed you're still sane two years later."

He ran a hand through his hair as he looked around the cluttered house. "I thought about Mel a lot. It got me through. Does your mother ever throw anything out?"

"Nope, and neither does Sam." Julie checked her watch. "He's supposed to be here." She raised her voice. "Sam?" She led the way through the kitchen and pointed. "The disks are on the table." She opened the door to the backyard. "Sam?"

Johnny heard a distant crash, but couldn't pinpoint the location through the fog. "Is there a shed back there?"

"Next to the greenhouse. My mother uses it for potting." Julie let out an irritated breath. "Transients moved into it one year while she and Sam were in Bermuda. They lived there for a week before my uncle discovered them."

"Weren't the neighbors curious?"

"Nah, they thought it was Sam and a friend, camping out."

A door slammed close by. Julie sighed. "That was either Mr. Dawson's garage door or someone's moved into the shed again. You got a minute?"

Not one he wanted to spare, but for Julie's sake, he nodded. "Weather's getting colder." He turned up the collar of his jacket. "My money's on the garage door."

Julie didn't draw her gun, but approached the shed with caution. When she tried the knob, the door creaked open. "Not a good sign," she said over her shoulder. "It should be locked. Anyone here?" She groped for the light switch. "Police. Sam?"

"You don't actually think he's hiding from us, do you?"

"Where's the damn switch? I don't know what to think. What was that?"

"A rat?"

"I don't hear you."

She found the switch at last and flipped it on.

It was a potting shed, all right, a good-sized one, with three long tables, dozens upon dozens of terra-cotta and ceramic pots, vases, clippers, fertilizers and, stacked against the far wall, massive bags of soil and peat.

"I don't see any backpacks or food wrappers, do you?"

"There's a broken pot at the end of this table." Johnny crouched to pick up the pieces. "That's probably the noise we heard."

"The simple answer, right? Okay, mystery solved. Let's go. Maybe Sam's upstairs in the shower and didn't hear us. I'll just… Johnny what are you doing?"

Brow knit, Johnny inspected the table beside him. He remained in his crouch as he eyed the eight-foot plank. "What is this, Jules?"

She bent over and whispered a humorous "We call it a board."

"Yes, I see that. What kind of board? From where?"

"No idea. Is something wrong with it?"

"It looks like barn board."

"Well, sure, it could be. My stepfather built this shed, and his brother had a grain farm close to the city."

Johnny thought back to the night he and Meliana had first gone to Charlie's apartment. "Charlie got a vibe from Meliana's slip, the one the rose was sitting on."

"In her dresser drawer. I remember."

"He saw a white rose. He said the thorns had been sliced off with a razor blade."

Johnny heard the catch in Julie's voice when she asked, "A flat blade?" and turned his head.

"Yeah. Why?"

She rubbed her knuckles up and down her throat, then glanced at the house. "My stepfather used a flat-blade razor to shave until the day he died."

"Three years ago, right?"

"Just over." She shook herself. "Means nothing, Johnny. Lots of men still use flat-blade razors."

"Barn board," Johnny reminded her. "Charlie saw a long plank table made of this stuff."

"Come on, Johnny, my brother wouldn't—" She broke off at his sharp look, and hissed out a breath. "What do you want me to say?"

He searched the floor, then the trash can. And found what he didn't want to find. "Thorns," he said, his tone flat. He dropped them back in the can and stared at the plank table. "We need to look in your mother's greenhouse."

"Hi, Mel."

At the sound of her name, Meliana ended her conversation with the heart surgery team and turned. "Hey, Sam. I thought this was your day off."

"It is. I left a book in my locker. The headaches are gone, so I wanted to read it."

"That'll take ten minutes."

He blinked at her. "Are you going upstairs now?"

"For a while. I need a break."

A grin broke out. "Then this is perfect timing." He handed her a small packet, tied with raffia. "A patient gave it to me as she was leaving. I passed her in Reception. Her name's Claudette. Her parents brought it home for her from France, but she doesn't like caffeine so she said I could have it."

"Except that you don't like caffeine either, so you really can't use it." She sniffed the wrapper. "Smells great. French roast."

"Some expensive brand, she told me. I figured you'd like it."

"Seeing as I'm a caffeine addict and all."

He sobered. "You're not offended, are you?"

"Because you gave me a packet of coffee?" She smoothed one of his dark curls. "I'm not that touchy, Sam. Look, if you're interested, Johnny wants to take me to Blue Lake for a while. You could come up and do some fishing with him."

He blinked again. "Don't you like to fish, Mel?"

"Not really. I can't eat something that stares back at me."

"You eat hamburgers."

"Hamburgers don't have eyes. Cows do. There's a difference." She smiled over his head at her watchdog. "Roney's fidgeting, and I have to check on a patient. Thanks for the coffee. Think about the Blue Lake thing, okay?"

"I will. Bye, Mel—oh."

She heard a small clink, and saw him bend to snatch up a key.

"Bike lock?" she assumed.

"Huh?" He reddened. "Oh, yeah. It's new. More secure." He almost tripped when he stood.

Roney started forward, but Meliana waved him off. Sam was embarrassed enough about his clumsiness without having it underlined.

Her cell phone rang. She smiled at Sam, regarded the screen and answered. "So where are you now, big brother?"

Mark chuckled. "I'm fogged in, like everyone else in Chicago, little sis. They're hoping for a window in the next hour or so. My flight's next in line to leave. Is Johnny there?"

Meliana told him about the copied witness accounts of Bianca Foley's murder, then added a wry "Trust me, anyone looking to give me a hard time today won't be feeling very well once they get a load of J. D. Roney."

"Regardless, I'd rather stay put. Call it cop's instinct. Something's about to break."

She started for the elevator. "And you called to tell me that so I'd feel more secure, huh?"

"Hey, what are big brothers for? Speaking of which…"

"There are two security people trailing along behind Roney, Mark. Any more of a train, and I'll start scaring the patients."

"Better scared patients than a dead you."

"Thanks for the reassurance." She held the elevator door for the guards and a man in an arm cast. "Listen, tomorrow's surgery was canceled, so I might give in and go to Blue Lake with Johnny." She glanced at the man in the cast. "Bianca Foley's death really freaked me out."

"Freaked all of us out, I think. There was a definite resemblance."

"The bullets were fired from the same gun he used at Charlie's place."

"Well, you had to figure. Look, go to Blue Lake if you can. It'll make me feel better to know you're there. And since Johnny's pretty much back to his old self…"

The way he let the sentence hang made Meliana laugh. "You're so subtle. I don't know what's right for Johnny and me at this point. Maybe separation's the key."

"You're dragging your feet, Meliana. I'm gonna check on my flight. Say hi to Jules for me. And stay out of trouble."

She ended the call with a murmured "Easier said than done," rehooked her cell and stepped off the elevator.

She'd look in on her patient later. Right now she wanted some time to herself.

At her office door, she pointed to an adjacent area. "There's a lounge with coffee and cookies, Roney. I'll be about thirty minutes."

Inside, she leaned on the door to close it, then tossed the bag of coffee onto a cabinet and headed for her desk. If she wanted to go to Blue Lake, she needed to clear her schedule. She also needed to deal with the guilt she felt over Bianca Foley's death.

Her e-mail indicated a new message. She opened it and shook her head as two large words jumped out at her. "Call Julie!"

Better than a death threat, she decided, reaching for the phone. She sat, swiveled and began to dial. Then stopped when she noticed her desk drawer was partly open.

Her eyes went to the door. She thought about alerting

Roney, but decided against it. Instead, she took a deep breath and pulled the drawer back.

Her fear returned in an icy rush. He'd given her another white rose.

A FEW HOURS LATER, Meliana stood in the downstairs hallway of Julie's mother's home with her hands in her jacket pockets and her head reeling. "I can't believe Sam would hurt anyone, least of all someone he likes."

"We found white roses in the greenhouse, thorns in the trash and flat razor blades in the downstairs bathroom cupboard, Mel." Johnny massaged her neck as he looked up the stairs. "Where do you want us to start, Julie?"

She came down, heavy-footed. "I've gone through his room, top to bottom. There's nothing but the usual junk inside. The FBI's sending another agent. He can do the outbuildings—shed, greenhouse, garage. You two, take your pick. You know the house, Mel. I have to find Sam before someone else does. I'll drop by the station first, give you a call from there."

Meliana hugged her. "I feel like this is my fault somehow."

"Why? Because he's obsessed with you?" Julie hugged her back. "No way. There's no fault on your part, and maybe not on his, either. He says he's not doing drugs, but I'm starting to think he's a better liar than I suspected."

Meliana sighed. "My spare office key went missing from the nurses' station. They didn't discover it until after I found the rose. Sam dropped a key on the floor while I was talking to him, Jules, but I don't know—this still seems really far-fetched to me. The best words I can think of to describe your brother are sweet and shy. Those traits simply don't tie in with death threats, explosions and poison."

"They can," Johnny told her. "You keep things bottled up long enough, sometimes you blow."

"Maybe, but—Sam?"

They heard a knock. Straightening, Julie gave her a weak smile. "Must be the fed." She opened the door and went rigid. "No damned way!"

"I was sent by the Bureau, Julie," Chris said. "Not my call."

Johnny set his jaw. Meliana wanted to groan. Bad to worse, was all she could think.

"Let it go," she advised Julie. "This needs to be settled. Sam has to be found. Do the second thing, and forget about the first for now."

Julie shot Chris a dark look, but nodded and handed Meliana a set of keys. "Don't let them start squabbling. And remember, you and Johnny do in here. Blackburn's outside."

"Gonna be fine," Meliana murmured as her friend left. "Shed, greenhouse, garage," she repeated to Chris. When he started to protest, she softened her tone. "It's how Julie wants it, and this is her mother's house. Still unofficial here, Blackburn, even from the Bureau's perspective."

Johnny offered him a cheerful smile. "I'll walk you out, make sure everything's unlocked."

Despite the situation, a spark of humor kindled. It was like watching two dogs face off over territory.

Meliana climbed the stairs to the second floor. The house was messy, crammed with furniture and knick-knacks. Julie's mother was a hoarder. So was Sam, she reflected, taking a peek into his room. The difference was, Sam's stuff was organized to a fault.

She went into the guest bedroom, saw nothing out of order and moved on to the upstairs office. This had to be Sam's domain, as well.

Everything stood in tall, neat stacks—papers, books, magazines, DVDs, games. Even his pens sat in a tidy line next to the monitor.

She checked the drawers and the closet. She hesitated, then tried his computer, but Sam had everything coded. Julie would have to bring in an expert to get past the barriers he'd erected.

Johnny poked his head across the threshold. "Any luck?"

"I slammed the closet door on my hand, but otherwise, nothing unusual." She shook her fingers as she spoke. "This is a geek's room, Johnny, not a homicidal maniac's."

"We're not done yet. Is there an attic?"

"I think you access it through the storage room at the back of the house. It's probably locked." She tossed him the keys Julie had given her. "Good luck finding the right one." Frustration set in as she gazed out the window. "Johnny, does Sam seem like a killer to you?"

Johnny came in, caught her hand and kissed her bruised knuckles. "There's no actual type, Mel. The face we present to the world can be real or a very good mask. How do you tell the difference? Maybe Charlie'd know. I sure as hell don't. Some people have the capacity to adopt multiple personalities—and I'm not talking about candidates for psychiatric care. I mean they can act."

But she couldn't, no matter how hard she tried, envision Sam as a homicidal stalker.

At least not the Sam she knew.

There were two bathrooms on the second floor. She only glanced into Julie's mother's. Jars and bottles littered the countertop and the rack above the toilet. Liz had more hair and skin care products than a drugstore. Who could use so much stuff?

Sam's bathroom was equally crammed. She moved on to the medicine cabinet—or tried to. She twisted the latch twice before she realized it wasn't stuck but locked.

Not good, her instincts whispered.

She went searching for Johnny and retrieved Julie's keys. There were at least twenty on the ring and it took her several seconds to find the right one. Even after she did, she still had to work to open the mirrored door.

Surprisingly, the shelves were almost bare. Two brown bottles and two clear ones sat on the bottom shelf. Meliana stared for a minute, then reached inside. The first bottle she picked up caused her stomach to pitch and her heart to give a sick thump.

"Oh, Sam…" She closed her fingers around the almost empty vial. "What in God's name were you thinking?"

Chapter Seventeen

"Steroids?" Julie croaked the word over the phone line. "Sam's doing steroids? But he—but—Mel, are you sure?"

"It's a testosterone compound, Julie, a popular one. I've seen the effects of it before, or rather the side effects—enlarged prostate, liver damage, heart attack, impotence, the list goes on."

"But…" Clearly Julie was stunned by the news. "He told me he wasn't doing drugs. I haven't noticed any added bulk."

"Sam wears baggy clothes, Jules, and he's not doing street-variety drugs."

"Steroids are sold on the street, Mel."

Meliana ran her thumb across the label. "These ones aren't. They're put out by ParMed, Tim Carrick's pharmaceutical company."

"This accounts for the aberrant behavior, doesn't it?"

"Absolutely." Meliana had already examined the other bottles. "Every one of these compounds is testosterone based. Cypionate, isocaproate, propionate. And the physiological side effects are equally radical. You've heard of roid rage, haven't you?"

"Heard of and dealt with. I know the deal, Mel. Intense aggression. Users become dangerous to themselves and to others."

"You have to find him, Julie. I don't know how long he's been on this stuff, but his behavior's only going to get worse."

"I'm about to check the local theater."

"Do you need help?"

"You're already helping, and anyway, I'm not alone."

"Roney?"

"Better. An out-of-towner we both know and love—" A loud noise caused her to break off. "What was that?"

Meliana had no idea. The crash had come from the far end of the house.

She heard a shout, then another sound like shattering glass.

"Something's happening," she told Julie. "I'll get back to you."

A thump reached her from down the corridor. She ran for the ladder that Johnny had left hanging and began to climb. She heard male voices. One was Johnny's. The other sounded as if it belonged to an adolescent boy.

"Now what?" she muttered, and shoved the trapdoor open.

She spied Johnny on one knee. He was watching someone. Meliana followed the line of his gaze to the side wall and had to set her teeth to stifle her reaction.

Sam stood there, clutching a baseball bat. His face was red and the veins on his neck protruded with each word he uttered.

"I don't want to hurt you. That wasn't the idea. I only wanted Meliana to know how I felt. I didn't mean for anything bad to happen."

Johnny knew she was there, but didn't look over. "Meliana knows how you feel, Sam. She's not angry."

The bat jerked higher. Meliana remained silent and motionless. "Everyone's angry," Sam shouted. "They're all looking for me. It's not fair." He stomped a foot. "I gave her roses. I gave her…" He did a double take when he spotted Meliana, and let out a loud cry.

Meliana took the last step into the attic. "Sam, it's okay. It is. Put the bat down, and talk to me."

His face got redder. The veins in his neck threatened to pop. "Where's Julie?"

"Looking for you."

"You see?" Spit flew from his mouth. "It's like I said—everyone's mad."

Johnny stood. "No one's mad, Sam."

"Don't lie to me." His shriek faded to a whisper and his face crumpled. "Don't lie to me."

"We're not lying." Meliana eased closer. "It's the steroids that are making you act this way. It's not you. We know that."

Johnny shot her a fast glance, then returned his attention to Sam. "Come on." He held out his hand. "Give me the bat, and let's go downstairs."

"Johnny!"

Chris's impatient shout triggered something in Sam. His features contorted and he hunched down.

The bat swung in a wild arc around him. Meliana jumped sideways as he bolted. "Sam," she called, but Johnny motioned for her to let him go.

Sam didn't stop. He stumbled down the ladder, howling and banging the bat as he went.

Meliana waited until he reached the bottom before tugging on Johnny's arm. "We have to follow him."

But Johnny held her back. "No, *we* don't."

"But he's—"

"Got weapons, Mel. A bat and a gun. Loose cannon, with weapons and a scary attitude. You're not the one who should be chasing him. Call Julie." He drew his gun. "Don't argue," he warned when she opened her mouth. "I don't interfere when you do your work. Let me do mine. Call Julie, and stay here."

Chris's scowling face appeared through the trapdoor. "What the hell's going on? Why did Sam try to deck me with a bat?"

Meliana punched Julie's number. "Sam's doing steroids, Chris." She turned her gaze northward. "And our neighbor in Blue Lake is his supplier."

"YOU HAVE A DEALER living next to you in Blue Lake, and you didn't know it?" Chris covered Johnny while he searched the backyard. "Man, that's bush league. I thought you had good instincts."

"If I followed them without question, you'd have

been a dead man long ago, Blackburn. Ten to one Carrick didn't make a profit off the first round of 'roids."

"What, the guy's a philanthropist?"

"In a way. Lightfoot says he gives out samples of his drugs."

"Good PR tactic."

"He's in a prime position to build a clientele."

"From samples to discount deals to dependency. The guy's a prince. Do you see anything?"

"Yeah, shadows. There aren't any footprints or broken branches. Sam knows the neighborhood. He probably slipped through a gap in a fence before we even got out here."

"Do you know where he hangs?"

"Julie does."

"You sure she'll want to find him?"

Johnny sent him a look of contempt. "Not everyone's as skewed as you. She'll search."

"Uh-huh." Unconvinced, Chris made a circle of the yard. "I'll go through the outbuildings again. You can do the basement."

Johnny didn't argue. He lowered his gun and returned to the front hall.

"Freeze, lady," he said when he spied Meliana.

She gave the doorknob she'd been reaching for a twist while he holstered his gun. "You had the same idea, huh?"

"Chris did. Is the cellar finished?"

"Johnny, you can smell the damp up here."

"Old houses have problems, Mel."

"Which is why I don't buy old houses."

He caught her wrist. "I'll go first."

His macho attitude amused her. "Be my guest. I don't think he's down there anyway. The door sticks. I'd have heard the hinges creak if he'd opened it."

Still, it was better to be thorough. Johnny led the way down a set of sagging stairs, and on through five cobwebbed rooms. But there was no sign of Sam anywhere and no indication that he'd been there.

"I talked to Julie." Meliana checked her hair for cobwebs when they returned to the first floor. "She's going to go through the neighborhood house by house until she locates him."

"Does she want us to help?"

"Actually, she suggested we get out of the city. She doesn't think he'll follow us even if he realizes we're leaving."

Johnny brushed a sticky web from her shoulder. "What do you think?"

"She could be wrong. Steroids misused can create monsters. I've dealt with several cases in Emergency. Sam's heavy into the testosterone compounds and those are the ones that cause overt bouts of aggression. Taken a step further, the side effects go beyond physical and physiological. People on serious 'roids have been known to commit murder."

Johnny studied her face. "Why would he do it, Mel?"

She dusted off her hands. "Charlie could answer that better than me. Sam's always been shy and awkward. He's not small, but he has a slender build."

"I didn't notice him bulking up."

"Neither did I, but like I told Julie, he wears baggy clothes—and I'm not sure adding bulk was his goal in any case. Steroids promote a sense of well-being that's difficult to top. Unfortunately, it can go the other way, as well."

"Thus the weird behavior." Johnny looked around. "We might as well hit the lights and go. Julie's right. There's not a lot we can do at this point. Seeing either one of us seems to set Sam off."

"Mmm." She appeared preoccupied.

He caught her chin and tipped her head back. "Problem?"

She met his dark eyes. "What's the deal with the roses? Did he really have a crush on me?"

"Ah." Johnny glanced upward, then blew out a breath and slid his hand around the back of her head. "It's a lot more than a crush. People have died here." He moved his head. "I found a scrapbook in the attic."

She sighed. "Of me?"

"Pictures of you. Poems he wrote but never sent. He also had a surgical mask, a garter, a piece of wedding cake and…"

Meliana closed her eyes. "Let me guess—a white rose?"

"Pressed and labeled. It's from your wedding bouquet."

THEY REACHED BLUE LAKE before eleven—not bad in Meliana's opinion, considering the evening they'd spent. Johnny unloaded the food they'd bought in the city. Meliana dealt with the dogs, the backpacks and the carryalls.

She ran her finger along the banister as she came down from the loft. "Eileen hasn't been here for a while. I thought she was supposed to come even when you weren't around."

"Maybe she's busy with Sheriff Frank."

"Don't be sarcastic. It could happen."

"So could teleportation, but I'm not holding my breath." He slammed the fridge door. "Is your cell charged?"

"Always, Johnny. You're the forgetful one."

"Only when it doesn't matter."

Meliana wandered to the window, slid her fingers into her hair and held it back. "It reminds me of an old horror movie out there. Even with the porch lights on, all I see is fog and the occasional branch."

"Be grateful we have power."

"I am, very grateful." She exhaled with gusto. "For what it's worth, I found out why Nick's been sucking up to me lately."

"Let me guess. His grandfather needs surgery and he wants you to botch the job."

"He'd use more than fine wines as a bribe in that case. Do you remember the lust Charlie said he felt when he handled the rose Nick gave me at the tasting party?"

"I remember the word *lust* coming up."

"Well, apparently Nick has a friend—also a surgical nurse—who works at General, and Nick's been working up the nerve to ask me to talk to the chief of staff about giving this nurse a job with us."

"Simple as that, huh?"

"Nick broke down and confessed before today's surgery. His friend's name's Ronnie."

"Is Ronnie a male or a female nurse?"

"No idea, but whatever the gender, Nick's definitely interested. Ronnie helped him put the roses together for the party. Thus the feelings of lust."

"That's one mystery cleared up."

"And Charlie's credibility validated." Meliana rubbed a damp palm down the leg of her jeans. "Johnny, why don't I think this is over?"

He summoned a vague smile. "I could give you a cliché answer about a fat lady singing, but I won't." Hoisting himself onto the sill in front of her, he ran comforting hands along her arms. "I can't see Sam following us here, Mel."

She stared into the fog. "Me, neither."

"Does he drive?"

"Not often and not well, but he's licensed. And his father's car's still in the garage. Julie takes it out from time to time. It runs."

"Good to know… What was that?" His head snapped up and he swung around.

"I didn't hear anything."

"Not hear. I saw a light."

She dredged up a smile. "If it's Tim Carrick, shoot him. He deserves it."

Johnny squinted into the fog. "Don't worry about Tim. We'll talk to Zack or Sheriff Frank first thing in the morning."

His intense surveillance brought goose bumps to Meliana's skin. "Was it a headlight or a flashlight?"

"I couldn't tell."

"I didn't hear an engine."

"You wouldn't hear a tractor over that old fridge."

Several uneventful seconds ticked by before Meliana relaxed enough to ask, "Do you have cable?"

"Did we have it before?"

"Yeah."

"Then we have it now." He turned back to her. "I didn't change anything, Mel. I wanted the place to be like it was when we were together."

Humor rose. "It fig—" It vanished when one of the hazier shadows shifted. Her gaze sharpened. "You're right, Johnny. Someone is out there. I saw a movement."

He hopped down and set his head next to hers, cheek to cheek. "Someone on foot, or another light?"

"Both."

He swore.

"Johnny…" She slapped a palm to his chest. "Don't go out there."

"You want to wait for him to come in here?"

"I'd rather be the one doing the ambushing than the one being ambushed."

"It doesn't work that way, Mel."

"I knew you were going to say that." She headed for her ringing cell. She spied Julie's number and picked up.

"Mel? Are you safe?" Her friend sounded frantic.

"I'm not sure." Meliana scanned the foggy yard. "We can't see much, but there might be someone outside. Have you found Sam?"

"Not yet. You're in Blue Lake, right?"

"Just. Julie, does Sam know how to use a gun?"

She could almost see her friend wincing. "Uh…"

"That's a yes. Did you teach him?"

"Only for fun. You know, target practice with empty cans and hand-drawn stick figures. Look, no one I've talked to has seen him. I'll check my mother's garage. If the car's missing, I'll be up there in an hour."

"Okay…what?" she demanded when Johnny dipped down.

"Our someone's skulking." He pulled out his gun. "Once around the perimeter of the house," he promised, and gave her a sound kiss. "My job, Mel."

"Stop saying that. Johnny heard footsteps," she relayed to Julie. "He's going to circle the house. I'll give him two minutes before I call Sheriff Frank and go after him myself."

Johnny cast her a narrowed look from the side door, but said nothing and slipped out into the night.

Meliana spun back to the window. "I hate this, Julie. If I let him go, he could get killed. If I go with him, I might distract him."

"Bolt the doors," Julie suggested. "Turn the lights

down and sweat it out. Okay, stay on the line. I just
pulled up outside my mother's place."

Meliana heard a squeal of tires followed by
slamming doors and murmured voices. Then she heard
Julie groan and felt the ball of fear in her stomach drop.

"Mel?"

"Car's gone, right?"

"For quite some time, too, or I'd smell the exhaust."
Doors slammed again. "I'm using the siren. Warn Johnny,
Mel. And if Sam is there, don't believe a thing he says."

I'M HERE, MELIANA. Can you see me? Hear me? Feel
me? I have the last piece of lingerie I took from you.
It's folded up inside my jacket pocket. You're going to
wear it for me, like you wore it for Johnny on your
wedding day. You remember that day, don't you? You
looked so beautiful in your long white gown.

But looks can be deceiving, can't they? You've
looked at me, many times. You wanted me to love you,
I know you did. Was it all a game for you? Other
women play games, but I thought you were different.
I thought you would love me back.

I won't shake tonight. I'm angrier than I've ever
been, but I won't let myself fall apart. I'm going to end
this dream gone bad, for all of us. When it's over, you'll
be dead in my mind.

You'll be dead period.

JOHNNY WENT FARTHER than he'd intended. He searched
the dock—probably not a smart thing to do—then

circled back to the woods. He passed the tree where they'd found Laura the night she'd been poisoned. He crossed the path where they'd met the teenagers who'd been making out. He walked through the clearing where he'd glimpsed the man in the plaid jacket.

He knew how to be silent, even in rural situations. He kept his eyes and ears alert and his gun drawn. There was someone here. Every ten seconds or so, he heard a twig snap or a stone shift underfoot.

When he caught the snapping sound again, he used a large evergreen for cover and crouched down. The fog was a curtain of swirling gray, but if he couldn't see the stalker, then the stalker couldn't see him.

Was it Sam? He aimed his gun skyward and kept his eyes moving. He'd gone fishing with the kid, watched baseball with him. Except he wasn't a kid anymore, was he? He hadn't really been one at their wedding.

A bush rustled to his left. Johnny snapped his gun down and spun on one knee.

"Drop it," he ordered. And fired when he spied a glint of metal.

MELIANA GAVE JOHNNY sixty seconds before she picked up the phone. Shannon barked and Lokie, sensing trouble, nudged her leg.

"Forget it, guys, you're not going out there." She listened. "Phil? Is that you?" When the mechanized voice droned on, she shook the handset. Of course there was no one answering at the sheriff's office. After nine, you left your message, and the person on duty responded whenever he happened to check in.

"Great system," she said to the dogs. She left a brief message, then redialed. "Sorry, Sheriff Frank. You're going to have to wake up and listen to me."

It took Meliana several minutes to get through to the man. He mumbled and muttered and finally, reluctantly, agreed to give up a portion of his night's sleep.

"Lock your doors" was the last thing he said before he hung up.

She regarded the dogs. "Does every law enforcement officer in this state think I'm an idiot? Even you two would lock the doors if you thought there was a killer stalking you."

Except he wasn't stalking her, was he? Right now he was going after Johnny.

"Hell."

Meliana glanced at the dogs again, then went to the closet for the gun Johnny kept there. She checked to make sure it was loaded, gave Shannon's head a scratch and pushed her firmly away from the door. "Watch the house," she told them both and, taking a bolstering breath, stepped onto the porch.

A light cut through the fog, swiping across her. A moment later Zack appeared at the bottom of the stairs.

Relieved, Meliana dropped the gun into her jacket pocket. "Did you get my message, or did Frank call you?"

"I retrieved your message while I was patrolling Lakeshore Road. What's going on? Where's Johnny?"

"He saw someone, heard something and took off."

She joined him in the yard. "We think it's Sam who's behind all this—leaving roses, poisoning apples…"

Zack shook his head. "Killing people? I don't know, Mel. Personally, I'd have suspected one of your dogs before him." But he drew his weapon as a precaution. "What makes you think it's him?"

"He's using steroids, courtesy of Tim Carrick."

"Uh…" Zack's gaze shifted. "I don't want to worry you, but I spotted a car on the side of the road as I was driving in."

Meliana scrambled through her memories. Julie's stepfather had purchased a Buick two years before his death. "Was it a silver-gray LeSabre with a dented rear fender?"

Zack's brows came together. "No, it was a red Camaro with tinted windows and a sunroof."

She whipped her head around. "Are you sure?"

"Positive. Why?"

Fear slithered in, cold and unbridled. Only two thoughts registered. Johnny was out there somewhere.

And Chris Blackburn drove a red Camaro.

Chapter Eighteen

"Drop it, Blackburn," Johnny shouted. "I'm a better shot than you."

A protracted silence preceded Chris's surly "In your dreams, Grand. You drop it, or I'm firing."

At what, Johnny wondered. Fog?

He lowered his weapon slightly. "What are you doing here?"

Chris's response came from his right. "Looking for you, old friend. I figured I'd find you roaming around. I had you pegged from the start. Separation didn't sit well with you, did it? It doesn't matter that she's finished with you. Your ego doesn't want to hear that, no way. So you come up to Blue Lake and let your mind take a slow slide. There has to be a way, something you can do to make her want or even need you again. If she needs you, she might give in. That's how it went down, right—in your head." Silence stretched out between them. Chris made an angry sound. "Come on, man, admit it, you're done. No matter what you do, I've got the upper hand here, so..."

A click next to his ear stopped him. "Throw it on the ground," Johnny warned. "Ah-ah." He pressed the tip of his gun to the side of Chris's head. "No tricks, no sudden moves."

Rage simmered as his former partner lowered his gun and threw it forward.

Johnny didn't trust the situation or Chris. You worked with a guy, you learned to think the way he did.

"Stand up," he said. "Slowly."

Chris remained in his squat. "What you gonna do, man? Shoot me in the head? You kill me, you'll never see the outside of a prison wall again."

"So I'm supposed to let you shoot me instead?"

He heard the smile in Chris's voice. "Sounds like a plan to me."

"Get up, Blackburn."

Chris half turned in his crouch. "No way you'll shoot," he said with a grin. And went for Johnny's knees.

"IT'S BETTER IF I GO ALONE, Mel." Meliana mimicked Zack's parting words. "I'm a cop, Mel. I have a gun." She kicked the porch door open and crossed the floor to the rear exit.

"He's headed for the woods." She peered through the window, then opened the back door and slipped out.

Nothing stirred except the fog. She heard Lokie whining behind her and thought of Sam. Was he here, too? Sam and Chris?

"And Johnny," she murmured.

She glanced at Shannon, set her hand on the gun in

her pocket. There was something nagging at her, some hazy thought she couldn't quite grasp. Nothing, absolutely nothing, made sense to her right now. Was Sam the stalker, or was it Chris? Sam was doing steroids. He had a scrapbook in the attic. Chris hated Johnny. His Camaro was parked at the side of the road.

Why?

"Damn." Reaching behind her, Meliana unlatched the door. She couldn't take Lokie, but Shannon was well trained. She'd be able to track Johnny in the fog.

A single gunshot shattered the stillness in the woods. Meliana's hand froze on the latch. She felt the blood drain from her cheeks. Again that hazy thought darted through her mind.

No more shots were fired. Had Chris hit Johnny? Had Sam? Or had Johnny fired the bullet?

The seconds stretched out. Meliana's nerves stretched with them. Just when she thought they would break, another set of lights cut across the trees beside the house.

"Doc Mel?" Sheriff Frank's voice reached her. "You here?"

She met him near the side porch. "Over here, Sheriff."

He seemed more concerned than cranky, which wasn't like Sheriff Frank at all.

"You're not hurt?" He took her by the arms to inspect her.

"I'm fine. Johnny's the one in danger."

"Johnny? Where's he?"

"Out there." She motioned toward the woods. "With Chris Blackburn and maybe Sam, and Zack."

"He's out…" The sheriff's jaw dropped. He closed his mouth quickly, turned and gave a shrill whistle.

The lights on his cruiser were immediately extinguished. The door opened and closed.

That's when it hit her. The haze in her mind cleared, and Meliana swung her head toward the front of the house. "One headlight," she whispered. She pulled free of the sheriff's bruising grip. "There was only one headlight!"

"GET OFF ME, GRAND." Chris panted. "At least let me turn my head. I can't inhale dirt."

Johnny's knees throbbed from the blow he'd taken. He wasn't sure he could stand, but he eased back and allowed Chris to avert his head. "Start at the beginning, Blackburn, and tell me why you came up here."

Chris squirmed without success. "I came to stop you."

"From doing what?"

"Killing Mel."

For a moment Johnny didn't move. Then he arched his brows and offered a disbelieving "What?"

"I talked to the witness who saw Bianca die."

"Which one?"

"The junkie. He said he saw the murderer."

"Yeah, I got that story, too. I also got a lot of laughing and gurgling."

Chris struggled again. "We dried him out, man. When I saw him, he was almost straight."

Johnny tightened his knees around Chris's torso. "You should be running a rehab facility."

"He said he talked to Bianca's killer."

Johnny frowned. "When?"

"Twice. The night she died and again today."

Johnny grabbed a handful of hair and yanked Chris's head out of the dirt. "What the hell are you talking about?"

"I'm talking about you," Chris snarled. "He told me the guy who did Bianca looked like you."

SHE'D SEEN A VEHICLE with one headlight. That vehicle was Zack's car. Meliana had noticed it when he'd driven up, but she hadn't been paying attention.

"Whoa, Doc. Whoa, now." The sheriff struggled to run and grab her at the same time. "Don't go off half-cocked."

She halted, spun and retraced her steps. "I don't have time for this, Sheriff. Maybe I'm wrong, I don't know. I'm not a cop. I don't have those instincts. But one way or another, Johnny's out there with someone who wants him dead."

"He wants both of you dead, Meliana."

Meliana's eyes shot up as a woman appeared through the fog. Her cheeks were wet with tears. Her hair hung in limp curls.

"You're not wrong." Her voice was strained and broken. "I've suspected the truth for some time now. I just didn't want to believe it. There's something very wrong with my boy. He's not thinking straight."

Meliana stared at her. "What's he going to do, Eileen?"

The curls began to tremble. "He's going to kill Johnny—then he's going to come back for you."

JOHNNY WAS TEMPTED to shove Chris's face back into the dirt, but he held off and gave his ex-partner's hair another yank.

"What do you do between assignments—sit around and dream up ways to turn me into a villain?"

Chris grunted. "Tit for tat, pal. You wanted me to be the stalker."

"I'm still not convinced you aren't."

"Ditto."

They were getting nowhere with this, yet Johnny was reluctant to let Chris go.

"You'd take a junkie's word over mine?" Johnny shook his head. "Man, you've got problems." But he released Chris's hair and relaxed his kneehold grip. He glanced toward Chicago. "Why would he say that?"

"Because it's true?"

Johnny's lips took on a faint curve. "You must like pain, Blackburn."

"You couldn't hurt me if you tried."

Unable to resist, Johnny leaned down. "Wanna bet?"

A twig snapped close by. Johnny's head came up.

"What was that?" Chris demanded.

Johnny gave his face a shove to shut him up.

Nothing moved. But there was something. Johnny felt it, like bugs on his skin. Chris wasn't the stalker, his gut instinct whispered, no matter how much he wanted him to be.

He gave his former partner a swat on the shoulder and motioned to the left. Chris nodded, holding still as Johnny released him.

This time it was a branch that cracked. Was it Sam? Although the evidence pointed that way, Johnny didn't buy it. Sam had always had a thing for Mel, a sort of lingering crush that everyone labeled harmless.

"What are you thinking?" Chris climbed to his knees.

Johnny had his gun out and his eyes moving. "What did the stoner say, exactly?"

"He said the killer looked like the fed he'd just finished talking to. Then he laughed and said it must be nice having that kind of power."

"The power to hide behind a badge."

"Hey, you wouldn't be the first."

"No," Johnny agreed. He strained to hear the smallest sound. "I wouldn't. Cover my back."

"I can't." Chris spoke through his teeth as he searched the clearing. "You kicked my gun away."

"You don't have a backup?" Disgusted, Johnny reached behind him for the second gun he'd stuffed in his waistband.

The branch cracked again. Johnny swung, but pulled up short as he spied the pained expression on Chris's face.

Zack had his gun pressed to the back of Chris's head. Despite the chill, he was sweating. And smiling.

"I'M SORRY," Eileen sobbed as she ran along in Meliana's wake. "I should have said something, warned you of my suspicions. But he's my son, my baby. I thought he was just going through a bad emotional time."

"He's a murderer, Eileen." Meliana kept a firm hand on Shannon's collar. "He's killed two women that we know of, and a morgue attendant." But he wouldn't kill Johnny, she promised herself. He couldn't do that.

Shannon kept her nose to the ground. "Can she find him?" The sheriff panted at her heels.

"I hope so. Johnny trained her, not me." She glanced back as they ran. "How could Zack be so messed up, and no one except Eileen noticed it?"

"He's been messed up most of his life, Doc. Started out a bad kid, seemed to get better but in fact got badder."

A shot blasted through the fog. Meliana stopped so quickly the sheriff ran into her. Farther back, Eileen stumbled to a gasping halt.

"That came from the woods near Tim Carrick's place," Meliana said.

Another shot rang out. Changing directions, she ran toward it.

"SORRY, GUYS." With all the fog and shadows, Zack's smile appeared grotesque. "Am I freaking you out? It's just that I enjoy watching puffy, overweight federal officers go all white and pasty. Pants still dry, Blackburn?" He jabbed the barrel of the second gun he carried into Chris's neck. "It is Blackburn, isn't it? You've got feelings for Meliana, too, don't you? You have my sympathy, pal. She'll smash your heart and all your dreams into little pieces. She did it to me and to sweet Sam." His expression hardened. "Put the guns down, Johnny. You won't use them, not when I've got your ex-friend and partner in such a compromised position. One twitch and his brains'll be splattered all over you. Very messy. Mel won't like it. Tidy, tidy is our Meliana. Do you know, the place where she stitched me up after I got cut a few years back is hardly even visible now? Twenty-six stitches, and all you can see is a little hairline mark. Amazing." His tone roughened again. "I said lose the guns, Grand."

Johnny held his stare, but let his hands fall and the guns drop.

Zack's smile returned as he leaned toward Chris's right ear. "You see? He's still your friend. Now me, I'd have let you die. One less competitor for Meliana's affections. But that's okay, because I'm going to kill you anyway. First you, then Johnny, then the prize."

Johnny's muscles were wired. If he was going to die, why not rush the guy? Maybe he could turn one of Zack's two guns back on him. At least Meliana would be safe.

"Brain's working overtime, isn't it, Johnny?" Zack screwed the tip of his gun into Chris's neck. "You're thinking, 'I can get him. I'm faster than he is.' But you know what? You're not. You're faster than this big lump, but even Sam could dodge him, and from what I've seen, the kid's a total klutz."

Johnny kept his arms loose at his sides. "You've known about Sam all along, haven't you?"

"Would've been hard not to. He was a walking rose garden."

"You used him."

"I used his roses," Zack corrected, "to my advantage. When I could."

"You put one of Sam's roses in Meliana's lingerie drawer the day you broke in to our house."

Icy anger crept into Zack's expression. "Her house, Johnny. Be very clear on that point. You were no longer in the picture. Yes, I put the rose in her drawer, after I took what I wanted from inside it. Sam left it on her doorstep. I just—moved it to a better place."

Johnny inched closer. "How did you get past the alarm?"

Zack laughed. "High-tech infiltration tactics. I sat in my car across the street one day and used binoculars to watch Meliana punch in the code."

"Why did you set the alarm off?" Chris asked.

Zack poked his head. "Felt like it. I'd seen you before, Blackburn, sniffing around like that dog Sam gave her. I knew you were a fed. I figured I'd give you a puzzle to work on. Except you didn't. You got moody and petulant, and you started in on Johnny. At least, that was the scuttlebutt I got from Julie. Dating her was a total brainstorm. I mean, after all, I couldn't be everywhere, could I? I still had a pissy part-time shift to work up here."

"But no paramedic course," Johnny assumed.

"Oh, I started the course, but I dropped out after a few weeks. Meliana was going to love me no matter what I did for a living. I didn't need to prove anything to her. Face it, Johnny, you don't know squat about medicine. In fact, you faint at the sight of a hypodermic needle. If she could marry a squeamish undercover agent, she could marry me." His mouth compressed.

"That's how it was supposed to go. But then you rode to her rescue, and everything fell apart."

Was Zack trembling? Johnny couldn't be sure. He was definitely twitchy. He kept jiggling his right hand and fidgeting with the gun.

When he caught Johnny watching, his eyes narrowed to slits. "Don't even think about it, pal. I can shoot you so you'll never father children."

"If you're going to kill me anyway, what's the difference?"

"It's called pain, Johnny." Zack adjusted his grip on the gun at Chris's neck. "I want you to suffer. That's important to me." He swiped the side of his other hand across his upper lip. "Maybe—yeah, maybe I'll kill Blackburn right now, and let you live a little longer. I have a final gift for Meliana in my pocket. I'm going to make her put it on before I shoot her."

Johnny eased himself a half step closer. "But if you kill me, you won't have to kill her, will you? Because I'll be gone and out of her life."

It was the wrong thing to say. Zack bared his teeth and jammed both guns into Chris's head. "Do you think this is a game, Johnny? Because it isn't. You screwed up your life and your marriage. You left her for two long years. She came up to Blue Lake whenever she could. You were gone, and she came to me. Then you came back, and you were a stranger. You split up. My turn now. Only I never got a full turn. You straggled back into her life and refused to leave." Sweat glistened on his forehead and chin. "I wanted her to kick you out again. I fantasized about it. But she didn't. That's when I realized what she really was. Not my lovely, sweet Meliana but a common, garden-variety whore."

Johnny glanced at Chris, who gave a subtle nod. The gap between them was less than eight feet. Zack was agitated, sweating. He was also working himself into a murderous rage.

"It's over, Johnny," he snarled. "Meliana blasted my heart apart, and now I'm going to blast hers. But just to be sure you don't interfere…" He raised the gun in his right hand.

Johnny ducked sideways and did a shoulder roll. Chris took off in the opposite direction.

Caught off guard, Zack jumped backward. He let out a shocked yelp, staggered backward several feet, then spotted something through the fog. He dropped to his knees. A slow smile spread over his lips as he took aim. And fired.

Chapter Nineteen

Johnny grabbed one of his guns when he rolled. He came to his feet in a low crouch just in time to see Zack jerk sideways. He knew the shot from the deputy's gun had hit someone. He heard a cry—a woman—pictured Meliana and went wild. So did everything around him.

He flew at Zack, knocking away the gun the deputy had managed to retrieve, losing his own in the process. Zack snarled like a caged bear. He got his foot up and narrowly missed connecting with Johnny's groin.

Chris shouted, "Let him go—I've got a shot," but Johnny wasn't listening. He'd spotted Meliana at the edge of the clearing. She was on her knees and bent over as if in pain.

His right fist caught Zack's jaw. The deputy stumbled backward, first into Chris, then into a tree. His eyes landed on the ground several feet away and he dived sideways.

"Johnny, the gun!"

Meliana's warning distracted him. Only for a split second, but it was enough for Zack to butt Chris in the stomach and grab the weapon. He came up, arms extended, facing Johnny and blinking sweat from his eyes.

"You're dead, Johnny Grand."

In his peripheral vision Johnny saw that Chris had lost his gun. Again. And his own was probably buried in a bed of rotting leaves.

"I'm gonna enjoy this," Zack hissed. He moved the barrel to Johnny's chest.

"Zack, wait!" Meliana's voice reached them from the edge of the woods. Johnny wished like hell he could see her. "Look at me," she said. "Look over here."

"I loved you." Zack spat the words at her. "I would have done anything for you. Been anything for you. But you chose him." He made a disgusted motion. "Move one muscle, Blackburn, and I'll blow Johnny's head off."

"You'll blow it off anyway," Chris retorted, but didn't move.

"Zack…" Meliana tried again. "Please look at me."

Zack's breath came in gulps. He yanked Meliana's white lace bustier from his pocket and tossed it at her. "I wanted you to wear this when I killed you. You had it in your drawer with your wedding garter. I have pictures of you on your wedding day. You and him. Sometimes…" His fingers squeezed into a frustrated ball. "Sometimes, if I squint my eyes just enough, I can turn Johnny's image into mine. We're similar, aren't we, Meliana. But only from a very long distance." His mouth took on an ugly smile. "Well, there's no distance now, and no doubt who's going to be alive when this is all over. You're going to watch me kill the man you love, Meliana." The smile became a sneer. "Have you ever watched a loved one die?"

"I have," she said, then asked softly. "Have you?"

"I don't love you. Not anymore."

"Look at me, Zack. Just for a minute, look at me."

"I don't love... Whoa." Whipping his head around, he drew back slightly, blinked, then frowned. "Whoa."

It was all the opening Johnny needed. He knocked the gun from Zack's hand and tackled him to the ground. Zack kicked and thrashed, but Johnny held fast.

"Get his legs," he ordered Chris, and, using Zack's belt, bound the deputy's wrists behind his back.

Fear rose like black bile, but he controlled it. "Mel?" He gave the belt a final, hard tug.

"I'm fine."

Johnny stood, swayed, then pushed the hair from his face and ran to her. He fell to his knees, winded and drained. But not too drained to haul her into his arms. "He didn't shoot you." He kissed her hair, her forehead, her eyelids. "I thought he'd shot you."

He realized he was trembling, but didn't care. She wasn't hurt. Zack hadn't shot her.

Meliana hugged him back, hard. "I thought he'd care," she whispered. "I can't believe he doesn't care."

"About what?" Johnny brushed the hair from her cheeks. He was still focused totally on her, and grateful that she didn't even appear scratched.

"Zack shot her," she said into his shoulder. She let out a deep breath. "Johnny, Zack killed his mother."

IT WAS A VERY, VERY LONG WALK back. Zack grumbled and cursed but didn't actually say anything. Chris held a gun on him. Johnny and Meliana remained a few paces back.

"What happened to Sheriff Frank?" Johnny asked.

Meliana sighed. "He stepped on a rock, turned his ankle and hit his head on a tree trunk. He probably has a mild concussion. He was unconscious for a few minutes."

"Or scared and faking it?"

"Or that. He knew Zack was having problems, but I don't think he actually wanted to confront him." She closed her eyes, pictured Zack's mother lying dead on the forest floor. "He'll stay with Eileen until an emergency team arrives, then go with her to the county hospital."

"Another morgue."

She wrapped her arms around his waist as they walked. "I couldn't see clearly through the fog. I thought he'd shot you, I really did."

"Same here." He kissed her hair. "You threw a stone at him, didn't you, just as he fired into the trees?"

Uncertainty crept in. "I wanted him to drop the gun. Instead, I messed up his aim. I don't know if I did the right thing or not. Maybe Eileen's dead because of me."

Johnny halted, turning her in his arms. "Not a chance, Mel. I was there. I saw. I heard. He fired before your stone hit him. His shot, his fault. All you did was keep him from firing again."

Her lips curved. "You have awfully good foggy night vision."

"Twenty-twenty," he agreed. His gaze traveled to

Zack's receding figure. "Look, I'm sorry Eileen's dead, genuinely sorry. I liked her. But I didn't pull the trigger, and neither did you. It was all Zack."

"She knew something was wrong with him."

"Explains the dinner she had with Sheriff Frank."

"And other, more private meetings. She thought he was reverting to his old ways—whatever that means. But she didn't know for sure until she actually worked up the courage to break into his house. She told me what she saw. It was all there, almost exactly as Charlie described it. White candles and dozens of pictures and clippings from the local newspaper."

"What about the marked bullet?"

"I imagine he had that in one of his guns. He planned to kill both of us tonight, Johnny. Instead, he wound up killing his mother." A shiver ran through her. "God, I hope the bullet he marked for me isn't the one that ended her life."

Johnny pressed his lips to her forehead, stared at the almost invisible outlines ahead of them and murmured a soft "Amen to that, Mel. Big amen to that."

Chapter Twenty

Julie couldn't sit still. It made Meliana tired watching her pace. "Sam didn't do it," her friend repeated in amazement. "He's okay. Fixated, but okay."

"Steroids, Jules," Meliana reminded her from the sofa.

"Yeah, I know, but that's a drug problem." She frowned. "Although he did lie to me."

"He probably thinks of it as medicine rather than drugs. After all, he got the compounds from Tim Carrick, and Tim's supposed to be a reputable pharmaceutical supplier."

"Good point, but Sam's still got some explaining to do."

Meliana flopped back against the cushions. "Sam gave me white roses and a white dog. It's a load off my mind, I have to tell you. Zack intercepted some of Sam's roses and used them for his own twisted purposes, but for the most part the flowers were well intended. It explains the discrepancies—why they'd be fine one time and crushed the next."

Julie gave a violent shudder as she circled. "God, I can't believe I let him kiss me."

"Don't think about it."

"How can I not? It wasn't that great an experience anyway, but now it's positively creepy. I knew he was a dud after the benefit, Mel. I just didn't know how extreme a dud. Can I pick 'em, or what?" She sighed. "Have things been happening in town lately?"

"Actually, yes. There've been several Peeping Tom reports. Also, kids cited for vandalism were allegedly being roughed up in the process. That was Zack's doing. The cars that were pushed into the bog were teen related. But Zack pushed Johnny's SUV and his own cruiser into the lake. Just for the hell of it, I imagine."

"Man." Julie shook her head. "He is sick. Really sick. Makes Sam look fine by comparison."

"I think Sam needs help, Jules."

"He'll get it," her friend promised. "From Charlie, I hope."

Meliana eyed her friend in mild amusement. "So you were with Mark tonight, huh?"

"Don't go there, Mel. Mark's New York flight never took off. I told you earlier I was with someone we both know and love."

"I thought you meant Zack."

Julie shuddered again. "Whatever made me think I wanted to trade city life for a quiet job up here? Where are Johnny, Mark and Chris?"

Meliana glanced sideways. "Over at Tim Carrick's place—reading him his rights, I imagine."

At last Julie dropped onto the sofa. She pulled a folded picture from her pocket. "Do you recognize this guy?"

Meliana studied the thirtysomething male. "Should I?"

"His name's David Ronson. He went to school with Zack. We ran into him at the benefit the other night."

"The old friend you mentioned."

"He became an accountant, bagged a job at a prestigious national firm. He'd been drinking before we bumped into him. When he recognized Zack, he embarked on a sloppy trip down memory lane."

"Which bored you, so you left."

"I shouldn't have." She slouched lower. "According to Ronson's wife, they talked about old high school antics—as well as several of the badass crimes they'd committed. David used to siphon gas from neighbors' cars. They both stole cigarettes and booze. Zack—" she slid her gaze sideways "—terrorized a girl who wouldn't put out."

Meliana's mind skipped backward. "Agnes's granddaughter, Alicia?"

"The very same. I talked to Ronson's wife on the phone while you and Johnny were outside a while ago. Zack dated Alicia in high school. She wouldn't have sex with him, so Ronson's wife figures he decided to scare the crap out of her. He crept around her backyard at night, tossed pebbles at the window, then hid in the bushes. He'd phone her, do the heavy-breathing thing and hang up—you know, the usual stalker stuff."

"He stalked his own girlfriend." Somehow Meliana

wasn't surprised. "This sickness has been festering inside him for years. How did we manage not to see it?"

"We weren't looking."

"There had to be some very big signs, Julie. I mean, Eileen and the sheriff obviously chose to ignore them, but as unbiased outsiders, not to mention trained observers, you'd think we'd have noticed something."

"What can I say? He was a good actor."

"That's Johnny's theory."

"Uh, Mel—" Julie tapped the photograph of David Ronson. "About this guy."

"You think if you'd stayed and listened to his drunken ramblings, you might have twigged to Zack's true nature sooner, right?" Meliana nudged her arm. "It wouldn't have worked. Zack would have whisked you out of there before his friend got going."

"Yeah, well, he used a different solution to shut the guy up."

"What did he do, threaten…?" Meliana trailed off, then swung her head around. "My God—Zack killed him?"

"And dumped his body in the Chicago River. I didn't recognize him when we fished him out because he was badly bloated and already decomposing. There was no ID. I was searching for Sam when Roney called and said they'd identified the John Doe from the river. As soon as he said the guy's name, I flipped. Luckily, I was almost here by then." She pushed on her temples. "My mind was all over the place, Mel. Sam, Zack—who the hell were we chasing down? As Mark pointed out, though, once we learned about David Ronson, Zack made a lot more sense than my brother. Thankfully."

Meliana slid her gaze sideways. "Sam never did make any real sense as a killer, Julie. Even on steroids, it was a hard thing to imagine."

They were silent for a time.

"So what's the deal with you and Johnny?" Julie asked out of the blue.

Meliana rested her head on the deep cushions and turned her gaze toward their neighbor's place. "I'll let you know," she promised. Then sighed. "When we figure it out ourselves."

JOHNNY AND MARK DIDN'T ARRIVE back at the lake house until after 6:00 a.m. The fog had thinned but seemed reluctant to actually lift. Mark hugged his sister, then staggered up to the sofa bed in the loft.

"Julie's in the guest room," Meliana told Johnny. "Sam's fine. She got hold of him and explained about Zack and the borrowed roses. Sam said he never meant to frighten me—he just wanted me to be happy, and flowers make women happy."

"And Lokie?"

"Apparently dogs make us feel safe." She smiled at the pair sleeping peacefully under the table. "When well trained."

Johnny raked a hand through his tousled hair. "She'll learn—if only from Shannon."

"Hey, I grew up with cats. Training's not really a word in the feline vocabulary." Because she needed to keep moving, Meliana went to the fridge and got him a soda. "Is everything settled with Zack and Tim and Eileen?"

"All done." He hoisted himself onto the counter beside her. "Zack's in the Blue Lake jail awaiting transportation to the city. Tim, wearing his favorite plaid jacket, is in the cell next to him, awaiting charges of theft, fraud and trafficking. And you already know Eileen's in the morgue."

She rearranged the hair on his forehead. "Did Zack say anything about her death?"

"Not really. Last I saw, he was curled up on a cot with his head buried in his knees. He was shaking so hard the cot was rattling."

"Did you go to his house?"

"Briefly." He worked up the ghost of a smile. "There's a lot of stuff to sift through. Pictures, clippings, clothing. Souvenirs."

She didn't like the sound of that. "What kind of souvenirs?"

"Things he stole from you. And a few things he took off his other female victims."

Meliana braced herself. "Were there many others?"

"Only the two we know of so far. Bianca and Elena. He lifted a scarf from Bianca at the charity benefit and a few pieces of lingerie from Elena."

"Pieces he replaced with mine."

"The guy's got big problems, Mel. Mentally, emotionally and now legally. He won't be killing any more people, women or men."

Meliana let her head fall back and stared at the high

ceiling. "Mark's thinking of transferring to the New York Police Department, as a sharpshooter."

"Really? Huh. My boss might have a thing or two to say about that." He shrugged at her quick look. "The Bureau needs sharpshooters, too, Mel."

In spite of herself a laugh slipped out. "You guys are so macho. It's like you're all on steroids. Did you and Chris come to any kind of understanding in the wake of this nightmare?"

"Yeah, we're going to keep our distance from each other."

"Surprise, surprise."

Crooking a leg, Johnny turned to her. "Tell me honestly, Mel." He leaned forward until their noses touched. "Do Zack and I look alike to you?"

Now she did laugh—and tug on his long hair. "In height and general build, yes. In coloring, both skin and hair, yes. In features, disposition and sex appeal, not even a little."

"So you'd never have confused him for me."

"That junkie really messed you around, didn't he? Chris told me about him," she added, then kissed his nose. "No, Johnny, I would never have confused him for you. Your stoned witness either has cataracts or there was a heavy fog in Chicago the day Bianca died."

"Could also be his brain's fried."

"Could be that." She glanced over his shoulder as Lokie yawned and rolled onto Shannon's tail. "So... how would you feel about training my beautiful white dog for me?"

His lips brushed her temple. "I'd have to be around her quite a lot to do a good job of it."

"Well, yeah, I kind of figured."

He drew back to search her face. "You're okay with me being around?"

She began unbuttoning his shirt. "I married you, didn't I?"

"Yeah, a thousand years and one alter ego ago."

"I'd say the alter ego's under control at this point, and in case you've forgotten, it was your idea for us to separate."

"No, it was my idea to get the hell out before I did visible damage to our already strained relationship."

"Semantics, Johnny." She slid the shirt from his shoulders, pushed his hair aside and took a bite. "I haven't so much as glimpsed John Garcia for weeks."

"And won't again. I'm done with long-term under-cover assignments, Mel. Two years was too damn long to be away from you."

"Uh-huh." She went to work on his jeans. "You know what Saturday is, don't you?"

"Our fourth wedding anniversary." He rubbed his mouth over hers. "Is that wood?"

"I was thinking Canary myself—as in tropical islands. Sun, sex and surf."

The smile that curved his lips was nothing short of wicked. "Sounds like a plan to me. I'll pick up the tickets, the sunblock and the dark glasses tomorrow."

"You've got a deal, Grand."

"No." He kissed her. "What I've got is you. It's all I've ever wanted. I love you, Mel. I always have."

"I love you, too, Johnny. Always have, always will." Smiling, she set her lips on the scar where the bullet had entered his shoulder five years ago.

"It had your name on it," he murmured. "In the best possible way."

She laughed. "There's a best way to get shot?"

"There's a best way to do anything." And lifting her onto the counter beside him, he set out to prove it.

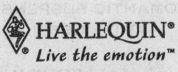

HARLEQUIN®
INTRIGUE®

WE'LL LEAVE YOU BREATHLESS!

If you've been looking for thrilling tales of
contemporary passion and sensuous love stories
with taut, edge-of-the-seat suspense—then
you'll love Harlequin Intrigue!

Every month, you'll meet six new heroes
who are guaranteed to make your spine tingle
and your pulse pound. With them you'll enter
into the exciting world of Harlequin Intrigue—
where your life is on the line
and so is your heart!

THAT'S INTRIGUE—
ROMANTIC SUSPENSE
AT ITS BEST!

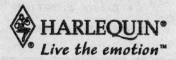

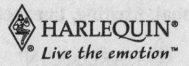

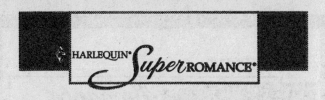
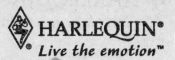

Harlequin Historicals®
Historical Romantic Adventure!

*From rugged lawmen and
valiant knights to defiant heiresses
and spirited frontierswomen,
Harlequin Historicals will
capture your imagination with
their dramatic scope, passion
and adventure.*

*Harlequin Historicals . . .
they're too good to miss!*

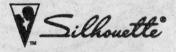